D1232846

The Wedding Column Murders

Jeffrey Metzger

www.darkstroke.com

Discover us online:
www.darkstroke.com

Join us on instagram:
www.instagram.com/darkstrokebooks/

Include **#darkstroke** in a photo of yourself
holding this book on Instagram and
something nice will happen.

To Nicole

Acknowledgements

I would like to first thank my mother Teresa for teaching me a love of reading and for introducing me to mysteries. I also thank her and the rest of my family for their love and support throughout my life.

My gratitude as well as my deepest love and admiration to my wife Nicole for being a patient spouse and a perceptive reader. And I thank Nicole, Teresa, Nick Perdiew, and Thomas Yannucci for reading early versions of the novel and offering helpful suggestions and encouragement.

Finally, a hearty thanks to Laurence and Steph at Darkstroke for helping make this book a reality. May The Wedding Column Murders be as lucky out in the world as it has been getting there.

About the Author

Jeffrey Metzger is a writer living in the deep interior of the American continent, where he occasionally has days when he sees more bison than people. He is an academic who teaches philosophy and political theory and has written on those topics, but The Wedding Column Murders is his first novel. He has begun work on his next novel, about a group of American Sherlock Holmes enthusiasts who travel to an English country house where they begin to be murdered. Like The Wedding Column Murders, it will be a traditional mystery with comic elements.

The Wedding Column Murders

Chapter One

Bella Jacobs

We are a supremely comfortable people. No more for us the sting of want, the calloused hands and the stooped back. True, we sometimes still eat our bread in the sweat of envy and greed, but that's where the real trick is worked. We have broken the yoke and shame of brute penury and, still more wondrous, have quieted that clamorous and uncanny hobgoblin we used to call the conscience. If we hear him at all it is gibbering toothless in the corner, doddering and muttering an ancient and opaque formula that means nothing to us. The tolling of the bell is as foreign to us as the muezzin's call to prayer, and who would have it otherwise? Anyone who still feels that obsolete affliction voluntarily turns themselves in to be drugged out of it, or at least suffers in a decent silence. And so we live our lives as a pleasant, self-regarding dream, warm and content and well-sated till we wake.

I think you of all people will understand me, and I'm sure you feel the same. So let me tell you my story from more or less the beginning, from when those murders began, or rather when they first broke upon the mind of the public like the first portents of a black, black storm.

At first the police were unable to see a pattern at all. When poor Charlotte Turner was killed it was shocking, but no one thought it any great mystery. The police were sure it was her fiancé, but he had been at a Yankees game with three other scions of New York's finest families. His alibi wasn't just airtight, it was pedigreed, or at least well-heeled. But they couldn't see past him to anyone else, so they were moving heaven and earth—discreetly, of course, as befit an investigation of a Speers—trying to prove he had hired someone to do it. I didn't envy them, having to balance the pressure from her family against the pressure from his, all the while trying to find the hitman for the billionaire class. And of course they never did, and people whispered (and a very few with the deepest pockets even stared), but no one thought there was anything more to it than that.

Then it was Jordan Wymark, but everyone had heard the stories about his adventurous sex life, featuring a quickly rotating cast of both women and men. If even a few of those stories were true the possibilities for sexual intrigue were endless, and the potential suspects all as shadowy as could be. There were rumors about some questionable business dealings, Daddy's bulging bankbook notwithstanding, and of course drug use. And then he was shot, and although shootings in Chelsea (indeed anywhere in Manhattan) are unheard of now, it still seemed like it might have been some kind of botched robbery. The police only had one suspect for Charlotte, half the city for Jordan, and so naturally they made no connection between the two.

Then Bella Jacobs was killed. It took a day or two, but someone with the police noticed that all three had been engaged, and that all three had their nuptials announced in *The New York Primrose*. The police were still making very careful runs at Charlotte's fiancé, trying to track down any movements of cash that might be unexplained payments to some third party, and discovering very little beyond how difficult it was to get even the most basic information on the Speers' finances. Some other set of unfortunates was finding out that you don't just poke your nose in at the Yacht Club and ask if Jordan Wymark was on the down-low or what kind of drugs he might have been buying and from whom. The connection through the *Rose*'s wedding announcements might have seemed as improbable to the average homicide cop as a leprechaun serial killer, but the poor saps working these cases were probably ready to jump at anything new, especially anything that seemed to point the finger at someone they'd find at Ray's Pizza rather than the Russian Tea Room.

I remember quite clearly when I first heard the notion that the murders might be connected, though other things made a much stronger impression at the time. Dad and I went to visit Bella's father, Max, a couple of days after she was killed. Years ago Max had bought a luxury apartment building overlooking Central Park. He had the entire top floor transformed into one gigantic penthouse that he and his family moved into. I had a hazy memory of going to a housewarming party when it was finally finished; I was maybe twelve. I had completely forgotten about all the time we used to spend there, but it came back to me as we waited for the elevators. The lobby of the building had been renovated and was almost unrecognizable, but it still had the same old-fashioned elevators, copper doors framed by dark marble, and a little light above the door that would glow and bing when the elevator arrived. Once we got into the elevator and the door closed behind us, it was quiet, and a flood of memories came back to me. The feeling got even stronger when we went into the apartment itself. The high ceilings, the thick carpets and cream-colored walls, the gold accents in the crown molding. Max was sitting on a sofa in an alcove in the main room, which must have measured forty feet across. I remembered the alcove well: it featured an enormous window looking out over Columbus Circle and Central Park. I remembered being an awkward teen at parties the Jacobs hosted, standing in that alcove, avoiding the other kids while I pretended to study the gold on the Maine Monument and carefully observe the traffic moving through the Circle. Only then did everything start to seem real to me, and I was overcome with emotion, but I was able to keep my composure as Max advanced to greet us.

Max Jacobs was older than my father, probably pushing seventy-five, but whenever I saw him now he always seemed more animated than I remembered him almost twenty years ago. Max was bald, with a powerful, aquiline nose and deep lines carved into his skin, running from either side of his nose down to his mouth. If a Roman Senator had been born to Jewish immigrants in Brooklyn in the forties, he might have looked like Max.

Max's newish wife, Davina, led us over to the sofa where he was sitting. He was looking pretty dejected, but when he saw us he got up. He came over and hugged my dad, holding him for a while, and when he finally pulled away both their eyes were moist. "Max," said Dad, as if he were going to ask him a question, but didn't say anything else. Then Max turned to me and shook my hand. "Ethan, thank you for coming, too," he said, holding onto my hand, his dark eyes fixed on mine. "Bella always liked you, always looked up to you for doing so well in school." This was an absurd thing for him to say, and for a second I felt like a boy being congratulated on a good report card, but then I was again convulsed by an unexpected wave of emotion and could barely control myself.

We all found seats, and were quiet for a few seconds. It was still light out, and the clear evening sky through the window behind Max somehow made everything both more poignant and more oppressive. Max was never one for small talk when there was something important to be discussed, so he started right in. The police had just been to see him, not an hour ago. They broached the theory that all three killings were related, and that the connection was the "Vows" column in *The New York Primrose*. Max was unconvinced.

"No way. No way in hell this was some kind of random attack. They went after Bella because she was Jewish. It's that son of a bitch von Clapp! Can you imagine something like this happening three years ago?"

Dad tried to calm him down. "Max, be reasonable. I'm sure the police know what they're doing. If they say there's some connection through the newspaper, it's at least worth hearing them out." Dad knew from long experience that when Max didn't like an idea his skepticism had roughly the force of a Category 4 hurricane. "What is their idea, that a serial killer has fixated on those announcements?"

"Or that it's class warfare. Today's Bolsheviks, apparently,

6

want to seize the Style Section of the *Rose* rather than the means of production. Bah," he snorted contemptuously.

Dad seemed to consider it for a moment. "Well, Max, it's terrible to consider, but I have to say that the theory does make some sense, whatever the ultimate motive might be. What are the chances that Charlotte, Jordan Wymark, and Bella would all be killed in a few weeks' time? Maybe there is a common thread," he said thoughtfully.

Max waved him away with both arms. "Turner, it was the fiancé, the Speers boy. God only knows what Jordan had gotten himself into. There is no connection!"

Davina sat on the couch next to Max but gave him his space. She was dressed all in black, like almost every other time I saw her, and with her black hair she really was striking. She gave a slight look of concern but overall seemed very placid, as if she was used to riding out Max's tirades and somehow hadn't grasped that the root of this one was something completely different.

"It couldn't have been Andrew Speers, Max. He was at a baseball game with friends. Afterwards they went out for drinks. Perfect alibi."

"Oh, his friends wouldn't lie for him?"

"Other people saw him at the game. They remember him, remember he was there all night. The people sitting right behind them. Really, he's in the clear."

"The coroner can't make a mistake about the time of death? He probably strangled her before he went out. And if he didn't there's contract killers. That's what the police think, you know. That he hired someone to kill her. They can't make any headway because it's the Speers, but believe me, he killed her."

"Why, Max? What motive could he have possibly had? I saw them together just a few weeks ago at Didier's. He was crazy about her. Like a schoolboy."

"Of course! Jealousy. I hate to break it to you, Doolie boy, but Charlotte was not closing out her accounts, not yet, anyway." He looked at me. "Ethan, you know what I'm talking about."

"Mr. Jacobs," I began, and may have actually blushed. I hadn't addressed him formally in years, but between the memories his home brought back and the way he addressed me, I felt like I was fourteen again. I was now embarrassed in addition to the confusion of other emotions, and couldn't have said anything coherent if I had wanted to. Fortunately, it didn't matter—Max wasn't inviting me to join the conversation.

"Think about it, Doolie," he said, turning back to my father and fixing him with a serious stare. "Charlotte Turner was strangled in her own apartment sometime around eight o'clock on a Wednesday evening. Jordan was shot somewhere off Seventh Avenue in the middle of the night. My poor Bella was poisoned at Evelyn Cravath's engagement party. What kind of person somehow gets invited into the Turner girl's apartment on a Wednesday night, strangles her in cold blood, then picks up a gun and stalks Jordan Wymark in the wee hours of a Friday morning, before finally getting invited to a party thrown by the Cravaths, were they use their expert poisoning skills and sleight of hand to murder Bella? There is no such person, Doolie! And the victims have nothing in common, except their weddings being reported in *The New York Primrose*, which has led to this cockamamie theory. All because the police have no clue!"

Dad sat there silently, apparently at a loss, so Max kept going. "And Bella's death was all von Clapp. The campaign he ran! He spent fifteen months playing footsie with this so-called 'alt-right,' and now every drooling, Jew-hating crackpot in the world has come crawling out of the woodwork like the deranged cockroaches they are. Well, I'll tell you this, Mr. I-voted-for-the-Nazi-so-I-could-get-a-tax-cut, I'm not going to sit here like a duck in a shooting gallery while the whole world goes mad. I'll move to Israel!"

"We're not moving to Israel," his wife said quietly, speaking for the first time since we all sat down. Max suddenly turned to her, surprised, then wary.

"No," he said, turning back to my father, "no, Davina's right. I've lived my whole life in New York City, I'm not going anywhere now."

His wife's comment seemed to have taken the wind out of his sails, at least for a moment. His face darkened and he seemed more withdrawn. Dad leaned forward, his elbows on his knees, almost like he was reaching out to hold Max's hands. "Max," he said, more softly now, "maybe you're right. Maybe someone else had a better motive. I know it's terrible to—"

Max shook his head, impatient and completely unsentimental. "You're talking about Micah. Bella had a will, it all went to charity. She hadn't changed it—I called the lawyer today. We had various arrangements for her, of course, but they all went to her alone, until she had children. Then, at most, he would have held the assets in trust for them until they were eighteen. But of course there were no children. Micah gains nothing, and he knows that."

Dad shrugged slightly. "You said Andrew Speers might have been jealous. Maybe…"

Max looked at him and nodded, his dark eyes now sad and knowing. "Bella travelled the world for ten years, more, had all the adventure she wanted. Painted on the banks of the Seine, dated an Israeli paratrooper, was engaged to that big-shot novelist I had never heard of. Now, she wanted stability. Watching her mother and I growing up, I can't say I blamed her…The point is, Micah had no reason to be jealous. She was way out of his league, but he knew that and had made his peace with it. Besides, he's not the jealous type. He has a steady but narrow practice at Cromwell and Sharpe. A few clients he does well by, but nothing to shake the world…no flash, no ambition. He'll probably be doing that until he dies. What's his motive?"

He kept his eyes fixed on my father while he was saying this. Dad presumably seemed unconvinced, because Max paused for a moment and an even sadder looked somehow shaded his face. "Alright, Doolie, let's talk turkey. So what if Micah was jealous, what then? First of all, he wasn't at the party. He went back to Cleveland at the last minute because his grandmother had a stroke. So, completely unplanned, he's not there. He obviously couldn't have done it. So what, he hires a hitman, like the Speers boy? First of all, he has no way of predicting his grandmother's stroke and knowing he'll be out of town. So if he hires a pro to poison her at this party, he has no reason to think he'll be in the clear. On top of which, he doesn't have the Speers' money, to hire someone who could do something like this and then just disappear. But even if he did, he has to worry about the shakedown afterward, when the killer has him by the balls. Micah is maybe the most risk averse man I've ever met. All of this is enough to convince me he couldn't possibly have done it, even if I thought he might want to, which I absolutely do not.

"But leave all that aside. I talked to Sydney Cravath. She assures me no one could have gotten in who wasn't on the guest list. If he put out a hit, there are easier ways, in any case. One of Micah's friends? He didn't have any there. He does alright, but he's not old money like that crowd. He's quiet, sticks to his practice, has a few old friends around the city, none of them at the party. I've looked at it every which way, Doolie." Here he gave a subtle nod, and his eyes got still softer. "I can't see any way Micah did this."

Dad sat there, his elbows still on his knees, his fingers pressed together. He was leaning forward, tense, afraid or just unable to say anything. "Doolie, what," Max asked, his voice husky, almost croaking. I suddenly remembered when I was younger, when we would go to parties at the Jacobs' and Max would have a few drinks and start getting emotional, his voice sounding like this. Then it usually embarrassed me. Now it hurt.

Dad began slowly, quietly. "You're telling me it must have been someone at that party. Surely there were people there who knew both Jordan and Charlotte—who even would have been invited in to Charlotte's apartment."

Max waved him off again, but this time less vehemently. He sunk back in the couch, but kept his gaze trained on Dad. "Who? Of the people who know the three of them, who could possibly want them all dead, and why? Besides, Charlotte's building has a doorman, cameras. You don't think the police

10

have looked at who was in there to see her that night? As for Jordan…you don't want to know half of what goes on down at Ossington—and you wouldn't believe the other half if I told you."

"Riverboat gamblers?"

"Ha! Riverboat gamblers can at least see some money on the table in front of them!"

"But I always heard that Jordan didn't really do much there. His position was more of a favor to Adam. And besides, surely a Wymark would be of more use to anyone alive than dead?"

"Maybe, Doolie, maybe. My name is Max Jacobs, not Sam Spade. These are just ideas I'm tossing out. But I'll tell you this, this harebrained police theory about a newspaper killer is nothing—just pure fantasy born of desperation!"

"Why do you hate this theory so much, Max? The police are just trying to find whoever did this."

"Because…don't you see? If that's true, or if Bella just happened to be murdered because she was at some fancy party, that makes it just…random. Meaningless. There needs to be some reason, however stupid or evil…" He choked out the last few words and sprang up from the couch, spinning around and turning his back to us. It was dark now and I could see him in the reflection in the window, his face buried in his hands. Dad popped up almost as quick, and went over and put his arm around him. After a few seconds Davina also got up. She went over and slid her hand onto his back. It seemed a little wooden, but when she turned back around her face was wet. Still, Max seemed to be taking more solace from Dad, until eventually he recovered himself and said he needed to go to bed. "I don't think I've slept since I heard," he said, and suddenly Davina burst out crying. Eventually a servant came in with some water and tissues, another absurd counterpoint to the wrenching emotion in the room, and as she stood there stone-faced, watching the four of us struggle with our grief, I couldn't help but feel like she was casting some kind of judgement on us. Max told us again that he needed sleep and, after Dad and he repeated about five times

11

apiece that they would call each other, we left.

Standing outside in the landing, waiting for the elevator, I got the sense that Dad wanted to talk, but I avoided his face, looking up at the sky blue above the elevators as if I was studying something. I hated to freeze him out like that, but I felt a clutch in my stomach and really worried that I was going to be sick. Dad asked me to drive home, and once we were out on the street and in the darkness of the car we both relaxed a little. "Why does Max call you Doolie?" I asked, trying to recall something else I had forgotten.

"It was actually from when you were kids," he said. "Bella couldn't say my name. I don't know how, but somehow she changed 'Ronald' into 'Doolie.' Max adopted it for himself and has called me that ever since." I gripped the steering wheel so tight it hurt my knuckles. Neither of us said anything else, and eventually we lapsed into the natural quiet of our own thoughts.

It was full dark now, and the night outside was warm and heavy, the first real summer night of the year. The streets were crowded, the people buoyant and relaxed. It seemed everywhere you looked there was a flash of color, a broad smile, a woman's bare shoulders. Watching these figures from the car I could feel the great distance between them and myself, as we drove in silence through the murky but vibrant streets.

Chapter Two

The Family Balfour Considers the Case

I decided to walk Dad in and stay with him for a bit when we arrived at the ancestral home. As we entered I saw Mother sitting in the windowsill at the far end of the room. She had drawn most of the curtains but had them open where she was sitting; a line of daylight was still visible on the far western horizon. The room was steeped in shadows and the furniture formed a melancholy assemblage of half-shapes, black and cream and mahogany blocks slowly being claimed by the darkness. At the far end, Mother sat with a drink in her hand, bathed in blue and purple light. I have to say the old girl looked rather elegant, but also somewhat small and fragile. Again I felt a flood of emotions, and went over to get a drink myself.

"Hello, dear. How was Max," she said, getting up and moving back into the room, taking a seat on the couch.

"He seems to be holding up pretty well," said Dad. "Better than I would have expected, really."

Mother nodded. "That's good. I tried to call Lilith today, but her assistant had her phone and wasn't letting anyone talk to her. Apparently she's just devastated, poor thing. I'm sure it's worse because the two boys live so far away."

"His wife wasn't very sympathetic," Dad said glumly.

"She's his third wife," Mother replied. "And thirty-four. Sympathy isn't part of the package."

"Marie."

"What? I like Davina, I really do. She has exceptional taste, just like Lilith. But you can't expect the depths of compassion from her. She's almost a child herself."

13

There was a long pause. "His only daughter," Dad whispered in a choking voice.

"Well, dear, sit down. Try to relax a little. Would you like a drink?" She looked over towards the liquor cabinet and saw me.

"Oh, Ethan! How nice of you to come in."

"Yes, sorry to make a bee line for the gin, Mother, but I'm afraid the visit with Max was a little rough for me, too."

"Well, a man ignoring me for the charms of the bottle... I'm afraid it wouldn't be the first time."

"I'm sorry, Mother, but no one's going to believe that."

She smiled, and I could tell she felt better about the fact that I hadn't greeted her immediately. I went over and gave her a kiss on the cheek. Dad was sunk into a chair, sitting stoop-shouldered and staring at the ground in front of him. It seemed the visit had been harder on him than I had realized. "Dad, would you like a drink," I asked. He waved me off absent-mindedly, so I sat down on the couch next to Mother.

"I'm sorry the evening was difficult for you, dear. But it was good that you went. How did you think Max was managing?"

"Pretty well, all things considered. I think he'll be okay as long as he has something like an enemy to focus his energy on."

"Enemy? Have they caught whoever did this, then?"

"No, unfortunately not. In fact, they seem pretty far from that. Max's enemy is the theory the police have that Bella's murder is somehow connected to Charlotte's and Jordan Wymark's."

"They think all three are connected? How extraordinary. How?"

I looked over at Dad, who remained withdrawn and uncommunicative. "Well, all three had their weddings announced in *The New York Primrose*."

Mother shot me a quizzical look. "But dear, that's ridiculous. Hundreds, thousands of people must have had their weddings announced during that time."

"Not in the *Primrose*."

"But what difference could that make?"

"Come on, Mother, don't play dumb," I smiled at her. I had poured myself a generous glass of the gin she had out, which was apparently some kind of specialty blend with a peppery aroma and taste. It burned a little and played with my nose, but I found it generally agreed with me. The first few sips gave me a needed kick, and now a warm feeling was settling in my stomach and spreading through the rest of my body. Mother was still pretending incomprehension. "You know the social prestige an announcement in the *Rose* carries," I said to her, and paused for a moment. "You may even have heard of the pressure that is sometimes applied to make certain an announcement finds its way past the goalie."

"Yes, it's a nice acknowledgement, but who on earth would kill over something like that? What's the theory, that disappointed conjugants are killing the couples they feel took their spots in the column?"

I gave Dad another quick glance. Mother hadn't really turned on the lights since we had come in, and he was sitting in the half-dark. He was still slumped forward, looking at the ground, and in the dark his silver hair looked thin, his temples knobby, his cheeks sunken. I reached over and turned on the lamp on the table next to me. "I'm not sure. Dad, do you remember what the police thought the motive might be?"

"Hmm? No, I...well, yes. Max seemed to think it had something to do with class resentment or something. Compared it to the Bolsheviks, didn't he?"

"Bolsheviks," Mother said, and sounded almost startled, as if she had looked up and seen a stern little man with a pointed goatee and pince-nez climbing through the window.

"Not actual Bolsheviks, Marie. But I thought Max said something about Bella and the others being targeted because of their wealth or social status. Ethan, wasn't that it?"

"Yes, I believe so, though he was more interested in demolishing the theory than expounding it."

"Then surely there would be a manifesto or something," Mother said. "Admittedly, I don't have much personal experience as a revolutionary on which to draw here, but I can't see how you'd set off a class war if no one even knows what you're up to."

Dad peeked over at her. He gave her an indifferent shrug, but he was starting to come out of himself. "Art for art's sake?"

Mother took a sip of her drink and seemed thoughtful. "I suppose it could be a personal grudge."

"Yes, I suppose so," said Dad. "Or just a lunatic with a fixation on the wedding announcements in the *Primrose*."

No one said anything for a few seconds. "Do the police really think there's a connection," Mother asked, and looked back and forth at us.

I stayed quiet, hoping to keep Dad talking. "I guess we don't really know. Like Ethan said, Max wasn't much interested in telling us about their theory, except to say it was hogwash." He paused for a moment. "I have to say, it makes some sense to me. I can't remember the last time someone from a family like the Turners or the Jacobs was killed by a stranger—much less three in three weeks."

Mother nodded as if she were agreeing despite herself. "Really, no one gets killed in Manhattan any more at all," she said. "I suppose a connection does seem reasonable—even inevitable."

"What if it's some kind of jilted lover," Dad said, raising himself up in his chair. "What if it has nothing to do with wealth or position or anything like that, and this is just someone who wants to take revenge on happy couples. Like Son of Sam."

Mother let out a low, pained groan and seemed positively grieved by what he had said. "I never thought the name of a serial killer would somehow inspire nostalgia in me. But here we are, I guess. I don't know how that time seems simpler and better than now, but it does. And not just for us," she added, as if heading off an objection that neither Dad nor I were eager to make.

"I'm being serious, Marie. Think about it: some poor, lonely soul somewhere out there in the city. Maybe his lover leaves him, maybe he can't even get that far down the lane.

He feels despised and abandoned—"

"So dramatic," said Mother.

Dad shot her a slightly annoyed look. "Well, yes, Marie. Since he's killed three people, I'm going to go ahead and say he might have a slight flair for the dramatic." Mother smiled. He was usually irritable when he started to pull out of his depressive moments. Apparently she had been more attentive than I had given her credit for.

Dad looked around the room. The sun was down now and, besides the small lamp on the table next to me, it was quite dark in the apartment. "Marie," he said, somewhat waspishly, "why are you sitting here in the dark? Turn on some lights." Mother shrugged and, with a bored air, reached over and flipped on the light next to her.

"Anyway," Dad continued, gripping the arms of his chair and straightening himself up, "imagine this lonely, dejected, alienated young man walking the streets. It's springtime, and he sees all these happy young couples around him. His despair and envy intensify. Then he looks in the paper and sees these blissful, beautiful people being treated like heroes for doing the one thing he most wants to and can't." Dad really was getting carried away here in a way that was unusual for him, but of course I said nothing. The emotions were obviously running strong within him.

"I don't know if they're quite treated like heroes," said Mother, but in a tone that suggested she found herself being persuaded.

"Better than heroes: celebrities," Dad said.

"I would have thought celebrities were something rather lesser than heroes," I said, for no particular reason.

"We live in a debased world, dear," said Mother.

"And of course something like celebrity is exactly what this sort of person would crave," Dad said. "All the attention and affection they've been denied. And the shallowness of the whole thing would never dawn on someone who would literally kill for it."

"I have to say, Dad, you paint a convincing picture. Though I don't know...lots of people are depressed and

17

lonely, but they don't go around killing people."

"You watch the news, Ethan. Shooting people is our new national pastime. Everyone these days seems to think they have a reason to do it."

I was about to remind him that only Jordan had been shot, but now it was Mother's turn to theorize.

"Well," she said, "if I were going to be convinced that there's a serial killer at work here, your version would have done it, dear. But I can't see that there's any connection at all."

"No connection? But Marie, that would be an almost impossible coincidence. You said so yourself."

"Yes, but I've reconsidered. I think one demented individual somehow doing all this is what's really impossible.

"You're giving your imagined serial killer far too much credit. Most of them are cannibals or necrophiliacs, and they're certainly not brilliant assassins, patiently stalking their victims until they can strike with impunity. Son of Sam went around shooting people in their cars. Even Jack the Ripper, supposedly the stuff of legends, was a barely literate little creep who just wanted to cut women open. He probably disappeared because he succumbed to syphilis and spent his last days a stinking, sore-ridden pest, gabbling and foaming at the mouth in a cell somewhere.

"A serial killer is no different—certainly no better—than a man riding the subway wearing a trench coat and no pants. They're both enslaved to their disgusting little urges, it's just that serial killers are more dangerous and so more frightening. But they're little more than animals, and in fact less intelligent than most animals. They're on the level of insects, maybe. They always do the exact same thing, for the same reason flies are always drawn to excrement. They can't help themselves. A creature like that would lack the imagination to select victims from the newspaper to vent his romantic frustrations on—much less would he be choosing them to make some point about income inequality, if that's the police's theory. Even if he did, he wouldn't know how to find such people, and he certainly wouldn't have the self-possession—much less the social connections and *savoir faire*—to infiltrate their private lives and kill them subtly enough to escape immediate detection. Can you imagine such a person bluffing his way into Charlotte Turner's apartment or Evelyn Cravath's engagement party? Of course not. I'd sooner expect to see a worm dance the jitterbug."

"So it couldn't be a serial killer because they're just not our kind of people," I asked, smiling.

"Tease me all you like, dear. But do you think someone who only knew Bella Jacobs from her wedding announcement would know who Evelyn Cravath is? He certainly wouldn't have any idea that she was getting engaged, even less that Bella would be at the party. And even if someone told him, he couldn't get in—and even if he did, how would he recognize Bella? In a room full of young women, he'd pick her out based on one or two photos he had seen in the newspaper?"

"Bella would be hard to miss," I observed.

"Fair enough," Mother said. "But my point stands."

"But Marie," said Dad, "you're missing the fundamental point. There's simply no way these three murders are unconnected. It's too great a coincidence. How did this person find Bella and target her? Who knows? Maybe he poisoned her before she entered the party. Maybe he was working for the caterers. But before you start tearing apart the how, you have to ask why. And it just isn't believable that three separate people came up with three independent reasons for killing these three the very same week their profiles were run in the *Primrose*—and then that each of the individual killers also had the opportunity. There must be a connection. And I think the jealous and forlorn lover makes more sense than the revolutionary who leaves us to decipher his message by hunting down last month's wedding announcements."

Mother was unimpressed. "As I said, dear, you're misunderstanding what a serial killer is. They choose the easiest opportunities—prostitutes, delivery boys, people parked in cars on dark streets or deserted parks where it's easy to escape. They don't haphazardly pluck wealthy people

19

from the newspapers and then carefully shadow them, waiting for the one chance to fell their randomly chosen target. Your version, for lack of a more appropriate word, is too romantic to be true."

"But it's the only possibility that covers what we know of the cases," said Dad, somewhat petulantly.

"What we know of the cases? But dear, we don't know anything at all. We know that three people were killed, and that the police think there may be some connection with the wedding announcements in *The New York Primrose*. Beyond that, we don't know nearly enough to start constructing theories and sketching some master criminal behind them all.

"Take poor Charlotte's murder—though perhaps it would be better if we didn't talk about," she said suddenly, looking at me.

"I appreciate that, Mother," I replied, "but as you know, Charlotte and I went our separate ways a long time ago. I had barely seen her for the past couple of years. And while it's not a pleasant topic of conversation, after all this I find my mind turning towards it, whether we talk it over or not."

"Well, then," Mother picked back up, "take poor Charlotte's murder. We know almost nothing, except that she was strangled in her apartment and that she seemed to have trusted her killer, since she apparently was sitting on her couch when it happened, not trying to escape or fend him off until it was too late. Or did Max know anything more after his interview with the police?"

She looked at us both. "I don't think he mentioned anything," I said. "He seemed convinced Andrew Speers was behind it, but I don't think that was based on anything he had heard from the police."

Mother gave a slight, satisfied nod. "So we know almost nothing about Charlotte's murder, but what we do know suggests that it was almost impossible that this was just some person who decided to murder her because he saw her in the paper. Such a person would have no idea about the back door in Charlotte's apartment—but I've already been over this whole side of it. But even more there's the fact that she was strangled. It's a terribly gruesome way to kill someone—brutal, ghastly, yet slow and horrifically intimate. It's simply inconceivable that someone chose her at random and was able to pounce on her while she sat on her couch and follow through strangling her without hesitation."

"And maybe Andrew could have killed her that way," said Dad, "but we know he didn't. Why would a contract killer strangle Charlotte rather than just shooting her? Who's ever heard of such a thing?"

"Because it's quiet, dear. Even with a silencer, a gun would be loud, and quite distinctive. And then the killer either has to take the gun with him, and risk being caught with it, or leave it there."

"A professional would have a gun that couldn't be traced."

"Which would make it perfectly obvious that the killer was indeed a professional, and point the finger very squarely at Andrew Speers, even if his alibi was the Queen of England."

"Bah," said Dad. "What a considerate sociopath who kills for money! Wouldn't want to inconvenience Andrew!"

"Regardless of what happened to Andrew, the killer wouldn't want to make it so obvious it was a contract killing. A mysterious gun would tell the police exactly what type of person they should be looking for, even if they didn't immediately have a name. These people like to be completely invisible, and leave no hint that such a thing may have happened."

"Have you had occasion to look into all this," I asked her.

"Not recently. You know, dear, that my two weaknesses are spirits and true crime."

"What about a knife," Dad persisted. "That would be much quicker and more reliable than strangling, but could also look like a crime of passion."

"With a knife Charlotte certainly would have fought back, or tried to get away, or most likely both. The killer could have been wounded, and likely would have ended up with her blood on his person. And I'm sure she would have screamed and raised the alarm.

21

"When you think about it," she concluded, "strangling is really the only path open to a professional killer in this case."

"But it's difficult, and prolonged, and hideous. You yourself just said what a horrible way it is to kill someone."

"We're talking about someone who has undertaken to kill in cold blood for money. Do you think the act of choking the life out of an anonymous stranger is going to be too much for their delicate sensibilities?"

This finally took the wind out of Dad's sails, and he slumped back down docilely in his chair. But I wasn't fully convinced. "But how did the hitman get into her apartment, Mother? It seems to me he faces the same obstacles as our mysterious newspaper killer."

"Andrew Speers would know about the back entrance— he's probably obsessed with it. He would have told the killer about it."

"But why would Charlotte let him into her apartment? And sit calmly on the couch before he approached and strangled her?"

"Andrew could have told her it was a friend of his who needed to bring something by. Or someone coming to plan something for the wedding. Or someone delivering flowers. Really, who knows? He could have told her anything that would have put her at ease about having a strange man in the apartment. The poor girl never stood a chance."

We all maintained a respectful silence. I wasn't fully convinced by Mother's theory, and I suspect Dad wasn't either, but no one could formulate a meaningful objection. She took a slow sip from her drink and looked into a dark corner of the room for a few moments. "So far as I can see," she said, "there are three basic options.

"The first is that the same person has committed all of these murders, for whatever reason of their own. I think that's ridiculous, as I'm sure I've made clear. The other is that the murders are totally unconnected, and the fact that they've followed each other—and each victim's wedding announcement in the *Rose*—so closely is pure coincidence. I have to admit, Ronald, that does seem a little far-fetched when I stop now and think about it. But there's a third possibility: Charlotte was murdered, and someone used that as a smokescreen for an unrelated murder they had already been contemplating."

"What, they just made up the *New York Primrose* connection on the fly," said Dad, obviously no more convinced by this theory than the previous one she had advanced. It was nice to no longer see him so depressed, but he could have been a better sport in our conversation.

Mother simply shrugged again. "Think about it. If you were looking for a victim of opportunity, you could hardly do better than Jordan Wymark. He's out late most nights, keeps questionable company, engages in various sorts of risky behavior. And sure enough, he was shot dead—maybe the easiest way for an untrained, unmotivated killer to strike—in an isolated back alley somewhere. A complete stranger wouldn't have any way of knowing about Jordan's social calendar. But an acquaintance might. Maybe the real question here is who wanted Bella Jacobs dead, and why?"

I had to admire her for spinning all this out, entirely on the spur of the moment. The events before us were beginning to seem very much like they could rearrange themselves in this new design she was tracing.

"Someone wants Bella dead," she continued. "Someone close to her, or maybe just someone who has a violent grudge against her father. Suddenly Charlotte Turner is killed, probably by her fiancé's agent, and Bella's nemesis sees an opportunity. As it happens, subjects of the *Rose*'s vows column have been killed for three consecutive weeks, but it doesn't even have to be that neat. This person knows Bella's nuptials are approaching, knows she'll be featured in the *Rose*. The very next week, it's Jordan Wymark in the Vows column. The nemesis sees the opportunity and seizes it. Obviously a nervy individual favored by fortune. So when they have a chance to poison Bella at a crowded party where no one expects to find a murderer, they take it. Now if the murders stop, people will think something has befallen our mysterious serial killer. In any case, how will anyone ever bring it back to someone who killed two of the three, and one of them for no reason?

"He may well never be caught." She paused for effect, or so I thought. "I have to say, it really does chill my blood a bit," she said, her voice rather different.

We all sat there quietly for a few minutes. The murders hung over us all, and as I got up and poured myself a little more gin I went back over the different explanations we had canvassed. None of the theories quite made sense, though none of them were actually impossible. It seemed too much to believe these three murders were connected by nothing more than coincidence, even leaving the *Rose* announcement aside. But then what did connect them? Mother was right about Dad's theory: the notion that some kind of misfit loner was executing these murders beggared belief. Her idea, meanwhile, was brilliant—much too brilliant to be true. It was all but impossible for me to imagine someone hearing about Charlotte's murder and just inventing the idea of the *Primrose* connection on the spot to camouflage their planned murder of Bella, especially since it was hard to see why anyone would want Bella dead. Still less could I believe in someone being cold-blooded and dogged (or just lucky) enough to kill Jordan undetected, then going on to poison Bella at the party. This would have to be a criminal genius, of the sort that probably doesn't exist, not someone who would kill her from jealousy or to spite Max. The police appeared to believe that the three were targeted because of their wealth and social status—though I couldn't remember now whether Max had specifically said that was their angle—the other obvious thing they had in common. But if there was some social or political motive behind the murders, why not publicize it? Were these killings leading up to something else, something that would cast them in a completely different light once it happened? If so, what could it possibly be?

Mother broke the silence. "I take it Micah was at Sydney's party," she asked quietly.

"Actually, no," said Dad. "He was called away at the last moment, back to the Midwest for a family emergency. Max is

24

convinced he had nothing to do with it."

Mother nodded. "I've spoken to him several times, including sitting with him at dinner. He really doesn't seem the type." Here I couldn't help but shoot her an amused look, though she didn't notice. "But then if he were going to murder his wife, I can imagine him using poison."

"Well, he didn't do it," said Dad shortly. "Look, Marie, I'll grant you that Charlotte may have been murdered by Andrew Speers. That's even the most likely explanation, when you step back and look at it by itself, without all of these other questions and distractions. And, let's face it, there are reasons why someone might want to kill Jordan Wymark as well. But why would anyone want to kill Bella? It makes no sense. No one hates Max that much, and if they did, they'd go after him. It's New York real estate, not a Shakespeare play. And how would the killer even know that she was going to be featured in the *Rose*'s wedding announcements? You think she's the reason Jordan was killed, but I don't see how you can even account for that."

Mother shrugged again. "Because the killer is someone close to her," she said, as if she was stating something too obvious to need pointing out.

Dad harrumphed. "I don't buy it. In that case, the murders are most likely just unconnected."

Dad, it seemed, was not going to be able to move on from Mother's rather unceremonious treatment of his Son of Sam theory. Mother, for her part, looked like she was done humoring his mood. I had gone from trying to draw Dad out of his funk to trying to preserve the harmony between two rather animated parental units, and decided to turn their attention away from each other. "You may not want to admit it, Dad," I said. "But Max's ideas might hold up here. If there's no connection to the other murders, as you just said, Bella could have been targeted because she was Jewish."

"But why would they target her," said Dad. "It's the same problem as the idea it was some kind of social protest—if you kill someone to make a point, you're really going to want to make that point. Besides, I'm sure there were other Jewish people at the party, if you're the poisoning type and you've somehow made it onto the guest list."

"But Bella was famous, remember? She had been a model —and her profile had just been in *The New York Primrose* the weekend before. A random assassin wouldn't know who else was there, much less how to recognize them if he somehow knew a few names."

"Make up your mind," Dad snapped. "Either the columns are part of the crimes or they're not. And if someone wants to attack Jews, there are far more straightforward ways to do it than to poison a retired model at a private party and then stay silent as the grave about the whole thing." After that outburst, however, he seemed to come to himself. "I'm sorry, Ethan— and Marie. I don't mean to be disagreeable about all this. I obviously have no idea. It's just been a very difficult night, in the middle of a very difficult year."

It was of course hard not to sympathize with him. Rather than dwelling on it, which was likely only to depress him again, I tried to playfully draw the conversation to a close. "Well," I said, looking sideways at Mother, "at least we can all agree that the murders clearly aren't over something as trivial as being left out of the wedding announcements in *The New York Primrose*."

"That's not trivial at all, dear. If it seems that way to you it's only because you don't pay attention to such things. Most things are important, if you think carefully about them—but that doesn't mean any reasonable person would kill over them. I mean, a baked chicken can be excellent, or poor, or indifferent. And those things are important, but if the police suggested three different people were killed because they couldn't bake a chicken properly, I think we'd all be a little skeptical."

We all laughed, rather hard and for a good while. "Alright there, Mother, I think that's enough gin for you." I was torn between changing the subject and reminding her that her first thought had been that disappointed couples were killing those who had taken their places in the Vows columns. But just then we were interrupted by a series of loud noises in the

26

hallway, out of harmony with each other and with the world around them. This cacophonous cascade of aggrieved commotion heralded the arrival of my sister Alana.

She slammed the door and came tramping down the hallway. When she entered the main room where we were sitting Mother wisely headed off whatever spontaneous ejaculation she might have sprung loose upon seeing me there. "Look, dear, Ethan has come for a visit. Isn't that nice?"

Alana glowered at me with a familiar mixture of hostility and distrust. It was her default way of regarding me and indeed most of the world. Her eyes narrowed as she asked, "What is he doing here?"

"Alana," said Mother, her voice almost a purr, perfectly blending tenderness and disapproval, "come sit down and talk with us." This was typical, my sister needing to be instructed in the most basic points of human sociability.

Alana came and sat in a chair. For a moment she was tense and watchful, but she soon slumped back and watched us through her still-narrowed eyes. "So if I'm not allowed to ask why Ethan is here, can I ask what you were talking about?"

Sadly, no one had anticipated this question. We looked around at each somewhat helplessly, then Dad, rather unadvisedly, volunteered the truth. "Ethan and I went to see Max Jacobs tonight." After a pause he added, "You know Bella was murdered earlier this week."

"Well," said Alana, "I'm sorry, but I'm just not sorry at all. She was always rude to me. Very stuck-up, even just... mean."

"She was never mean to you," I said. "You were just envious of her because she was so much more accomplished and better looking than you."

"It doesn't matter if she was mean to you," mother interjected, nipping our exchange in the bud. Alana glared at me bitterly but Mother wasn't about to allow either of us to run wild. "It's a terrible tragedy, and very difficult for the family. We don't want to even think about what they must be going through." She looked at neither of us but lapsed into a judicious but vigilant silence.

"Well," said Alana, "I don't want to talk about it anyway —how depressing. I just had a wonderful dinner with the girls. We took some great pictures that are doing really well on Insta. I can't wait to see how my account blows up in a couple of weeks." She paused for a moment, basking in this thought, then turned to me. "What about *you*, Ethan? You're also going to have an eventful summer. Do you have anything lined up for when Balfour and Son closes up shop for good in a few weeks?"

"Alana," said Dad sharply. "If you're going to talk like that, you can go to your room."

Alana looked hurt and stunned for a moment. She had never quite figured out how upsetting the whole losing-his-life's-work thing was to Dad, because of course she hadn't. I, meanwhile, refrained from commenting on a twenty-five year-old woman about to be married being sent to her room. Dad's emotions were still apparently fairly raw, and he sat turned in his chair, glaring at Alana, who for her part was still too confused to find her way to her usual posture of indignation. I saw my opening and decided to seize it and press my advantage.

"I'm looking at several things. And you? Of course you won't be getting a job, but I'm sure you'll want to begin your days of wedded bliss in your own home. What neighborhood in Brooklyn are you thinking of?"

"For the last time," said Alana, gritting her teeth, "I am *not* moving to Brooklyn."

"Oh, come on," I replied. "You'll be the envy of all your Vardlinian classmates."

"First of all," she said, her anger rising still further, "we're not 'Vardlinians.' We're Vardleyites, and our mascot is the Brewer."

"Well, you do all tend to come out of Vardley duller, fatter, and full of gas, so I suppose that is appropriate."

"Oh," Alana returned, choking with emotion, "now you're going to make fun of my IBS? Things like this are exactly why I don't want to talk about it publicly."

"Well," I began, but Dad wasn't having it.

"Both of you stop it," he said. "I am *not* in the mood for any of this, especially tonight. Ethan, I'm surprised and disappointed you don't know that, especially after being there with me. And you, Alana…" but his voice trailed off and he just gave her a rare reproachful look.

"Fine," said Alana, "I think I *will* go to my room." She got up and stormed down the hall, slamming the door to her room behind her.

The three of us sat there in silence for a moment. There was a longstanding, tacit agreement not to discuss Alana's manner of being in the world, and we had all resolved ourselves to stick to that agreement. In this case, however, the silence couldn't be complete. Dad was still looking down the hall to her room when he began. "I don't know that Max ever said this straight out, but I don't think that police theory about the murders was for public consumption. I'm sure Alana wouldn't intentionally spread something like that around"—here I had to bite my tongue, because that's exactly what she would do, and exactly what Dad was thinking she would do—"but I think it's best if we keep this discussion to ourselves. It would only upset Alana, and she has enough on her mind with the wedding approaching."

We all agreed, but the topic still held us in its grimly wordless grip. After my abortive quarrel with Alana I didn't think it was for me to break the spell, but eventually Mother said something.

"If there is some connection to the *Primrose* columns…"

"Yes," Dad said gravely, "I was thinking the same thing. Alana's will be printed in less than two weeks."

"Well," I said, after observing a moment of suitably stony-faced quiet, "didn't we agree that the notion of a single killer was too fantastic? Probably the police will arrest someone for one of the murders soon, maybe in the next day or two. Whoever is responsible and whatever their reasons, surely we can't be looking at three undetected murders."

"But we are," said Dad, with a note of urgency. "Whatever that theory was and however serious the police are about it, they wouldn't have floated it to Max if they were about to make an arrest for one of the murders."

"I'm afraid Ronald is right," said Mother. "If it comes to this, we may have to prevail upon Alana to withdraw her profile."

"I'm not sure that's possible," I said. "They talked to everyone a week or so ago, didn't they? The columns are written at least a week out. I'm not sure how much control the subjects have over what happens after they're interviewed."

"And that's assuming Alana would be willing to make the request," said Dad. "We all know how much she's been looking forward to this. She said she's making a big announcement in the profile, but she won't say what it is."

"But surely if she sees the possible danger," I said.

"But is there really any danger," said Dad. "Would she pass up a chance to have her day in the *Primrose* Vows column because of an improbable theory that doesn't have anything but coincidence and speculation to back it up?"

"Perhaps," said Mother, "there really is no danger and we don't have to worry about it. If we can't find a shred of evidence to convince Alana she could be in danger, maybe we don't need to be convinced either."

"Of course we need to worry," said Dad. "I hope more than anything that there's nothing to this theory, but we can't just ignore it and hope for the best."

"This all seems so unreal," I said, and we lapsed into silence again, though of a very different kind.

"Yes," said Mother eventually. "It's hard to know what to think or believe, especially tonight. You two have had quite an evening. What you both need, what we all need, is rest. We should give ourselves a day or two to chew over this theory, and see what we think about it and what Alana should do in a day or two. And who knows? Maybe the police will arrest someone tomorrow."

Chapter Three

Talking With the Detectives About Love, Money, and Murder

I went home that night and had trouble falling asleep, but when I finally did I slept deeply and didn't wake with my alarm. I got into the office late to find a message waiting for me from the police, who wanted to talk to me since I had known all three of the victims. I was to call the Homicide Division and ask for a Detective Thomas Allison. I called the number given and, somewhat to my surprise, Allison himself answered. He asked me to come to the police station to speak with him and his partner, and I told him I would be there as soon as possible. I explained things to Dad; he had noticed my tardiness and was grouchy that I was leaving almost as soon as I got there, but he recognized that I needed to go.

I set off for the address Detective Allison had given me, which turned out just to be a nondescript building on the edge of Midtown. I was actually met by Allison's partner, Steven Leo, a youngish black detective who led me into a small interview room then left to get Allison. I was surprised at how clean and almost clinical the room was. Apparently television had conditioned me to expect something dirty and ratty, complete with an ancient coffee pot burning Sanka in the corner. Leo returned after a minute or two with Allison. The two of them sat opposite me but seemed to make an effort to adopt a friendly posture.

Allison was probably in his forties, somewhat short and not so much squat as plump. He had dark hair and a round, honest face with broad features. His face, indeed his entire manner, gave the impression of a slightly gruff and clumsy sincerity, but his eyes were distant, blank, even hostile. Detective Leo, on the other hand, was tall and fairly lean, with close-cropped hair and a pleasant, jowly face. He looked sleepy, and his eyes were hard to read, but despite his overall lazy, disengaged manner he seemed to follow the conversation closely, though with an oddly ironic air that was hard to figure out. Where Allison seemed to telegraph his personality, or at least what he wanted you to believe was his personality, Leo was reserved and objective to the point of being inscrutable.

"Thank you for coming down here, and for doing it so quickly, Mr. Balfour," Allison began. "We really appreciate your willingness to help us in our inquiries. As I mentioned on the phone, and as of course you already knew, three of your friends have been killed in the last few weeks..."

"Yes, I do know who you mean, Detective. But I'm not sure I would quite call any of them friends."

Allison raised his eyebrows. "Well, sir, you were at least friendly with them all. You were in contact with each of them shortly before they died."

"Oh, my. Was I?"

"Yes, sir." Allison's gruff demeanor gave the lie to his steady attempts to be polite. He seemed a little like a bear riding a tricycle. "You visited Ms. Charlotte Turner the evening she was killed," he said, glancing at a pad of paper in front of him, "you called Mr. Jordan Wymark an hour or two before he was killed, and you were at the same party as Ms. Bella Jacobs on the night she was murdered."

"Well, yes, I was there, along with maybe a hundred other people."

"Yes, sir. We're trying to talk to everyone who knew all three of the victims. To see if they can help us see anything they may have had in common."

"Oh, I see. Well, I think you'll find there are a fair few of us. If I can say this without being insufferable, we all tend to be part of a certain social circle...and not a terribly wide one. So everyone in it tends to know everyone else."

Allison smiled slightly. "Yes, we have noticed that, sir. But as I said, you seem to have been rather close to all three of them, or at least closer than most. Perhaps you know of something or someone that may have connected them, something a little more than just being part of that circle."

I thought to myself for a second and nodded. "That's interesting, Detective. I had heard that you were convinced there was a connection and had definite ideas about what it was. But it sounds as if you're unsure if there is one or what it might be?"

This caught him off guard and he seemed irritated for a moment. "Well, Mr. Balfour, of course we're not at liberty to discuss every idea we've had with the public. But there's obviously a connection, whether that connection explains the murders or not. We've had only three murders in Manhattan this year, and all the victims knew each other. That's remarkable any way you look at it, sir."

"Yes," I said, "I suppose it is. But I don't think these have been the only three murders in Manhattan this year, Detective. I believe a few weeks ago a woman was killed in Washington Heights."

Now both detectives started and looked at me. I'm not sure Allison believed me, but this certainly wasn't what he was expecting.

"We—Balfour and Son, the company I manage with my father—were looking to buy a building there. I think the poor woman was actually found inside the building we were considering. Of course I didn't just forget something like that. But I'm sorry, Detective, I'm being pedantic. You are of course quite right that the three murders you've mentioned are connected, and I'm sure this is quite unusual."

Allison nodded a little but didn't seem to relax. "You didn't strike me as a guy who sat in his kitchen and listened to the police scanner, Mr. Balfour. But you're right—I wasn't even thinking of the whole island, just this area south of 110th Street, where all the victims have been killed."

There was something settled about the way he said this, and I felt I had to return to his question and answer it. I had been able to surprise them for a moment but the advantage was short-lived.

"Yes, of course," I said. "I'll try to help you as best I can, Detective. And you're right that I did know all three, and even had contact with them all not long before they died—though that is a rather grisly thought. But I can't say I thought of myself as very close to any of them."

"Well, Mr. Balfour, you did visit Charlotte Turner on the evening she was murdered? And—forgive us for being too nosy, but it came up in our inquiries that you used to date her."

I smiled, and may have blushed slightly, remembering Max Jacobs' comment to me the night before. "Yes, we did date, but that was many years ago now…seven, eight? She travelled for a few years after we broke up, and I really haven't seen her much since she came back to New York after that."

"But you were at her apartment last week."

"Yes. She and Andrew were going to move into a new apartment after they were married. She wanted me to help her decide on carpets and tiles and things. But when I arrived, it turned out the decorator hadn't sent any of the sample books. So we agreed that she would call me when they did arrive, and I would come back then."

He frowned as if something bothered him. "So you hadn't seen much of each other for a while, years even. Then she calls out of the blue and asks you to help her pick out carpet? Did she say anything about why she wanted your advice?"

"No, but I imagine it was because she always admired my mother's taste. I think she was probably going to pick a few favorites and have me take them to my mother to ask her advice, but as I say, none of the samples were there."

"Ah, I see. So none of the samples were there, so you just left? You didn't stay for a drink or to catch up or anything?"

"No, I probably wasn't there more than ten minutes. I think she would have been glad of the company—Andrew was out at a baseball game, as I'm sure you've heard. But I'd been rather busy at work. I was preoccupied and had a headache that night. I was glad to get out and get some fresh air walking home." I paused for a moment. "I believe her apartment building has security cameras. But I also hit my arm on the desk on the way out. The doorman was very apologetic about it. He might remember."

Allison leaned back in his chair a little and put up his hands in a profession of innocence. "Oh, Mr. Balfour, you're not a suspect or anything!" He laughed a little, and Leo even managed something like a smile, though he maintained his wry, detached attitude.

Having assured me in his official, polite tone that I wasn't a suspect, Allison suddenly switched to a conspiratorial half-whisper, leaning forward again, "Although frankly, with a whodunnit like this, I do appreciate the alibi!" and he laughed again. I relaxed a little.

"Did Ms. Turner say she was expecting anyone else that night," Allison asked, returning to form.

"No, she didn't. I imagine she wanted other people's advice than mine on her decorating choices, but I don't know who. As I said, we really hadn't kept in touch."

"Did she seem concerned about anything? Or excited?"

"No, I can't say that she did. To be honest, Detective, I was tired and a little irritated at having gone over there for nothing. I hate to say it, given what I know now, but I'm afraid I was probably a little rude. I doubt I did much to inspire confidences."

Allison nodded sympathetically. "Was this visit planned for a while?"

"No, actually. She only contacted me that day. That's part of what annoyed me so much, that she pressed me to come over when she knew the samples weren't even there yet."

Leo spoke up. "So she invited you over when she didn't even have the samples yet?"

I shrugged. "I think she was expecting the decorator to send them over that afternoon. She even seemed to think they might arrive while I was there."

Leo lapsed back into a bemused silence but Allison continued. "I don't mean to beat a dead horse, Mr. Balfour, but did Ms. Turner seem like maybe she was worried or nervous at all? Maybe there's a reason she wanted you to be there? Did she say or indicate anything like that? Or did anything about her behavior maybe suggest that?"

"Oh, God," I said, and started up in my chair. "You think —"

Allison again raised his open hands, this time in a calming motion, almost like a priest pronouncing a blessing on me. "No, Mr. Balfour. We can't discuss ongoing investigations, but it looks like Ms. Turner knew her attacker and let them into the apartment. There's no reason to think you would have stopped anything by staying. We're just trying to find out everything we can. Look at it from every possible angle," and again he smiled in a way that seemed forced and overly friendly.

"Still, it's terrible," I said, and let the sentence trail off. No one said anything for a moment, as I was at a bit of a loss and Allison maintained a respectful silence. Then something occurred to me. "Detective, I'm fairly certain Charlotte's building did have security cameras. Have you seen anything on those?"

Allison flashed a quick smile; this one seemed natural and spontaneous. He nodded a little. "The residents of Ms. Turner's building value safety, but they also value privacy. There's a back entrance without a camera. Of course the residents know about it, and no doubt many of their friends and associates do, but it's meant to be kept something of a secret. So while we can't tell you anything about what might be on the film we have seen, I'm afraid that wouldn't tell the whole story in any case."

Now I returned Allison's sympathetic nod, trying to indicate that I completely understood his reticence though I actually found it rather annoying. I looked back and forth at both detectives. "I'm really sorry I can't tell you anything worthwhile, gentlemen, especially in light of the questions you've put to me. I really am mortified to look back and think how callous and unobservant I was. But at the time, the whole trip just seemed to me like a pointless annoyance at the end of a long and stressful workday."

"That's perfectly understandable, Mr. Balfour. And really, you've been very helpful—and may continue to be. Do please try to keep thinking about it. Something else might occur to you, even something small or seemingly insignificant. If it does, just give us a call. Moving on, then," he glanced at me for approval, and I nodded slightly, though I wasn't sure what else there was to say, "you and Mr. Wymark were close?"

Ah. So we weren't just going to discuss Charlotte. "Oh, no. I wouldn't have said that at all."

"But you called him the night he died," said Allison, politely but just a little more than firmly.

"Yes, that's true. As I said, we were part of the same general social circle. Our families knew each other, but not terribly well." I thought for a moment. "You know, Jordan was always a very outgoing and charismatic fellow, and he always had people around him. The Wymarks are one of the really great old New York families and, if I can be a little crass for the sake of helping you with your investigation, they're tremendously wealthy. He never lacked for well-wishers, let's say. But there always seemed to be quite a crowd of them, some rotating in and out more quickly than others, and none of them ever seemed to get very close to him. So maybe, now that I think about it, maybe I was about as close as most people got to him."

"Did he not have any close friends?"

"Oh, I really don't know. Maybe some old friends from Andover or Princeton, or maybe from the water polo team. Keith Halwood, if he's still in town? Robbie Sloan, maybe? Wynn Aldershot?"

"Was he close with his family?"

"His fiancée, I imagine. Otherwise, so far as I know, he wasn't terribly close to anyone else in his family. No ill will or anything, just not particularly close. Certainly not his father, not really his brother or sister. He was a little wild for a Wymark. Nothing improper, of course. But not wonderfully close with any of them."

Allison nodded as if he already knew all this. "Why did

you call him that night?"

"I had been working late, and felt too wound up to sleep. I knew Jordan tended to be a night owl, and a few weeks before he had seen me at a party and invited me out with him as I was going home. So I thought he might be up. And, as I said, he had a natural charisma and was always good company."

"And did you get through to him?"

I grinned slightly, as I suspected the detective knew the answer. "Yes, we spoke briefly. He was wide awake, and seemed to be out on the town, but he said the rest of his evening was spoken for. He said I should call him back on the weekend, and also invited me to a party at their house in the Hamptons."

"Do you happen to remember exactly what he said? That his evening was spoken for?"

"Oh, no, I'm sorry. That was just my phrasing right now— I had the sense he was out but was otherwise engaged. Let me see if I can remember…I believe he said something like, 'Tonight's not going to work, but you should call me this weekend.' Sorry, I know that's not very exciting. Then he made the invitation to the Hamptons, though it was a little unclear to me when the party was going to happen."

"Did he sound…inebriated? Anything like that?"

"Not really. There was some background noise, so I can't be completely sure, but he wasn't slurring his words or anything."

"What kind of background noise?"

I thought for a moment. "I hate to say it, but I don't really know. It may have been music, or indoor background noise, or it may have been traffic and street sounds. I'm sorry, I just wasn't paying attention."

"Perfectly understandable, Mr. Balfour. Anything else you remember about that night, anything he said?" He paused for a moment. "Anything else about Mr. Wymark that might be relevant?"

"Well," I said, and now I paused. "As I said, he was fun-loving and adventurous. I'm sure you and I have both heard

38

other things about him, but I really don't know how true any of them are, or whether they'd be at all relevant to your inquiries if they were."

"Mr. Balfour," he said, and looked at me very seriously, "I understand completely. But this is a murder investigation. And, if I may say so, we have been very discreet, but very thorough. I doubt you could tell us anything we don't already know. And definitely not anything we haven't heard before."

"Yes, of course, Detective. This is not the time for being coy. Well," I said, shifting in my chair a little, "of course Jordan had a great *joie de vivre*, and one heard that it embraced certain recreational substances."

Suddenly Allison's face lit up. "That's great! What was that? *Shwab da zeebra*?"

"No," I said, and couldn't help but laugh. "*Joie de vivre*. It's French. It means 'joy of life,' that he really loved life. I'm sorry, I don't mean to be affected."

"No, no, nobody wants to be affected," he said with what seemed like mock seriousness. "But that's great! What was it again? *Joya de viva*?"

"*Joie de vivre*."

"*Joie de vivre*. That's great. You see, Leo, I'm learning something new here." Leo gave us a sleepy, enigmatic smile. Allison was animated now. "And I suppose that these, what did you call them, recreational powders can give you a nice *joie de vivre*?"

Again I had to laugh. "Well, yes, I suppose so. But if every young financier who bought a little cocaine was gunned down in a back alley somewhere, I think the city would look rather different, don't you?"

"I think it might," he said, and chuckled, his disingenuous manner starting to return. Then he gave me another serious look. "Of course he may have had other secrets. Things that might have been more explosive, especially for a man about to be married."

"Really, Detective, you want me to be forthright, I'm sure you can manage the same."

"Alright," he said, nodding at me quickly. "Maybe with

his great *joie de vivre* he couldn't stick to just one woman. Maybe not just one gender."

I had to smile. "Yes, of course I had heard those stories, and I believe at least one of them was true, though that was in the distant past. But honestly, Detective, why would Jordan hide being gay? Or, what I think was more likely, bisexual?"

Allison shrugged. "Family pressure. Religious parents, grandparents. Maybe he wants to have an old-fashioned family, or has some public image he's worried about. I worked Vice for a few years. Lots of wealthy men, gay or straight, like to go trolling for pros. They like having a secret, or the contrast with the rest of their life. Sometimes, they get shaken down. It can get dangerous."

"Yes, I suppose it could. But I would have no way of knowing if anything like that was happening, though so far as I know Jordan never sought professional help. And, for what it's worth, I really doubt he ever needed it."

"Didn't have to be a pro," Allison said nonchalantly. "Could have been someone he was seeing, a bit rough, maybe a criminal background."

"Yes, I suppose that's possible, Detective. But I really have no idea. We never talked about anything like that. But I will say that Jordan was not really the kind of person who would keep dark, elaborate secrets. That was part of his charm, he was very open. Not always terribly reflective or concerned about how his actions might be affecting others, but not one for maintaining a secret life. And, for that matter, if I had to guess I would say he hadn't been with another man since his adventurous youth, though again I really can't tell you anything definite."

"Man or woman, what would his fiancée think? Did she know about his *joie de vivre*?"

His persistence on this subject was annoying me, but again I couldn't help but be amused at his almost childish delight in his new phrase. "Oh, I haven't the foggiest. I met her once or twice, but barely spoke to her beyond pleasantries." I paused and thought for a moment. "Detective, you have to understand that Jordan really did possess great charisma, great charm. I didn't really know his fiancée, but she seemed sharp enough. It's entirely possible she had at least some idea of what she was getting and was perfectly fine with it. I doubt the idea will shock you."

"No. But, again, we have to try to look at it from every angle, especially in a case as dark as this one. And really, Mr. Balfour, I can't overstate how helpful you're being. I know I'm getting your hackles up, insisting on asking these kinds of questions, but it's going to be very difficult to catch the killer if everyone insists on keeping secrets."

"Yes, of course you're right, Detective. But I really hadn't kept up with Jordan in any kind of intimate way, and can tell you very little about his life now. I'm sorry," and for some reason I looked at Leo, who responded with a pinched but sympathetic smile.

"I understand," Allison said seriously. "Again, please let us know if you remember anything else. Ms. Bella Jacobs, then?"

"I'll tell you what I can, Detective Allison, but again she was little more than an acquaintance at this point."

"Your families are friends? Or do I have that wrong?"

"My father and Bella's father are definitely friends, yes. And they're old business partners, though I think it's been a while since they really worked together on anything. We used to spend time with the Jacobs when I was younger, but Bella and I went our separate ways in high school. I went away for school, Bella went to Trinity. Then she went abroad for college. Oxford, Paris, Jerusalem…it seemed like every time I saw her back in New York, she was studying at some new university in a different country. She eventually got a degree, maybe from Oxford. She lived in Europe for a while. When she did eventually move back to New York, I barely saw her."

"Did you see her at this," he looked down at a pad of paper in front of him, "Cravath party at all?" He seemed uncomfortable pronouncing the name.

"I did, yes. We spoke for a few minutes. I congratulated her again on her marriage, and we talked a little about the upcoming honeymoon. Apparently it was a rough time for her husband to get away from his work at the firm."

"Did you notice anyone around her, anyone behaving strangely?"

"Well, she got a rather frosty reception from Evelyn Cravath," I said, momentarily forgetting myself. I was plainly taken aback but also somewhat gratified to see another moment of genuine emotion from Detective Allison, whose eyes widened slightly as he leaned forward.

"I'm sorry, who was that? And frosty how?"

"I'm sorry, Detective, I shouldn't have said anything. It was Evelyn Cravath's party—it was her engagement. Bella was very beautiful, and I think Evelyn maybe thought she was trying to show her up. Which of course was nonsense— Bella hadn't done anything special that night...though I'm afraid Evelyn's basic intuition as to how the two compared was correct. But of course it was nothing. Evelyn was just being petty, and I'm afraid I was just being gossipy to even mention it."

"It made an impression, Mr. Balfour," Leo put in. The longer the interview lasted the more I received a certain impression from Leo. He seemed somehow both inattentive and precise in a way I found unsettling, all the more so as my attention was mostly focused on Allison and I felt Leo watching me silently.

"Yes, I suppose it did, but only because I was being a little malicious. I'm sure it was nothing that would lead Evelyn to want to harm Bella, especially at her own engagement party. And even if she did, I can't imagine she came to the party with poison secreted somewhere inside her dress, just in case someone outshone her." Leo nodded obscurely, but Allison still looked interested. "Besides, she was surrounded by guests all evening. She couldn't have poisoned Bella's drink even if she wanted to and somehow had the means."

"Her drink? What makes you think it was her drink that was poisoned?"

"Well," I said, "I suppose there was food there, if I think about it. But most people just had champagne, I believe. I'm pretty sure I saw Bella with a glass at some point. Of course it's possible she had something to eat, but I guess I thought it would just be much easier to poison a drink. And I thought Bella said something about leaving early to have dinner elsewhere."

"You see, Leo," Allison said, smiling, "this guy's a natural detective. Okay, did you see Ms. Jacobs talking to anyone else? Anyone else hanging around her, maybe?"

"Yes, I did see her talking with Hannah Sloan and Evie Kittredge at one point. There was another woman in their group, someone I didn't recognize. I don't remember seeing anyone suspicious skulking about. And I can't imagine Hannah or Evie had anything to do with hurting Bella."

"Mr. Balfour, you keep saying things like that, and I understand it's difficult to imagine people you know being cold-blooded murderers. But the fact is that someone at that party murdered Ms. Jacobs. And the only thing more unlikely than Mr. Wymark's pretty fiancée shooting him is his murder being a random attack."

"Yes, I suppose you're right," I replied. "Still, I'm afraid I really didn't notice anything strange or unusual, Detective. I was tired and distracted after another long day at work, and mainly just wanted to congratulate Evelyn and get out as soon as I respectably could." I remembered seeing Sydney Cravath prancing about and thinking she looked like a botoxed gazelle, but I decided against sharing this detail with the detectives. "And then I was happy to see Bella and wanted to congratulate her as well. But mostly I just remember a haze of smiling faces, and my being anxious not to get pulled into conversation with any of them. I got there relatively early, had a quick glass of champagne with Bella and a few others, then made my way to Evelyn Cravath and did the same. I probably left within half an hour."

"But," I added before Allison could say anything, "I've only heard as rumor or speculation that Bella was actually poisoned at the party. From what you've said it sounds like that was indeed the case?"

Allison gave me a stony, guarded look that lasted about a

second. "There's no point in being cagey about this," he said. "Yes, we're pretty much certain she ingested the poison that killed her at the party. But please, Mr. Balfour, don't repeat this. You have to trust me that if we want something to remain a secret—or at least unconfirmed—we have good reason for it."

"Of course," I replied. I thought for a moment, during which Allison seemed to be watching me, then said, "I understand the Cravaths have said that no one could have gotten into the party without being on the guest list. That may have been true for would-be gate-crashers trying to get in through the front, but of course there were caterers and others coming in through the service doors. I imagine a…I'm not sure what the term is, professional killer? would have known how to get in that way."

"Mr. Balfour, if you could try to help us close a few doors, rather than opening new ones."

"I'm sorry, Detective, I'm just—"

He raised his hands in a show of peace. "It's fine, Mr. Balfour, I'm just joking. You're probably right, a professional would know how to get into a space like that. But if a pro wanted to target Ms. Jacobs, there'd be much easier ways to do it than sneaking into a swanky party to slip her some poison in front of a roomful of people. Besides," he added, "we can't just have every murder be a contract killing. The odds of that happening are pretty much zero."

"Not every killing," I asked, remembering what Mother had said the night before. "So you think Charlotte…?"

"Mr. Balfour, we truly do appreciate your help, but we really can't tell you anything about an ongoing investigation."

Still, I wanted to press, and pretended it came to me in a flash. "It's Charlotte, isn't it? With the camera-free entrance. It would have been the easiest thing in the world for Andrew to tell her a friend was coming over to pick something up, or the samples were being delivered, or anything like that. Then the killer comes in through the back door, Charlotte lets him in thinking it's the person Andrew sent…which, after all, I suppose it would have been."

Allison's face was completely blank but his eyes seemed amused. "Mr. Balfour, you are a sharp one. Again, we cannot share the details of an ongoing investigation with you or any other member of the public. But you are a sharp one, I will say that."

I was slightly embarrassed by this compliment and looked down at the table. We were all quiet for a moment, and I assumed the interview had run its course. "I don't suppose then there's anything else I can help you with?"

Somewhat to my surprise it was Leo who picked up the thread. "Well, Mr. Balfour, there may be." He leaned forward a little and looked at me. "Of course we're just a couple of working stiffs," he said with a strained smile. Allison was staring at his notepad with a brow furrowed so deeply it looked like he was trying to decipher ancient Sumerian on a clay tablet. So apparently it was Leo's turn to be false and condescending in the hopes of lulling me into speaking too freely. "It's hard for us to really understand the unwritten rules in your social circle, as you put it. What life is like for the victims and for their friends and families. What motivates people, why someone might like or dislike someone else. What people in that world really want…what they're really afraid of."

"Well," I said, shrugging casually, "you seem to be after something in particular. I'll answer whatever questions I can, but I'm not sure I can paint the whole picture for you." I hesitated for a beat then added, "even aside from the fact that your question makes me feel rather self-conscious. I certainly have no desire to put on airs about some of the people I may know…still less to tell tales out of school about any of them."

Leo looked a little shocked, and Allison sprang back into action to try to smooth things over again. "No, of course not, Mr. Balfour," he said, as if he were trying to save a business deal that was about to go down the drain. I wasn't really that irritated, but was happy to have them both on the back foot.

"It's nothing like that," said Allison, chortling softly as if the whole thing were an amusing misunderstanding. "We have some specific things we want to ask about. Open knowledge, but not public, if you understand what I'm saying.

"It's like watching a baseball game, Mr. Balfour. Imagine you're watching but you don't really understand the game. So you can't tell if the pitcher is pitching around a hitter, or can't find the strike zone. We're not asking you to steal signs, just help us understand the game a little better."

"I'm afraid I'm at something of a loss with this analogy, Detective."

"Well, that's my fault," he said, still apologetic. "The bottom line, Mr. Balfour, is that you know the world of people who get their engagements written up in the *New York Primrose*—if you don't mind me saying that. And, after all, you did know all three victims. And since, if I can be a little blunt, you seem like a pretty sharp cookie yourself, we'd like to ask you some general questions. Nothing scandalous, just things that people like yourself all know but feel like they shouldn't talk about. Which we understand, of course. But now there have been three murders, and maybe it's time not to worry about all that."

My advantage didn't last long, because I couldn't tell if Allison genuinely thought I was insightful or if it was just flattery. But in any case I was of course eager to hear what ideas they might have and what direction they might be taking the investigation. So I softened my body language a little and said, "Of course I'll try to help in any way I can, Detectives," and even made a conciliatory little smile and nod toward Leo. He returned the gesture and I was happy to see his smile was friendly but not at all cringing or cowed. I really wasn't in the least upset with him, except maybe for trying that gambit when it was obviously so unsuited to him. Leo seemed like a natural outsider, intelligent but quiet and detached. His attempts to invite confidences by being self-deprecating and folksy just made everyone uncomfortable.

Allison's bull-in-a-china-shop routine, on the other hand, actually seemed pretty genuine, and it was disarming. He picked it back up now, giving me a series of quick, serious nods. "Thank you, Mr. Balfour, thank you. Now if I can just dive right in—and please do forgive me if I'm too blunt!" he said, and looked at me with a flash of comic light in his eyes, "can you tell us a little about the situation of the victims and their families generally? How did they look in the eyes of high society, if you don't hate that term too much."

"Detective," I said, "I wouldn't have much energy left for anything important if I went around hating terms. I'll tell you what I can. But I'm not entirely sure what you're asking."

"I don't think there's any way to be tactful about this, Mr. Balfour. Status-wise, money-wise," here he seemed to get a little uncomfortable and just blurted out, "how do the Turners look, for instance?"

"Well, they're an old family," I said, almost purring my words in an effort to sound reassuring.

"Came over on the Mayflower, right?" Allison put in.

"Well, yes… some a little more than others. But in any case, they owned vast tracts of land throughout the Northeast. They sold some over the years, and still collect a handsome rent on others. I believe they also got involved with one or another of the utilities here in New York, at the very beginning when they were set up. That's been very good to them, and still is."

"In a family like that, Mr. Balfour—and I don't mean to be too crude and unwashed here, but please forgive me if I am— every generation, the family fortune gets divvied up. Sooner or later, the shares start to get smaller, no? Maybe there's conflict over something like that."

"Depends on what the fortune was to begin with," I said. "And how well you manage it."

"The Turners?"

"A very large fortune to begin with, managed very well down through the years."

"So, and I'm sure you can appreciate how delicate this all is, Mr. Balfour, but there's no reason to think anyone in Ms. Turner's own family might have…" he caught himself up, apparently still trying to be diplomatic.

"Wanted her out of the way? I doubt it, Detective. So far

47

as I know, the family fortune was quite healthy and well-distributed, and Charlotte didn't take an active role in any of the family investments or businesses. So I can't imagine her being at cross purposes with anyone who had anything serious to lose, not wealth, not personal ambition."

"So it sounds," said Leo, "like the Turners are almost royalty in this world. If anyone is going to attract envy, even hatred…"

"I don't know," I said, "Charlotte tended to be a little retiring and awkward. She enjoyed all the benefits of being a Turner, of course, but she hardly carried herself like a queen. And to the average person, I doubt there would be anything setting her or the rest of the Turners apart from any other obviously wealthy family in New York."

"That's part of what makes this world tick, isn't it," asked Allison, with a kind of eager curiosity that appeared genuine. "Just to know it's there, know a few of the people and a few of the rules, that's already exclusive?"

"Yes, I suppose that's a fair way of putting it," I said, once again a little uneasy with the general air of inquisitiveness. "In any case, I doubt that the relative status of the Turners can throw any light on this, or at least none that I can see."

"But to someone who knows these distinctions, she might attract some kind of special hostility?"

I nodded vaguely, a little confused by Allison's doggedness on this point. "I guess that's possible. But that would hardly explain the other cases."

"Oh," said Allison and looked at me eagerly again, apparently overestimating my desire to talk about these subjects.

"I don't think that would explain the other murders."

"Why not," Allison asked. "The Wymarks are also a very wealthy family, also very old money. Or so we've heard," he said with a comic air of knowing his place.

"So they are," I replied, "but the Turners and the Wymarks are hardly families of the same standing."

"We were kind of led to believe they were on basically equal footing," said Allison.

"I wouldn't have said so," I answered. I didn't want to continue on the theme but Allison was wearing me down. "The Wymarks have what you might call some skeletons in the family closet."

"Skeletons! This is getting exciting, Leo. What are these skeletons?"

"Well, not a skeleton, but the money isn't nearly as old as the Turners', for one. Its provenance is also a little suspect, or at least could be to a family like the Turners. Of course there's that line about the foundation of every fortune being a great crime, or something like that, but the Turners' crimes are at least old enough to have faded from memory."

"And the Wymarks," Allison asked. He had this wry, slightly comic grin on his face during this part of our conversation, maybe because he was aware of how awkward it was for me, maybe because he just found the whole topic and need for decorum around it absurd.

"Well, there was some profiteering during the Civil War. They were hardly the only Wall Street family to do that, of course, though you don't hear much about any of it in the various museums they help fund. But even more than that, they made their fortune in the opium trade—twice. In the 1830s or thereabouts, one of the patriarchs made a fortune selling opium in China. After the Civil War, the inaptly named Victory Wymark lost most of the family's wealth speculating. He died shortly after; the family has always thought it was suicide. His son made back the loss and more, chiefly in the same way…of course no one wants to talk about this now, but he was probably at it for a decade or so."

Allison seemed unimpressed. "Ancient history, most folks would say."

I shrugged. "Part of being an old family is remembering and caring about such things. More recently, Adam's own brother, Charles, was disgraced in the '80s in an insider trading scandal."

"Every family has one."

I smiled. "Fair enough, Detective. My point is just that if the Wymarks are old money and, say, Max Jacobs is new money, they're not old money in the way that the Turners, or Speers, or Sloans are. But I should probably hasten to add that none of the Wymarks carry themselves as if they're particularly concerned with any of that, Jordan least of all.

"But the bottom line, Detectives, if I can cut to the chase here a bit, is that I don't think there's really much of anything linking the Turner and Wymark families, beyond the somewhat superficial fact of having a good deal of wealth, and having had that for at least a century or two. People who know this world wouldn't see the two families as very similar. Not in rank or stature, if I can be a little vulgar about it, or social profile, financial activities, even basic family temperament. And if someone did bear both families ill will, and was close enough to both to get at their grown children, Charlotte and Jordan would seem like the last members of either family to inspire such feelings. Charlotte was quiet and unassuming. I'm sure you know children from such families tend to be a little clueless, but Charlotte was generally kind in situations she understood. Jordan, on the other hand, was almost universally loved. Charming, good-looking, generous in the most natural and appealing way. Of course someone's resentments don't always make sense to other people, but allowing for that, I really can't imagine anyone targeting either of them because they had a grudge against the family."

Allison had his head down and was taking notes while I talked. There was a moment's pause before he realized I had stopped speaking. Then he went back into his serious nod. "Thank you, Mr. Balfour, this kind of insight is really very helpful." He finished whatever he was writing and looked back up at me. "You mentioned Max Jacobs."

I had indeed. I had grown bored with the interview and was tired of humoring their fishing expedition. Allison seemed to sense this and to be willing to accommodate my efforts to move the interview along.

"It sounds like," said Allison, "most people in your social circle would consider the Jacobs another step or two down from the Wymarks."

I winced a little at his phrasing. Allison started another

anxious apology but I waved him off. "It's alright, Detective. I want to help you catch this killer, so let's talk turkey. Just understand this is a little embarrassing and difficult for me. And please, if you happen to repeat anything I say to anyone 'in my social circle,' as we're saying, please be a little—no, a lot—more delicate than we're being here."

Allison assured me that of course he would. I had my doubts, and I stole a quick, slightly amused glance at Leo, who was gazing at me calmly but seemed to understand. Maybe he would remind Allison when the time came. In any case, I started in on Max.

"Well, detectives, you may know that of all three of these families, I am and have been closest with the Jacobs. As I mentioned earlier, Max and my father were business partners for years.

"So let's look at the family, since you're interested in that angle." I paused for a moment, trying to think of all the relevant facts and how to express them. "I suggested earlier that, for someone who might want to make a reckoning of such things, the Turners were of greater social status than the Wymarks. I wouldn't even try to fit the Jacobs into that system. First of all, there's not really a family, there's just Max. And of course he's Jewish. There might have been a time, not so long ago, when that mattered to people who had opinions about the furnishings at the Knickerbocker Club, but during my lifetime caring about such things has been seen as tacky, and now, in the age of von Clapp, morally objectionable. But perhaps more to the point, he was born poor and made all his money himself—but what a lot he's made. And again, gentlemen," here I shifted in my chair a bit, "I will try to be as blunt as I can, although the words seem to stick in my throat. But…Max is a billionaire. Worth far more than Adam Wymark, probably more than the entire Wymark family, probably worth more than any one member or even one branch of the Turner family. So…" but here my ability to be frank reached its limits, and I just trailed off and let the detectives figure things out for themselves.

"So," said Allison, rushing to my rescue, "while Mr.

Jacobs might lack certain social and pedigreegial graces, he's got more money than most of the bluebloods can dream about."

"You express yourself, Detective, in a way that I wouldn't try to imitate—or contradict. But I'm afraid it all comes back to the same thing. If you want to understand these murders in terms of the rules or mores of my social world, there's really not much connecting the three victims, or their families."

I tried to say this with an air of summing things up, but of course I could only do so much to move the detectives along.

"I understand, Mr. Balfour," said Allison. "Let me ask you this, and please take your time thinking about an answer. Can you think of anything then, anything at all, that would connect the three victims?"

"Well, of course all three had been featured in the Vows column of *The New York Primrose*," I said and looked very hard at Allison, who to my surprise put his head down and nodded. Leo seemed as impassive as ever, though I could really only catch a glimpse of him out of the corner of my eye.

"And what does that tell you, Mr. Balfour," Allison asked. His discomfiture had only been momentary, and he turned the situation around brilliantly.

"Beyond the bare fact of the matter, very little, I'm afraid. So far as I know, the police have received no communication about the matter"—of course he gave away nothing here—"so there's no obvious reason why that would tie them together. On the other hand, three murders in three consecutive weeks does seem a bit much to be a coincidence. But then if it's not a coincidence, what's the motive? Just a madman killing people featured in the *Rose*'s Vows columns?"

Allison looked grave and set his hands on the table. "As I mentioned earlier, Mr. Balfour, we can't discuss our investigation. If we thought anyone was in imminent danger, of course we wouldn't sit on that information. But I'm afraid I can't say anything more than that. But if you can think of any reason those three might be connected, or why their profiles in the *Rose* might be related or might in any way stand out, please do let us know."

I nodded and made a motion to get up and leave, but apparently Allison wasn't finished.

"You've been very helpful," he said, "with your 'social circle,' as you put it, Mr. Balfour. But Mayflower families aren't the only ones with money in New York, especially these days."

"Yes, that's right," I said. I didn't add anything else, because I wasn't sure what he was driving at.

"New money, I guess you'd call it."

"Yes, I guess you would. And certainly there's some of that in my 'circle,' as we've taken to calling it. Though a lot of those people make their fortune here then go buy a sports team in Nashville or Minnesota or wherever and live there. Or of course they move to California and start investing in tech."

"Yes," said Allison, "'tech,' that wonderful, mysterious continent that just keeps giving us new marvels and riches." His irony here was so subtle I almost missed it. "One day Leo and I might even hope to invest in tech.

"But let me ask you, Mr. Balfour, these new money folks. They float into the city from wherever, make a bundle, and then…are they ever eager to get into these old money circles? Have you ever known anyone who wanted into the Yacht Club but didn't have the right manners, and went away with hard feelings?"

"I'm sure that has happened at times, but I'm afraid I can't think of anyone in particular, recently or any other time. The Turners and such hardly have the cachet of English aristocrats in the nineteenth century. I imagine the whole idea of 'old money' seems stodgy and irrelevant to someone from Utah who's made a billion dollars managing a hedge fund."

Leo spoke up. "Of course it's not just wealthy Americans in New York."

"No, that's true," I said. "These days the real money is as likely to be Chinese, Arab, or Russian as anything."

"And maybe some of these folks want that old money

53

respectability," said Leo. "Maybe a little more keenly than a hedge fund manager from Utah?"

"Yes, maybe," I said. "Though really, I don't think they care. They have their world and we have ours, and I don't think they have much interest in joining ours, Yacht Club or no."

"They just think all that is kind of quaint," asked Leo.

"To be perfectly honest, Detective, I don't think they think about it at all." I paused and thought for a minute. "Though, I suppose that as long as we're just spitballing, there might be another angle there. Perhaps the issue wasn't with envy from outsiders, but with the insiders' need for cash flow. And, well…"

"Maybe your associates went looking for a new line of credit," said Allison.

"Maybe from a network of investors that you may not know much about," I said.

"We've thought about that, Mr. Balfour," replied Allison, "especially in Mr. Wymark's case. We haven't found anything to suggest he was in any trouble along those lines, but we'll keep looking." I was surprised to hear Allison be so forthright, but after all he was just ruling out a very long shot.

"Yes," I said, "that sounds right. To be honest, I doubt that would happen, even with Jordan. He was kind of wild, but not really reckless in that way, and in any case the Wymarks are doing fine and it's hard to imagine him needing to go in debt to Russian mobsters or what have you. Just thought I would mention it, since we're sort of throwing things against the wall and seeing what sticks."

"We appreciate that, Mr. Balfour," said Allison. "And we appreciate your time. In complicated investigations like this, you never know what kind of odd fact or angle on something might lead you on to something that breaks the case. A lot of times after an interview like this, people will think of something later that seems relevant. We've covered a lot of ground here, so if that happens with anything at all, please get in touch. You've been very helpful today, and we'd be very glad to hear about anything else you might think could be important."

He and Leo both handed me cards, which I dutifully tucked away. "Now, sir, I believe we've taken enough of your time. Thanks again for being so quick to come down here and so helpful with our questions."

"Of course, Detective. Anything I can do to help catch whoever might be involved with all this."

I shook their hands and left the interview room, eager to leave but not to get back to work. Coming out onto the street felt very good. The air was really warm, even hot, and there was no doubt it was summer. I hadn't realized how stale the air in the interview room had been, but now walking out in the heat, a warm breeze moving the green leaves on the trees planted along the sidewalk, I felt like I was reemerging into life from some kind of underground crypt. I decided to walk around the area a bit before heading back to the office.

The police had given up almost nothing, which I suppose was to be expected. They certainly seemed open to the idea that the murders were connected by the *Rose* columns, or maybe by some hazier sense of resentment about class or status. But they seemed just as ready to believe each murder had its own separate motive. Max said they had a theory, but it was hard to tell if that was something he had half-fabricated or had actually forced out of them.

As I thought about it, though, things started to take a certain shape. The decisive thing seemed to be Allison saying that they would be handling the matter differently if they thought someone was in immediate danger. Surely then they didn't believe whoever was featured in this week's column might be targeted. Or were they trying to set a trap for someone? And for obvious reasons not telling me so as not to spread any alarm among my "social circle"? But that was absurd. They seemed interested in a possible connection but didn't appear to have any real reason to think there was one. In fact, the more I thought about it, the more it seemed they must not have thought there was any real relationship between the killings, through the *Rose* or otherwise. Setting some kind of trap, or just waiting to see, was far too great a risk to run, especially given the people involved.

Still, this was all fairly speculative on my part, and I was not at all confident in my abilities to read either man's mind. But at the very least I was glad that we hadn't gotten into my own family's financial history, which we would have no doubt parsed in excruciating detail—how my mother's family fortune had been divided through the generations until she was the last van Horne left in New York, married to my father, while the others all absconded to Virginia and California; how my father was the only child of an only child of a venerable Manhattan family, made a great fortune with Max Jacobs in real estate in the 1980s, and had latterly managed to lose it all when he tried his hand at the new financialized economy. I thought for sure we were headed down that path when we started talking family histories, but Allison wasn't interested, or felt like he had to hold back, or perhaps just already knew. Small mercies.

I eventually made my way back to the office and worked late to try to catch up, though there was no catching up on everything we had to do at that point. For hours I watched figures strut and fret their hour upon the stage before dissolving into nothingness, annihilated as they collapsed into a bottomless pit of debt and loss. Eventually I left and had a quiet dinner alone at Stefano's. By the time I got home it was basically time to go to bed so I could get back into the office the first thing next morning.

But I couldn't sleep—despite the hours of tedious, draining work after my meeting with the police I was still tense from it, and everything seemed uncertain and dangerous. So I got up and turned on the television. A white guy pushing forty was being interviewed somewhere. "I said, 'Why doesn't the Vatican just give all its money to the poor?' 'Why doesn't Jake Beilzobos,' she said back. 'That's different,' I said. 'He made his money by providing a product. That's how the marketplace works.' 'Well then,' she said, 'in that case the Catholic Church got its money by providing spiritual goods and services.'

"And I tell you, Billie, that changed everything for me. I

said, 'My God, you're right.' And I let it go. I'm not religious myself—it seems a little kooky, to be perfectly honest, and I've heard that if you're at all serious about it there's absolutely no money in it, no return on investment. But I see the whole thing in a completely different light now."

I turned the channel. There was another white guy sitting in another chair somewhere, also being interviewed. He was older, tanned, salt and pepper hair brushed back and shirt open. He looked generous and relaxed, and although I couldn't help envying him for that I also couldn't help liking him. He was talking to a smaller man wearing a suit and glasses who was peering at him like a mole trying to make sense of sunlight.

"Now, John Eaton was one of Andrew Jackson's most important advisors and friends," said the moleman. "And in this film, you made him black."

"Yes, we did," said the other man, smiling serenely. "Any time you're making a film, or really just telling a story, you have to start by asking two very simple questions: who is the audience, and what do they want? Today, we live in politicized times. You have to take that into account when you're thinking about the audience—remember, who are they, and what do they want? In these political times, you have two basic groups, left and right. Ah, but they don't agree on anything, so you can't possibly come up with a story that will make them both happy, right? Wrong. What do they want? The left wants more diversity, so you make him black. But then will the right get angry? No, because what are we presenting, racial tension? No, there's none of that. Eaton is Jackson's friend, his ally and counselor, and no one mentions race. The left loves that, and so does the right. Why? Because you're giving them an America, an American past, without racism. It's the world they're always saying it is, the world as they want it to be. And both sides love this, by the way, they both want to believe this. So you make them both happy, and it couldn't be more simple" he said, beaming his secret at the other man.

"But in these politicized times, what about the Jesus folks?"

"Ah," said the salt-and-pepper mane, leaning back and smiling wisely. "We did some research and, you know, there don't seem to be any of them out there anymore, at least not enough to matter. For all intents and purposes, they're just right-wing. And you can ask anyone, anyone who's involved in politics, entertainment, anything where you need to understand and reach an audience and they'll all say the same. The religious groups, the so-called Christians and such, they're gone now. In fact, it's not clear that they ever actually existed."

I changed the channel again. A basketball game was on. I find the NBA confusing now, it seems like half the teams have yellow uniforms. So I had no idea who was playing, but hoped the game would help me fall asleep. The team with bright yellow uniforms brought the ball down the court; the point guard drove into the paint, then snapped the ball out to a forward who was standing alone about twelve feet from the basket. He flipped the ball up and, as we used to say when I was younger, *swish*. The team with yellow lettering and piping on their dark jerseys brought the ball down; their point guard moved to his left in a series of feints and dashes before eventually passing the ball to someone curling up behind him. The ball moved from one end of the perimeter to the other in a series of languid passes, back and forth like a pendulum, before in a quick, inspired flick it again found its way into the hands of another open player who executed another perfect jump shot. So it went, back and forth, the ball changing hands in a series of passes and shots, some crisp and premeditated, others more frantic and improvised, but almost always finding its home at the bottom of the basket. It was like watching money circulate among the people in "my circle." Everyone knew what to do with it when they got it, and when it passed out of their hands it was only temporary, only a matter of time before it came back to them and they made good with it again. All except for us, of course. We had managed to bounce the ball right off our foot and out of bounds, and now we were being sent into the crowd, into the upper decks, to pay two hundred dollars for a seat in another zip code and another twenty-two for a hot dog that tasted like pocket lint and was crawling with e. coli.

The steady rhythm of the men moving up and down the court and the almost flawless jump shooting should have been soothing, but I didn't feel myself getting tired. Watching it all I knew this was what we wanted to be as a country, what we wanted to think of when we thought of America. The health, the vitality, the broad smiles and the fluid, effortless energy, the mind-bending athleticism, at times stunningly violent and sudden, at others effortlessly, achingly elegant—this was everything we wanted to believe we were. Who cares about the stories of violence and abuse trailing behind almost every player out there? Who cares about the infinite, ravening maws of poverty and murder that they escaped from, the neighborhoods turned into hell on earth for the profit of the Sinaloa Cartel and Smith and Wesson, the numberless souls swallowed up in them, all the ciphers who didn't make it to be one of the ten men standing under a scoreboard that weighed more than a family of elephants and cost more than most the country would ever see to raise their children?

Eventually there was a time out. One guy was standing on the baseline, bouncing the ball at shoulder height; another guy wanted to talk to the referee under the basket. They were so at ease, so apparently unaware of anything other than goofing around with the ball or wanting to tell the official about a foul he missed. I envied them. Outside the night was dark and dead, but beneath the coat of silence I felt like there was something sinister and empty, something stalking the deserted streets, watching the traffic lights change for no one, coiled and merciless in the sleeping shadows. I realized there was nothing out there, or nothing more than the passing time, my envy and regret at somehow having lived through all the doors shutting around me and not noticing once. Somewhere out there in the darkness, I felt sure for a moment, there was a time when I could have become a man wearing a yellow uniform, running up and down wooden courts and sinking graceful jump shots, and been perfectly content with all that.

But that time was gone now, it was being smuggled away somewhere out there in the dark, harder to find than the monster I imagined lurking between the brownstones. The game came back from commercial but I couldn't take it, the men almost all somehow younger than me, so sure of themselves and their purpose and what they were doing chasing that little bit of rubber over a polished floor. I stood up and went to the window. There was a slight breeze moving the branches of the trees along the street; I thought I saw something glide and glint behind them. The stop light changed, but there was no one there. The wind blew a little harder, and I went back to bed.

Chapter Four

An Evening In Chelsea

It's a little dreary, when you think about it, the way we can never really escape the fog of ourselves. Other people float up to us like bodies from the bottom of a lake, made of our memories, hopes, disappointments, pains, and pleasures—which is ultimately just to say that they're made of our fear and desire. In most of us fear is stronger than desire, and we always have reasons not to act, but in some few desire is stronger than fear.

And so I think about you, watching all this, taking sides, coming to play your own role in it. I think it has something to do with me, and that in my telling of it you find something of yourself revealed. But perhaps I flatter myself, and your reasons for all this are entirely your own. Either way, do you know what it is that is moving you, fear or desire?

I didn't sleep well that night after talking with the police, but at least that made it easier to get up and pass through the doors of the fast fading Balfour and Son the next morning. As I approached the office I saw Dad coming toward me on the sidewalk, his shoulders stooped and his head bowed. It saddened me to see him so downcast, but in fact I had been making my way along the sidewalk in much the same posture, still mulling over everything I had said and heard during my interview with the police. From a distance we must have been a strange sight, approaching each other with nearly identical deportment, neither one seeing the other, mirror images except for about thirty years.

When we were finally within a few feet of each other I called out to him; otherwise I think he would have walked right past me without noticing.

"Oh, hello, son," he said, rather distractedly. "I'm leaving the office."

"Yes, so I gather."

"Yes," he said, shaking himself out of his ambulatory brown study. "We might have a buyer."

"Oh?" I lit up a bit at this, but it didn't seem to be taking any weight off his shoulders.

"Yes, a group of Russians might want to buy the whole operation. I'm off to meet their representative now. I'm glad to see you coming in, but there's actually nothing for you to do now. If they buy us out, they'll want everything. The whole thing is happening rather quickly, all this week. So no need to press on with the filings just now. You can hang out in your office until I get back—unless you have something else you need to do."

"No, that's good. I'll see you when you get back. Good luck," I added, rather uncertainly.

"Yes, thanks. I hope it will be good news, and sooner rather than later." And he went off, his head dropping again at once, just as abstracted as when I had first caught sight of him.

I went up to my office and thought I would check the *Primrose* to see if there was any news about the murders, and about the role the paper itself might have in them. The detectives seemed to be playing that angle down, but if word hadn't leaked out the paper itself might have noticed. There was no mention of it anywhere, but given my mood and preoccupations that morning, a particular story did catch my eye.

In Texas, A New Church Takes Gun Enthusiasm To Another Plane

Strange Fruit, Texas. A new church in this Texas town literally worships guns. And it's gaining followers.

The Church of the Gun was founded last year by Jim Vaughn and Dale Brodie. Worshippers gather in an empty room with at least one gun, and often several, displayed at the head of the room. Congregants prostrate themselves before the guns, sing songs to and about the guns, and express spontaneous enthusiasm by shaking, jumping, and running around the room, in much the same manner as Pentecostal Christians. There has been some talk of moving the ceremonies to an actual shooting range, though some members of the church have expressed reservations about people in the throes of enthusiasm handling loaded firearms. Most, however, have condemned these skeptics for their lack of faith in the gun.

"We just figured it was time to stop talking and start doing more to show our respect and reverence for our guns," says Mr. Vaughn when asked about the origins of the church. "It was time to give them the pride of place they deserve."

Mr. Brodie agrees. "It just kind of came together one day. There was probably another negative liberal media story about a shooting or something, and we just felt we needed to bow down and pray to some of our guns. Then we thought, 'Hey, I bet a lot of other folks feel this way, too.'"

Membership in the church begins with a simple profession of faith: "I do not own the gun, the gun owns me. It is my master, my lord, and my savior. I submit to the gun completely."

The church has had surprising success in a region that is often known for the strength of its conviction in a certain strain of American Protestant Christianity. The Church of the Gun has incorporated some aspects of evangelical worship, but few worshippers seem to see any tension between being Christians and worshipping instruments of death.

"Being a Christian doesn't mean being weak, being crucified or something like that," explains Mr. Brodie. "It means shooting someone who wants to take your TV, and being proud of it!"

"Jesus invented the AR-15," adds Mr. Vaughn vehemently. "And anyone who says otherwise is just fake news!"

Things between the two founders were not always so harmonious, however. When trying to decide on songs the congregation could sing, Mr. Brodie suggested Lou Reed's

"The Gun." Mr. Vaughn thought it presented firearms in too negative a light, but Mr. Brodie thought any mention of guns should automatically be taken as positive, indeed reverent. "He had me on the ropes there for a minute," recalls Mr. Vaugh. "But then my nephew looked this Lou Reed fella up on the internet. Turns out he's some Jew from New York who has sex with other men. Well, I said to Dale, 'So what, Dale, are we going to sing hymns written by some homosexual New York City Jew?' That brought him around right quick."

In consultation with the congregation, Mr. Vaugh and Mr. Brodie considered commissioning hymns from the country star Bucky Beauregard. There was some question about whether or not to use church funds for such a project, but when Mr. Beauregard heard about the church, he volunteered to write the hymns for them free of charge.

"Bucky's life has always been centered on the four F's: firearms, flag, family, and faith," said a spokeswoman. "He was happy to help with such an inspiring project to give our guns the veneration they deserve."

Mr. Beauregard's representative also shared some lines from a song he is working on for the church, tentatively titled either "Hymn to Gun Almighty" or "How Great Guns Are."

'Bout all I love more than the red, white, and blue
Is the feel in my hand of my ol'.22
I love dirt roads and family, but then even more
Love to praise the AR-15, glorify that .44

So come on, everybody, let's teach them liberals a lesson
Dig deep and buy more guns from ol' Smith and Wesson
And if you got that open carry, go on and flaunt it
And buy more guns and ammo, that's how Jesus would want it

Some of these lyrics give evidence of another unique feature of the new church: it will accept, and indeed encourage, corporate sponsorship. Representatives from both Mr. Beauregard and Smith and Wesson declined to comment on whether the gun manufacturer had "provided the singer *with any promotional consideration," as the representative from Smith and Wesson put it. But Mr. Vaugh and Mr. Brodie confirm that their church already features corporate logos and other forms of advertising from several firearm companies, including Smith and Wesson. The duo also confirm that they are looking into including advertising from other companies, foremost among them Walmart and Chick-fil-A, though they will not say whether they are already in contact with these companies.*

The church is attracting younger members as well. One young man, who asked to remain anonymous, spoke at length about the importance of guns to his life and his admiration for the church and its founders. "Someone told me about a guy in the early Christian Church who castrated himself to show how important his faith was to him," the young man said. "They asked me if I would be willing to do the same." His face grows solemn as he discusses a subject to which he has clearly given serious thought. "I chewed it over for a bit," he says, "and although I would hate to give up porn, I think I have to do it for the gun."

I was delivered from this tale of heartland idiocy by a knock at my office door. It was Maura Collins, Balfour and Son's resident publicity maven. We had little use for her at this point, and even less means with which to recompense her, but she was staying on to help us close things out.

"Glad I caught you," she said.

"Oh, I'm not going anywhere," I said, motioning at the piles of paper on my desk.

"I might be able to help with that," she said. "I wanted to invite you to the opening of Inez's art show tonight. Free booze and a little food," she added, raising her eyebrows. "Doors open at seven. It's in Chelsea."

Instantly I thought back to the last time I had been to an art gallery in Chelsea, and the attendant circumstances. It had been one of Alana's friends, also named Alana if I was remembering correctly, a Vardlinian in spirit if not in fact. She had done some kind of "visual installment" at a gallery there, which was basically just a screen playing some video she had shot in Thailand. It was supposed to be about the production of cheap clothes, so there were a couple of t-shirts and, for reasons that escaped me, an old shag carpet strewn around the table and floor in front of the screen. She filmed a cart carrying linens somewhere through the streets of Bangkok, then another carrying clothes to a market somewhere in the same city. A child was riding in the first cart, smiling sardonically at the camera. It was also in the second cart, but the image was crudely superimposed on the actual film. These scenes were interspersed with one-second clips of people shopping for clothes at a department store in New Jersey. It was about four minutes of this on endless loop.

Alana was fairly good friends with the *auteur*, so I had something of a behind-the-scenes view of the actual production of the film. The other Alana had initially wanted to go to Bangladesh but had been scared off by tales of poverty. She chose Thailand because it was the only country in the region any of her friends had been to, though she later bitterly regretted her decision when she realized no one associated Thailand with cheap clothes (I think I myself spoke to her twice and both times managed to ask, "Are you sure you don't mean Bangladesh," which produced a delightful agitation). But she found spending time in Bangkok "deeply triggering," so she made several trips to Hong Kong during the few weeks she was there, staying at a luxury hotel each time. Then there was the question of the child, whom she couldn't find for the second segment of filming. So when she returned to New York she asked a friend to help her edit the child into the film of the finished clothes in the cart. The final result was rather less than convincing, which led to several deeply acrimonious exchanges on social media.

In the event, several people thought the poorly edited child looked unearthly, and concluded that the film was making a point about the human cost of cheap textiles. Indeed, this was the point made in the brief write-up the installation received in one of the free weeklies, written by an intern hoping for a job with the media company owned by Alana's father. The overall production costs of the four-minute film ran into six figures (most of which went to the jaunts to Hong Kong), but it was a small price for Alana's father to pay for such a masterful critique of capitalism.

I was recalling all this in my mind and, I'm sorry to say, probably not listening at all to Maura as she ran on merrily, presumably describing her fiancée's work. Abruptly I just blurted out, "I don't want to go to—" I stopped myself, but it was too late.

Maura stopped mid-syllable and looked at me, her lips pursed in sudden surprise. "What's that?"

"Chelsea." Maura blinked at me, perplexed. "I don't want to go to Chelsea. I mean, it's not that I don't want to. I'm just not sure I'm dressed for it. I'm sure everyone there will be quite fashionable, and I'll be dressed like the working drudge I am."

"Oh, don't worry about that," she said, and waved her hand anxiously. She seemed uncomfortable so I went ahead and told her the story of my last visit to a Chelsea art gallery, trying not to make it obvious I had been ignoring her. I really did appreciate Maura, and hoped to continue working with her after we had finished at Balfour and Son. But the truth is I didn't really want to go see Inez's show, though it had to be better than Alana's. Inez, I recalled, had been in the military and had even deployed to an active combat zone. What if her work was about the grim reality of war or some such, and I had to try to manage a serious and compassionate reaction? But there was nothing for it, and I resigned myself to go as I launched into my own tale, making a mental note not to joke about having PTSD regarding Chelsea galleries. As I explained my aversion to Chelsea Maura relaxed a little, but still seemed somewhat uneasy, maybe even offended. I tried to assuage her by telling her about my meeting with the police the previous day and how I hadn't yet recovered my usual cheerful disposition. As I expected, she asked several astute questions but didn't seem overly interested in the matter. The conversation did, however, seem to put us back on better terms. I told her I was looking forward to the opening that evening and promised to take her and Inez out for a drink afterwards.

Maura left my office and I killed time for an hour or two, careful not to subject myself to any more of the world as it appeared in the pages of the *Primrose*. Eventually Dad appeared in the doorway with a hangdog look on his face. The Russians were not interested and it was back to work, though to what end I really couldn't see. So I went about my undertaker's business for the rest of the day and into the early evening, then got ready to leave for the party. I had a couple of Tom Ford jackets in the closet of my office; the lighter one, rather serendipitously, perfectly harmonized with the cream-colored shirt I was wearing. I put it on and went to tell Dad I was leaving for the gallery. He frowned.

"I know I gave you the morning off, but we need to make up that time now. I need you to help me get through all this work. There's no time for gallery parties, especially when you were gone half of yesterday."

"Dad, I could hardly refuse to meet with the police. And I'm not going to this party tonight for the open bar. This is Inez, Maura's fiancée. This is important to Maura, and making an appearance is the least I can do after everything she's done for us."

"Tell that to our creditors," Dad said grumpily, and bowed his head back down to the splayed mass of papers on his desk, like a vulture hunkering down over a carcass.

That brief encounter with Dad, and in fact the earlier one with Maura, left me feeling irritated and on edge. I realized this was falling as hard on Dad as it was on me, but I still really didn't appreciate being caught between dueling guilt trips. But I resolved to put on a good face as I entered the gallery, which was a small, square room with high ceilings. There were only a few people there; Maura and Inez were in the corner talking with a few men. I approached the video screen, which was in an alcove in the back of the room, to take in Inez's work unobserved by her or Maura.

The lighting in the main room was a little low, but it was much darker in the alcove. What light there was had an odd but subtle blueish tint to it, though it seemed to be very gradually shifting back and forth along some spectrum. The screen was set into the wall, and there were various grayish forms moving across it. They seemed eerie and spectral in the blue light. Sometimes they briefly looked like faces, decrepit and sunken or contorted in agony or sorrow. Other times they would, for just a split second, resolve themselves into what looked like scenes of violence, or freakish mass convulsions. Or was this all my imagination, a kind of animated Rorschach test? A strange robotic voice was intoning the lyrics to some kind of text or song, with echoing effects that were only enhanced, or perhaps created, by the visual effects in that small space. I could only make out stray words here and there, but the metallic voice seemed to be telling a story about a judge and a trial and fighting and dying.

Over the screen, "Johnny 99" was written in small, black lettering. Under the screen, written in separate columns on either side, were two short quotations. The first was from a *Washington Post* column by George Will; it opined that Bruce Springsteen was not a "whiner" and that songs about closed factories didn't seem to diminish the dime store patriotism Will heard in "Born in the U.S.A." The second, by Greil Marcus, was about executions and lotteries and the rich living as gods and nihilistic murders as acts of rebellion in a world where wealth and status had annihilated every other value. The whole thing gave me a creepy, uncanny sensation, as of course it was meant to, but this was accompanied by another feeling, maybe even more unpleasant, that I was somehow irritated that Maura's fiancée had talent, certainly enough to produce an effect in me. Suddenly I heard a voice behind me.

"What do you think, Ethan?" It was Maura. I turned around, somewhat startled, and she was standing there smiling quietly at me.

"Oh…interesting. Quite the sound effects. I was just wondering if someone had slipped me some LSD earlier."

Maura frowned at me, and seemed almost irritated. "You can't treat everything as a joke forever, Ethan," she said, and looked at me steadily. I realized that she wasn't so much irritated as disappointed with me. This made me feel oddly flushed and not a little irritated myself, though I tried to hide it all under a look of surprise. I wasn't sure how to respond, and fortunately didn't have to, as just then Inez joined us with two middle-aged men in tow.

Inez was an astonishingly beautiful woman, though she kept her hair short in a way that sharpened her features and made her seem, at first glance, more striking. I had met her once or twice before, and she was friendly to me in that exaggerated but clipped way people have with someone they barely know themselves but who is close to someone important to them. "Hello, Ethan. It's so good to see you here," she said with a fixed smile as she reached out her hand to me.

"Yes, thank you so much for inviting me, Inez," I said, grasping her hand and, I hoped, smiling more naturally than she. "I was just admiring your work. I found it unexpected and powerful and, to be perfectly frank, a little disturbing— but I mean that in the best way." I was conscious of Maura standing beside me as I said this, but I couldn't turn and see her reaction, if any.

"Oh," she said simply, and gave a little laugh and looked down, embarrassed but genuine for the moment. She then introduced me to the two men with her, who were the gallery owners. One was named Gus, the other Alfie. They were both wearing white dinner jackets and black ties, which was a little ridiculous for Manhattan in early June but seemed somehow appropriate in the setting. Alfie was tall, with a thick mane of brown hair, rather tan but with a somewhat unnatural hue. His body was lean but his face and throat were a little fleshy, and he had a tendency to look over the heads of the people he was talking to, staring off into the distance, sometimes with a slightly wild look in his eye. Gus, on the other hand, was shorter, hair and beard buzzed down to a silver stubble, blue eyes peering out from behind dark-rimmed glasses. He spoke with a British accent and wore a constant, slight ironic smile. I instinctively liked him better than Alfie, but there was no question Alfie was pulling the dinner jacket off much better than Gus.

They both praised Inez and talked about what an honor it was to be launching what would doubtless be a breathtaking career. Then almost instantly, and rather to my surprise, the conversation switched to Jordan Wymark's murder.

"Did you know there was a shooting just a few blocks from here recently," said Gus. "A fatal shooting," he added significantly, and raised his eyebrows at us. His eyes had a kind of questioning, searching quality that made me a little uneasy, though I was also interested in what he had to say about the shooting.

"There's been all kinds of talk about it," Alfie said with some enthusiasm, as if it were all just a good bit of gossip. "This wealthy young man who was killed—well, he wasn't unknown to some of the boys down in our neighborhood. Someone heard from the police that there might have been a romantic motive to the whole thing. Or maybe he was lured into the alley to be robbed, and somehow or other ended up dead out of it. Of course," he added with a sudden, lurid thrill in his voice, "it's terrible to think someone might be targeting gay men. It might even be a serial killer!"

"Yes," Gus cut in, evidently unimpressed, "but a couple of very wealthy young women have also been killed now. I've heard there may be some connection between the murders, though everyone is apparently very reluctant to say anything publicly."

Again I was aware of Maura's presence next to me, and this time a little more anxious. The last thing I wanted was to have my personal connection to the matter dragged into the middle of this conversation, and Maura knew me well enough to know that. But if she was upset or irritated by any of our exchanges that day, she chose not to act on those feelings. "Ethan may actually have known one of those women," she said vaguely.

Alfie instantly shot me a look of rapt attention, while Gus

just raised his eyebrows archly and waited to see what I had to say. Inez had grown quiet and seemed to fade into the background behind the two men.

"Yes, I did. I actually knew all three of the victims, though none of them very well."

"Oh, my," said Gus. "So maybe you did it."

"You never know," I returned. "But really, I'm afraid I don't know much at all, perhaps less than you. There's this theory floating around about the Vows column in *The New York Primrose*. Apparently each victim had been featured in one of the previous week's columns."

"Ah," said Gus, "a good populist murder. About time, I say."

"No need for something so far-fetched," said Alfie, "when the obvious facts are staring you in the face."

"I have no idea if there's anything to it," I said, a little defensively. "I've just heard people mention it."

"Yes, of course," said Alfie. "I'm the same way, I can only speak about what I know. And I am quite convinced of this: the Wymark boy may have been killed because of his wedding, but it had nothing to do with the newspaper announcement."

"Surely you don't think the *Rose* columns are just a massive coincidence," said Inez.

"I've heard even the police think there's a connection with the columns," said Maura, with admirable brevity.

"Ah, but my dears, the police are no match for our very own private consulting detective here, Alfie Sandborn. Though I'm not quite sure I can see you in a deerstalker hat, Alfie," said Gus, and looked up at his thick mop quizzically. The rest of us laughed.

"You can all laugh at me," Alfie said, becoming somewhat shrill, "but I know what I believe: that it was no accident that the Wymark boy was killed where and when he was."

"No one's laughing at you, Alfie," said Gus tartly. "But what are the chances that the members of three different billionaire families are killed in three weeks and they're not connected?"

"What are the chances that they are," Alfie shot back defiantly. "First of all, they're not even all billionaires. Only the last one was. The first one didn't have nearly as much money as her, and Wymark was way behind both of them. Still a very comfortable family, obviously. But people are being blinded by the fact that they were all from wealthy families—in fact they had nothing else in common. The last one was a Jewish girl, not just a model but a legendary beauty, whose father made all his money in our lifetimes. The first one was supposedly from a Mayflower family, or descended from Martha Washington, or some claptrap like that. Wealthy, very old money, but a very low profile. No one had heard of her until she was murdered, poor dear. Then Wymark was from a much younger family, people who made all their money in finance and still lived rooted in that world. He was a playboy and a hedonist and frankly quite reckless in everything—completely unlike the two girls, who were nothing like each other.

"And the first girl, Jane Brown or whatever unbelievably dreary name she had, was murdered in her own apartment. Strangled on her couch, we've all heard about it. Obviously it was someone who knew her, the motive was personal. Her fiancé, what's his name? Beers or Stabbs or something?"

"Speers," I put in.

"Yes, that's right, Speers. Anyway, he's a horrid little brute. You know Olivier," he said to Gus, "he works at Malcolm Warfield's, where this Speers boy buys his suits. Olivier says he's a dead-eyed toad. Mark my word, he's behind his fiancée's murder, even if the police can't bring it home to him."

"Alfie, dear, you've never even met either one of them," Gus said, smiling.

Alfie turned and gave him a long, incredulous look. "I've met both of them a thousand times. They're the most ordinary people in the world, even if they have the most extraordinary sums of money. She's vain, easily distracted, and likes attention. He's jealous, none too bright, and easily offended. This same sad, dumb, tawdry little story plays out

73

every day. It makes you want to just hide your face in your hands and go off to live on a mountain somewhere."

I smiled inwardly at Alfie's characterizations of Charlotte and Andrew. They were superficial but highly apt. But he wasn't done. I couldn't tell if it was just his pique at the way we reacted to his initial comments, or if he had actually thought all this out, but it turned out he had quite a case to make.

"And think about the alternative," Alfie continued, the rest of us leaning in, listening rather more attentively now, though he gave not the slightest indication of noticing. "Whoever was invited into Sue Drab's apartment and strangled her while she sat on her couch supposedly wants the other two dead for some reason? If it's a random series of murders, the killer just picking them out because of their wealth or their status or the fact that their weddings were announced in the *Primrose* or something, there's no way he could have gotten into Little Miss Clod's building, much less her apartment. The last one, meanwhile, Helen of Troy, was poisoned at some exclusive, high-toned party—we don't have any idea who did it, or why, or even if she was the intended victim!"

Gus was looking at him appreciatively now. "Alright, Alfie, you raise some good points," he said. "So then who do you think did it?"

"There is no 'it,' Augustus, that's what I keep trying to explain to you. The last murder, the Abrams girl, or whatever her name was, is the only mystery, and in that case we don't even know enough to speculate on a motive. The first girl, Maude Clod, was obviously killed by her little yacht-set sociopath fiancé, or maybe a lover or someone else close to her if you don't like my theory. No one else could have gotten close to her like that. And Wymark was killed a stone's throw from here in a little back alley, not strangled or poisoned but shot. There's only one reason you get killed in a back alley on the fringes of the gay village—maybe two, if you think it could have been a drug deal gone horribly wrong. Either way, that's obviously not who killed the Jones girl on her couch, and it's just as obviously not who poisoned

Aphrodite at her champagne party. And, like I said before, that's the only real mystery. Who killed *her*, and why?"

"So who did," Gus asked brightly.

"How should I know? Maybe that really was a case of someone striking out at the ultra-wealthy. Maybe one glass was poisoned at random, and she just happened to pick that one up. Pure bad luck for the poor thing."

"That's terrible," cried Inez.

"But why only poison one glass if you wanted to strike a blow against the rich," I asked. "Everyone at that party was wealthy. Why not poison all the glasses, or at least a few?"

Alfie shrugged. "Maybe the killer's hands were shaking and he spilled most of the poison. Maybe he has some oddball fixation on numerology and can only kill one person at a time. Or maybe next he'll kill two people at once, then three, and so on until he's caught. But that's the thing about having a *genuine* mystery—almost anything might be the solution!

"But, so far as that goes, maybe she was indeed the target all along. Maybe it was an old rival, tipped over the edge by her recent wedding, who saw this as an opportunity to kill her. I mean, from what I understand the girl had absolutely everything, and you know that doesn't always inspire the most generous feelings in people, especially other women— I'm sorry girls, but you know it's true. Or maybe her new husband was also jealous. Or maybe someone stood to gain financially. Just a small fraction of that immense fortune would be enough to move quite a few people to murder, sad to say."

"You know," said Gus, "you might really be on to something here, Alfie. Three murders, three different methods. Serial killers never do that, do they? Don't they always kill in the same way? Methodically, compulsively."

"Yes, exactly. And if he has a gun and is willing to use it, why not just stalk them all and shoot them here or there?"

"Well, perhaps not all of them had Wymark's proclivity for skulking around dark alleys late at night," said Gus. "It's easier to quietly poison someone than to quietly shoot them."

"Yes, maybe," Alfie replied. "But a serial killer targeting him because he saw his picture in the paper wouldn't have any way of knowing that. He just happened to decide to stalk Wymark with a gun, and was rewarded by finding him in a dark alley one night? By himself, for no apparent reason, just standing around there? And these other, completely different methods just happened to work for the two girls? The most versatile—and the luckiest—serial killer in history.

"Let's be honest, Augustus, you and I know what's happening here, even if these children don't. The police have always been a problem for gay men, and the fact that they're not as bad now doesn't make them good. Half of them are making jokes about Wymark's death being a homo-cide, the other half couldn't care less, and won't care until there at least three or four more murdered men. If this is someone targeting gay men, there's nothing that says this is his first victim. He could have murdered several already, and is just getting more aggressive and impetuous now. You know I hate to even think this, Gus, but let's not forget about Toronto already. This could easily be another case like that. Though, I grant, it's certainly within the realm of possibility that it was just some terrible impulse or accident, birthed in the course of an unsuccessful drug deal or argument. I certainly hope that was it."

Gus looked like he was about to say something in response, but just then a stylish couple came up to them. Gus and Alfie both greeted them warmly, and were almost instantly pulled away from our little group, trailing excited questions about Berlin and someone named Dieter in their wake. Inez also went off to greet other people, who were filing in in greater numbers now. Maura and I talked for a few more minutes, then Inez called her over to introduce her to someone. I milled about for an hour or so, making small talk with various strangers, then the event ended. Inez, Maura, Gus, Alfie, and I reconvened in the middle of the room as we watched the last few people leave. The strange metallic sounds were still coming from the alcove, even more unsteady and distorted now, and they made a weird, menacing counterpoint to the ebbing sounds of celebration. I suggested we all go out for drinks to continue Inez's big night, but Gus and Alfie had a late dinner party they had to attend. I wanted to take the girls for more champagne to somewhere nice in the Village or Tribeca, but they were strangely insistent on just finding the nearest bar (maybe because Maura was worried about keeping me out late—always the good soldier). Maura went to a back room with Gus and Alfie to get something while Inez, somewhat to my surprise, drifted outside. Left there alone in the middle of the now empty room I felt somewhat awkward, then a bit uncomfortable when the sounds from the alcove asserted themselves. I followed Inez outside.

I came out into the street and found Inez standing by herself, gazing into a window. I walked up to her and saw she was looking at a nativity scene. I looked around, trying to find the desecration, but it wasn't an art gallery but an actual pawn shop that had somehow survived on this street in Chelsea—and even more strangely had a nativity scene in its front window in June. I looked at Inez to comment on it and saw her eyes were bright and her cheeks wet with tears. I started a little and she seemed only then to realize I was there.

"I was just thinking of my mother," she said. "When I was little we would put up a nativity scene like this. Every year she would tell me and my sister how wonderful it must have been, how the angels had sung to Christ in heaven but now the Blessed Virgin was singing songs to the baby Jesus that the angels had never known."

Uncomfortable with this display of emotion, I tried to steer the conversation back to small talk. "Does your mother live with you here in New York?"

She seemed to shake her head without moving. "She died. Years ago."

Just then, and to my relief, Maura came out of the gallery. In my exaggerated enthusiasm to see her I waved and asked how I had lost her on the way out. Inez turned away and composed herself, though I somehow sensed it was entirely for my benefit, which caused me some kind of strange discomfort that soon turned into vague annoyance. Maura didn't seem to notice any of this and we set off down the street, Inez keeping her face toward the buildings we passed, looking for a bar in the neighborhood.

We found a place a couple of blocks away. In that generally fashionable area we somehow lighted upon an establishment that seemed like it was designed to embody the lowest common denominator between frat boys, tourists, and hopeless drunks. We sat outside at a table on the sidewalk, but it was still grim. Inez asked for a strawberry daiquiri and the waitress just stared at her blankly. We ended up getting a pitcher of beer for five dollars.

The waitress left us and we exchanged a few banalities about what a pleasant summer evening it was, then fell into a kind of collective absent-minded silence. Maura was looking back down the street toward the gallery, seeming rather more thoughtful than Inez or me. "You know," she said, "it's so sad the way Alfie sees everything through the lens of the struggles of the gay community. He was so convinced that the police have these three murders completely wrong, just because they can't take a murder in the gay neighborhood seriously."

"Oh, let's not drag all of that back up," I said. "Tonight should be about Inez and the triumph of her debut."

"Actually, I've been talking about my work all night," Inez said, somewhat shyly. "I'm more than happy to discuss something else—unless there was something you wanted to say about it, Ethan."

"No, nothing beyond what I said before, that I found it challenging, in the best possible way." She smiled, but in a forced, hurried way that suggested she didn't fully believe what I had said. Our interactions remained stilted and awkward, which I found a little embarrassing but mostly flattering, since she seemed solicitous of my good opinion.

"Well, then," Inez said, "we could talk about 'the case,' if you'd like. Unless of course you're tired of the subject, Ethan. Or it upsets you," she suddenly added, the thought apparently having just come to her and somewhat shocked her.

"No, it really doesn't, though it's very kind of you to think of that, Inez. It is of course sad to see them all taken like this —each one was so lively in their own way—but it's a long time since I was close with any of them." Inez nodded and seemed to relax a little.

"Well, I wasn't even suggesting we bring the murders back up. I was just thinking how sad it was that Alfie seemed to see everything in terms of the injustices of the past, and to be convinced they would never end. Perfectly understandable, but sad."

"Yes, but if it comes to that, I don't think he was really doing that at all. I think he made rather an interesting case that the murders aren't related," I said.

"You do?"

"Sure. What evidence do we have that there's any connection at all? It's not even circumstantial. There is nothing tying these three murders together other than those newspaper announcements—and there's actually nothing tying the murders to those announcements! And if you look at it the way Alfie was—that we have obvious explanations for the first two murders, even if no one can yet make an arrest, and Bella's murder is the only mystery—the entire thing looks totally different."

"I suppose," said Maura. "But three weeks straight now someone from those columns gets murdered? What are the chances that's just a coincidence?"

"Well, and what are the chances that three premeditated murders were committed by the same person, and there's no evidence linking them? Forget evidence—there's not even any superficial similarity between them. Just this one odd fact that they all had their weddings announced in the *Primrose*, which doesn't seem to throw any light on the case at all. Alfie was certainly right about that."

Out of the corner of my eye I noticed Inez quietly working everything over in her mind. I suspected she had been fascinated by the subject ever since it first came up. "You know," she said smiling, "if this were a murder mystery, the newspaper announcements might be a ruse. The murderer might just want to kill one of the victims for his own personal reasons, and be killing the others to mislead the police."

"Yes," I said, "that is an interesting thought. But then it takes us back to the same issue: why is there nothing connecting the murders, if they were all committed by the same person? Where—or what—is the killer's signature?"

"Besides," said Maura, "once they stop the police would realize something was amiss. They'd blow whatever cover they had created for themselves. It'd be self-defeating in the long run."

"If they stopped after just three murders, it probably would be," I said. "But if this goes on a little longer, then stops, there might be any number of explanations. I mean, serial killers have stopped or disappeared before, haven't they?"

Inez nodded. "That's right. Jack the Ripper, the Zodiac."

"'The Zodiac,'" Maura said and raised an eyebrow at Inez. "Have you been working on your cryptograms?"

"Or doing oppo research on Ted Cruz," I said.

Inez grinned. "I have another theory, this one maybe a little more fantastic. What if it's a conspiracy? What if there are multiple murderers acting in concert? That explains both the *Primrose* connection and the fact that each murder is so different from the others."

We all stopped and thought about this for a moment. "What, each soon-to-be spouse has partnered with another to kill their intended," said Maura rather doubtfully. "Inez, I think maybe you've been watching too many old movies." Maura seemed clearly to think herself the more practical-minded of the two, a fact she was willing to express with something bordering on condescension. Both of these things surprised me, especially given Inez's military experience, but she seemed to take it all in good humor.

"Well, maybe they are partnering with each other," Inez answered. "They are, after all, all members of a fairly small world. And the other members of that world seem to be pretty good at keeping secrets. But I was thinking more like a political conspiracy, a group of assassins who are targeting the city's economic elite."

"You know I love your imagination when you're using it to create art. But I think it's running away with you here. This is New York in the twenty-first century, not Russia in the 1870s."

"Maybe they're not as different as you think," Inez said quietly.

"Is it really that preposterous, though," I said. "Inez is right, it does explain how the murders could be connected but still so different." I thought it over a little more. "I'll admit I find the idea of a secret society of assassins a little hard to believe—I mean, strangely self-effacing revolutionaries, aren't they? And I can't imagine any of the bereaved as murderers, much less the kind of pitiless psychopaths that could kill a random acquaintance in cold blood...and I certainly don't think all three of them fit the bill. But really, what are our options for tying these murders together? What is a better explanation?"

"There's at least one other possibility," said Maura. "What if the killer is just very good-looking and seductive? He could have lured Jordan into the alley that way. And could have somehow gotten into Charlotte Turner's apartment—maybe she was seeing him, or maybe he just got into the building and knocked on her door with a sympathetic story and a charming smile. That might have been enough, especially if I've understood some of what you've said about Charlotte. Good looks and charm might have also been enough to bluff his way into the party where Bella Jacobs was poisoned."

"Yes, that's all plausible enough," I said. "But if he's such a charmer, why is he killing everyone? It kind of blows up the theory that he's doing this out of envy if he can just grin his way into anyone's bed."

Maura shrugged. "I can imagine that a budding serial killer might have trouble holding down a healthy relationship. But really, who knows why he's doing this? Millions of people are lonely and they don't become murderers, so who knows why he might be fixated on killing these people?"

"And that's only if he's some kind of lovelorn outsider," added Inez. "Maybe he is targeting them for their wealth and status."

"Yes," I said, and thought it over for a few moments. "That certainly would make sense—all the good looks and charm to work his way into the edge of that world, but never the money or family to really be a part of it." I mulled it over a little more and took another sip of cheap beer. "That makes sense...really all of it does. If he wanted to thin the ranks of the one percent, good looks and charm could certainly give him the access to do so. Then again, as you point out, Maura, good looks and charm don't mean he couldn't be a lonely, alienated serial killer. And, I have to say, Alfie really had me going. Maybe the murders really are unconnected, and it's all just a big coincidence, and the only real mystery is who killed Bella and why. And, after all, there are plenty of theories that would cover that, even if we have no idea which one might be more likely at this point.

"I'll let you in on a little secret, ladies, and I trust I can rely on your discretion—I would say your 'absolute discretion,' but it's really not that much of a secret. The police definitely aren't telling me everything, but my sense from talking to them is that they really don't have any clear theories or ideas, mainly because they don't have any evidence to base them on. They wanted to talk to me to see if I was aware of any connections between the victims or families—social, financial, anything. They seemed to me, if I can be somewhat blunt, to be grasping at straws, and I can't say that I blame them. I certainly wasn't able to find any connection for them, beyond those announcements in the *Primrose*—which at this point could be everything or nothing.

"But, after all, any time the residents of certain zip codes start getting murdered it's going to catch the police's attention. I suppose it's possible that all that pressure has pushed them into focusing too much on that one angle."

Suddenly Maura sat bolt upright in her chair, her eyes wide and a stricken look on her face. My blood ran cold just glancing at her. "What if it's a cop? That would explain everything."

We all sat there for a moment or two in silence, though I don't think Inez or I found the thought nearly as chilling as Maura did. "Yes, that would explain some things," I said. "But there were no police at Evelyn's party. I'm almost sure of that."

"He could have come in on the pretext of some security issue," Maura said, "and poisoned her drink in the catering area."

"But how would he have made sure it actually went to her," I asked. "The champagne was poured out into glasses that were lined up on a table at the edge of the room. Whoever poisoned it would have had to either give her the poisoned glass or somehow know which one she would take, which is impossible. A uniformed cop might have gotten in somewhere briefly, but if he had been walking around the party handing drinks to people, I think we would have noticed."

"It could explain how he got into Charlotte's apartment," said Inez. "And it would make it very easy to shoot Jordan, and probably to get him into that alley."

"Yes," I said. "Though you may be underestimating how much attention a uniformed police officer would draw, especially in Charlotte's building. There especially, it would have made more sense for the killer to just pose as a plainclothes detective. That certainly would explain how he got into her apartment, and why she was apparently sitting calmly on her couch when he began strangling her."

"And he could have been wearing a uniform the night he shot Jordan Wymark," Inez said. "It's not that unusual to see uniformed police on the streets later at night like that. Most people just ignore or avoid them. But it would have given him a good reason to be carrying a gun, especially if he couldn't get away from the area before he was seen. No one who saw a cop carrying a gun would have thought anything of it. I don't know if anyone reported seeing anything like that, but it certainly would have been a good way to set up the shooting and to get away afterwards."

"Yes, exactly," Maura said. "And it would all be much easier to do, to pose as plainclothes and as a uniformed cop on the street, if he actually was a cop. That explains it all."

"Not Bella's murder," I said. "If the police I've been spending time with are any indication, they would not feel comfortable at something like Evelyn Cravath's engagement party. And if one of them did and found their way in, Bella would hardly have taken a drink from someone she had never met before."

"What if someone served it to her? Brought it around on a tray, or whatever they do at parties like that?"

"There were no servers. All the food and drink was laid out at one end of the room, and people just took what they wanted."

"Are you sure about that? There wasn't a single person going around serving drinks, or collecting empties?"

"Well, no, I can't be absolutely certain, of course. But there would never have been just one person in any case."

"But that's just it," said Maura, "you don't know. And no one would have noticed if there had been only one person anyway. In the abstract, we know it wouldn't happen, but no one is paying attention to things like that when they're at a party. Certainly Bella wouldn't have thought about it if he brought her a drink. Somebody comes up and offers you a glass of champagne, you're hardly going to stop and count how many other waiters there are in the room before you take it."

"Yes, I suppose," I said. "But how would he have made sure no one else got the poisoned glass?"

"Maybe he poisoned it just before handing it to her. Some lethal bit of legerdemain."

"Yes, I suppose it's possible, I'll grant you. And, really, probably no more unlikely than any of the other scenarios we've considered. But it just doesn't feel right to me, for whatever reason."

"It is strange," said Inez. "We're almost making this person into some kind of superhero, able to pass anywhere, convince anyone of anything, perform any physical act. And really all they're doing is something ugly and wicked."

We all sat there in silence for a few moments after that. The air was still warm and the street had grown quiet and empty. The night was pleasant and peaceful, but we all seemed uncomfortable as we sat around the wobbly metal table on the sidewalk.

"Well," I finally said, rousing myself, "even if he is a cop, that only explains how he's doing it, or doing some things. It's not really the key to the murders, or an explanation of what unites them. And I still think there's something to what Alfie said, that they may not be linked at all."

"I agree it's an intriguing idea," said Inez. "But the coincidence just seems too great to me. Why do you find it convincing?"

"Well, as I said, it seems highly unlikely that one person is committing all these murders and there is no hint of similarity between them. And I think Alfie is right: if we drop the obsession with the wealth of the victims, we have two murders that are easily explicable, if a little banal and tawdry. And then one really bizarre and opaque mystery, the solution of which will probably seem obvious to us if we ever arrive at it."

"Yes," said Inez, "it's true that if Charlotte and Jordan were just killed by their lovers, that would be almost disappointing. Maybe that's why we want to believe there's some grand purpose for these murders, rather than just squalid little acts of jealousy and stupid rage."

"Maybe," said Maura. "But I don't think the explanation for Wymark's murder really is so clear. I don't find Alfie's theories for that convincing in the least."

"Why not?"

"Well, where's the evidence that it's a lover? A lover would have killed him indoors somewhere, not in a back alley at the edge of the gay neighborhood."

"Maybe he took Jordan there to kill him, so the evidence

wouldn't be in his apartment," said Inez.

"A pre-meditated crime of passion?"

"It's not inconceivable," I said.

Maura scowled. "I don't buy it. And why would Wymark have gone along with him?"

"Maybe the mystery man suggested it as something adventurous," I said. "To be frank, I could easily see Jordan going in for something like that. Or maybe it wasn't a spurned lover at all, maybe it was someone he had just met that night. They retreated to a more private setting, argued over something, and his new acquaintance ends up shooting him."

"Yes," said Maura. "Welcome to the newly gentrified Chelsea, where gay men regularly go cruising with pistols tucked into their belts, which they use to shoot someone they just met."

I smiled. "Alright. Maybe it wasn't sex at all. To be honest, I doubt that it was, whatever Alfie may have heard through the grapevine, though I wasn't nearly close enough to Jordan to say that with any confidence.

"But then maybe it was a drug deal gone wrong. You have to admit a drug dealer is much more likely to be carrying a gun."

"I really don't. Someone selling recreational drugs in this part of the city is no more likely to be armed than someone looking for love. And even if this person was armed, we're supposed to believe that Jordan Wymark, this charming, well-off, sensual young man, in the course of what must have been a fairly routine purchase for him somehow gets involved in an argument that escalates to murder? None of these scenarios are even the slightest bit plausible."

"Well, you're no fun at all," I said.

"Look, Ethan," said Maura, "I can understand this must be difficult for you, especially with your sister's wedding approaching. But let's be serious: when was the last time someone you know was murdered? But three of them are in three weeks, and it's supposed to be a coincidence? Of course they're related."

"There is one other alternative," said Inez. "Remember Alfie thought it could be a serial killer targeting gay men. Does that really seem any more doubtful than a serial killer targeting people profiled in the *Rose*'s wedding section?"

"By itself, no. But when you have two other people murdered in the same week they're featured in the Vows column, I think it's pretty outlandish to bring in a second serial killer to explain Wymark."

Maura seemed to be getting irritated, and it felt like our speculations had run their course in any case. "Well," I said, "I'm sure one of us is right—but then again, maybe not. Maybe if we ever find out what really is happening, it will be something none of us has guessed, maybe something even more fantastic than anything we've come up with tonight."

"Yes," said Inez, "and I suppose in the meantime we'll just have to wait and see. If it's a serial killer at work anywhere here there will probably be another killing soon, and maybe then the pattern will be clear."

"Yes," cried Maura, with sudden vehemence, "that's what's so terrible about all this! Whether it's someone picking their victims from the wedding announcements, or a rogue cop, or a serial killer stalking the gay village, there will be more murders!"

"Yes," I said, "it is disturbing. But, after all, the only way we can try to stop the murders is by figuring out who is doing this and why. Not that it's really for us to do—I'm sure the police have the matter in hand."

It was time to call it a night. "You know, Ethan," Inez said cautiously as we waited for the check, "Maura tells me you'll probably be moving on from Balfour and Son soon." I had to commend her powers of euphemism, and hoped my face didn't betray me.

"Yes," I said. "I'm actually kind of hoping to start a luxury brand. Maura may have told you about it, as I'd like her to handle the social media side of it. She seems a little reluctant, though."

"I wrote for various luxury brands when I first moved to New York," Maura said. "You're basically just trying to manipulate insecure douchebags. You're better than that, Ethan."

"Well," said Inez, artfully ignoring the thrust of what Maura had said, "maybe you could look at something with the police. You certainly seem suited to it."

"And he's already got himself an internship," said Maura.

"You're both being too kind. I just helped the police with a few questions they had about the bizarre and insular world of New York's old money families. I'm sure it won't go beyond this."

"You never know," said Maura. "I could certainly see you as some kind of private consulting detective. And don't worry, Gus was wrong. You don't need to wear a deerstalker cap."

Chapter Five

Spider Man, Royal Blood, and
a Sympathetic Vagabond

So for a few days that week the murders seemed to take over my life. Then they disappeared from sight again just as quickly. There was nothing in the news about any connection between the cases, through the *Primrose* columns or otherwise, and there were no reports on any of the individual cases, either—chiefly because there was nothing to report. Another Sunday came and went, and another round of wedding columns was published. Despite the hullabaloo the police made about the insight I was giving them into my "social world" they weren't in touch again, not even to ask about the couples profiled in the new batch of announcements. New York was enjoying the summer, and I did my best to enjoy it along with the rest of the city. On Sunday of that week we had a splendid thunderstorm. I dashed out into Central Park to see the dark, moving sky, then hid under a tree during the storm. I felt a kind of joy I hadn't known in years, so long that I couldn't even be sure it had ever happened, though I was sure the feeling wasn't totally foreign.

Then on Tuesday it was Jake Danforth's birthday, which he was celebrating with a massive party at the Old Hundredth. On the way there that evening I stopped by the ancestral home to drop off some documents to Dad.

I walked in on some kind of row between Dad and Alana, with Mother apparently making half-hearted attempts to mediate but mainly just looking bored and irritated. She did, however, brighten up a bit when she saw me come in.

"Ethan, dear, how nice to see you. Would you like some

dinner? It might still be warm."

Alana, who was sitting on the couch with her arms folded, scowling at Dad, turned to me and contorted her face into a rictus of bitterness that was impressive even for her. "He doesn't need to eat anything. That's our food!"

Mother rolled her eyes in a way that involved her entire body. "Ethan is always welcome here, to eat or to do anything else. Now behave yourself, and Ethan, you help yourself to what's left of dinner."

"That's alright," I said. "I'm not staying long anyway. I just came to drop these documents off for Dad on the way to Jake Danforth's party."

Now it was Dad's turn. Like Alana, he seemed to turn on a pivot, his entire upper body ridiculously stiff and his chest thrust out like an oddly belligerent songbird. "Another wild night? I suppose you'll be in late again tomorrow morning. Ethan, we really can't have this."

I was in no mood for any of this. "Don't worry, Dad, you'll be fine," I said. "President I Have The Clap will get you another tax cut."

"Ethan," mother said, "I wish you would stop making that joke. You've always been so clever—you should be above such cheap little digs."

"Well, I'm sorry, Mother. But our economy—our entire society—is set up so that certain people never have to want for anything. If they somehow managed to bungle their place in this perpetually renewing Ponzi scheme, they need to be insulated from hearing so much as one unkind word. Otherwise—"

Mother interrupted me. "Thank you, dear. It's always nice to have another installment of your one-man show, 'The Marxist Who Went To Choate,' but please not tonight"

It looked like the old girl was not quite as happy to see me as I might have hoped. It was then that I noticed she didn't have a glass in her hand.

"Mother," I said, "why don't you let me get you a drink."

"My doctor said I need to cut back." Apparently her annual checkup had yielded some unwelcome information.

"It seems I'm at the point in my life where I need to start giving up anything pleasurable, or else risk a general rebellion by my body."

"Well, what about just some soda water and lime? Just something to hold in your hand."

She gave the liquor cabinet a long look, her face an eloquent mixture of thoughtfulness, despair, and defiance. "I think I'll just go lay down. I have an unusually bad headache this evening."

Alana was still hunkered down on the couch, sitting with her arms folded and her body bent up like she had been screwed into the spot. "I'm going to my room, too," she said.

"Alana," Mother said firmly, "do not slam your door."

So Alana got up and flounced into the kitchen. Mother got up, apologized to me briefly, then headed into her room. Dad followed her, mumbling some explanation or other.

Suddenly Alana's cell phone rang out with a message from its place on the coffee table.

"Ethan, read me that message," Alana called out in a peremptory voice. I was annoyed but resolved, for some inscrutable reason, to keep the peace.

"What's the security code," I asked her.

"I don't have one. They never work for me, and you know it" she said with rancor.

There was a long list of perfidious objects and processes that "never worked" for Alana. As part of my sudden intention to be kinder to her, I tried to imagine what it would be like to make one's way in such an uncooperative—nay, malevolent—world. But then I was distracted from these edifying reflections by Alana's phone pinging with another message as I picked it up. I tapped the message icon and was confronted with the following artifact of our civilization:

YAAASSSS KWEEN

My boss trying to mansplain my job to me lol

"I'm sorry," I said, "I don't speak Vardlinian. These scrawlings appear to be some kind of pidgin dialect, presumably meant to approximate written English." I considered too late that these words may not help along the good will I meant to engender between us.

She appeared in the kitchen doorway and glowered at me. "I am not a 'Vardlinian.' Stop calling me that."

"But surely four or, in your case, six years in Schenectady leave a lasting impression upon one's soul. Do you so soon repudiate your time on the blessed isles?"

"First of all," she said, gritting her teeth, "Vardley is in Poughkeepsie, not Schenectady— "

"I'm sorry, no," I cut her off. "You're quite wrong about that."

She came storming out of the kitchen and snatched the phone from my hand. It seemed my attempts to be amiable were something less than a runaway success.

Around the apartment there were a series of black and white photos of the city Mother had taken years ago. I suppose they were nothing special, but I always liked them and thought they looked rather elegant. There was one of the Chrysler Building just outside the hallway leading back to the bedrooms. On her way to her room Alana stopped and looked at the picture, then stooped her back and threw out her arms like a tent revival preacher and shouted, "Stupid Empire State Building! What's so great about it?" She proceeded back to her bedroom but mercifully—or perhaps merely prudently—refrained from slamming her door.

I was left alone in the living room. I looked around for a moment, sighed sympathetically to the empty furniture, then turned and left.

The Old Hundredth was already quite crowded by the time I arrived. The place was mostly dark, lit by a kind of eerie light alternating between red and blue. There was music playing but the large, open dance floor was mostly being used for milling about and conversation. I made my way across it to the bar at the other end of the building, not seeing anyone I knew on my way. The bar was also crowded, and I heard snippets of conversation as I walked along, looking for an open spot to order.

"I mean, who's to say what's right or wrong?"

"You can't argue with the Laffer curve."

"So then he got all weird, said something about a generation of vipers, and left."

"So what if she's pregnant, you just get rid of it. Six hundred bucks and…

"I just don't know if I could ever be married. Sex workers are my therapy."

I found an open area and leaned over the bar to order. The barman saw me and approached, greeting me with a dramatic downward nod accompanied by a deep grimace, as if trying to squash some unreasonable optimism on my part.

"Limited selection tonight, bud. Just champagne, gin fizzes, and water."

"I see. I guess the water is sparkling?"

"No, still." He seemed confused.

I decided to stop looking for patterns and order. "I'd like some champagne, please."

"Wise choice, bud. They got good stuff tonight."

I got my drink, tipped the barman, and turned around to scan the crowd.

Halfway across the room I immediately caught sight of Reggie Chapman, who apparently thought it was meant to be a costume party. He had come dressed as Spider Man, but when he arrived and found everyone else in evening wear, saw no reason for this to dissuade him from enjoying the festivities. He had pulled the mask off and let it droop down his back like a hood. The red and blue of his costume shone garishly in the unnatural light, and he looked like a member of some misbegotten medieval order of arachnophile monks.

He saw me, smiled broadly, and set off in my direction, holding his glass of champagne aloft in front of him like a torch lighting his way. "Anyone call for a web-slinger?" he cried out as he approached.

I wasn't sure how to answer that, so I merely raised my glass a few inches in response.

"Hello, Balfour! You're looking well!"

"Thank you, Reggie—so are you," I returned, for some reason raising my glass again in exactly the same manner. "It seems the radioactive powers agree with you."

He laughed a little without showing the slightest sign of embarrassment. "Yes, don't know where I got the idea, but I thought this was meant to be some kind of costume party. Freddie might have told me, but I suppose it is rather a good joke. Freddie's here, you know, and so is Cousin Georgie—or at least he was. Were you here for his entrance?"

"I don't know."

"Oh, you'd know, old boy. He rode in on a horse. I don't know what convinced him that would be a good idea—or for that matter, where the horse came from or how he got it into Midtown. But he rode in on the thing like Caesar returning from the Gallic Wars. Well, you see the merry revelers thronging about you—I'm sure you can imagine the result. The poor animal stared at them for a few seconds and then panicked. He threw Georgie, who I don't think had ever sat on a horse until today. Fortunately the security detail—which is considerable, by the way, so don't get any bright ideas about starting a ruckus, Balfour—but the security detail seems to count at least one or two horsey men among its number, and they were able to get the noble creature under control. It was led off along with Cousin Georgie, neither one, I'm afraid, capable of feeling any shame in the matter."

"Astonishing!"

"Yes, I don't know what he was thinking. Someone said the horse was a gelding, so perhaps Georgie thought he would be a more docile creature. But it was obviously too much for him in any case. I just hope he didn't kick anyone."

"Yes, a horse could kill someone if it kicked them in the head!"

"Oh, the horse, yes. I was actually thinking of Cousin Georgie—he still throws little tantrums when things don't go his way. But you're right—the horse would be far more dangerous. Good thinking, Balfour."

We both turned and looked back at the large entryway to the main hall, as if any casualties the horse had claimed might just now be presenting themselves. Seeing nothing remarkable we turned back and, after a few seconds of friendly silence, our talk turned inevitably to the murders.

"No doubt you've heard about this rash of deaths," Reggie began.

"You mean the murders?"

"Do I?" He cocked an eyebrow but I just looked back at him, unsure of his meaning. "Surely you've heard these are just suicides," he asked.

"Suicides?"

"Yes, of course. It's the only thing that makes sense of all this, old boy."

"Well, I've heard nothing of it, so please tell me."

He rolled his eyes as if someone had been very rude not to tell me. "Yes, of course. Here it is: there's a pact among some of our contemporaries to help each other commit suicide. The deaths have to look like murders, otherwise the insurance won't pay out."

"Insurance?"

"Yes, they were all in debt, you know. This is the perfect, cleanest solution. The question is, who came up with it? I can't imagine any of the poor deceased doing so, except maybe Bella. But I suspect we'll know once the whole thing is over."

My mind reeled for a moment, but it all seemed impossible. "But they weren't in debt. Were they? And if they were, their families could have easily bailed them out."

"No sense in getting upset about it, old boy. It's just the way of the world. Let's see, there was Charlotte Turner. The old Turner fortune is spread quite thin at this stage of the game."

That wasn't my information, but there was no point in arguing with Reggie about that. "But she could have married Andrew Speers. They're still going quite strong."

"Yes, exactly—her only hope was to marry Speers, so you see why she chose death. Then there was Jordan Wymark. No doubt you heard about his problems with the market. Ossington and all that."

"Yes, but again, the family—"

He cut me off with a sad shake of his head. "Not for a long time. Adam likes to carry himself like some patrician old lion of Wall Street who emerged victorious from the great struggles of yore, but he's never understood enough to break even. That wasn't a problem when there were only a few houses where clever young men could work and Wymark and Hathaway was one of them. But those days are long gone, old boy, and Adam's hurting as much as anyone. He was very late to get into hedge funds, and then somehow picked the wrong ones when he did."

This was uncomfortable territory but I was too incredulous to worry about it. "But you knew Jordan, Reggie. He loved life and knew how to get all the pleasure he could out of it. He'd never go in for something like you're describing."

"Quite right, old boy, but there it is. He'd had his day in the sun and knew it. One shot and it's over quickly. What kind of life," he continued, seeing I wasn't convinced, "do you think awaits a playboy who has lost his fortune? Jordan knew, and he made his choice. But I can see this is upsetting you, Balfour, so look at it this way. He did the honorable thing. Adam and the rest of the family are in the clear now for his various debts."

"Yes, but what about Bella? Old Max is going stronger than ever. There's no way she needed money, even if she was somehow in debt."

"Ah, Bella. No, it wasn't money for her. She was still heartbroken over a photographer or something who had thrown her over years ago. Never got over him…some Italian fellow, of course. Thought it might help to marry the family accountant or whoever he was, but naturally it didn't. Again, don't take it hard, old boy. She helped the others, though we'll probably never know who exactly. And maybe the whole thing ends with her."

I was flabbergasted by everything he said and could barely make any reply at all. "But what about the wedding announcements in *The New York Primrose*?"

"Yes, well, what about them? Are you plighted now, Balfour? Bully for you, old boy. Afraid I missed the announcement. We'll be celebrating you next."

"No," I said, "the murder victims. Each of them had been

featured in the wedding announcements in the *Rose* the Sunday before they were murdered. Surely that can't be coincidence. That's the theory I've heard, that some insane killer is picking his victims from the newspaper." I stared at him but he just gazed back at me with mild curiosity, apparently completely unaware of what I was talking about. "You haven't heard any of this," I asked him.

"No, can't say I have, and I'm afraid I don't see much in it now that you've told me about it. There are a dozen or so people featured in the *Rose*'s wedding announcements every weekend. One of them is killed, but what about the rest? Where's the pattern?"

"I think one body a week is pretty prolific for a serial killer!" But he continued to stare calmly at me, apparently too polite to press his disagreement. "You don't see a pattern," I demanded.

"No, old boy, I really don't," he said with some sadness. "What I see is a lot of people unable to support themselves in the style to which they're accustomed. Old money is rather like nostalgia—it just isn't what it used to be."

We were back on uncomfortable ground, all the more so since Reggie seemed to know about everyone's finances. But we were distracted from all this just then when Reggie was accosted by his brother Freddie, who had Ronnie Highgate in tow. It was something of a coup for the Danforths to have a member of the British royal family at the party, and I have to admit I was somewhat impressed when he joined Reggie and me. That feeling, however, quickly wore off. With his drawn face, long nose, and the dark, dark circles under his eyes, he looked like a consumptive weasel. Despite this he approached wearing a simper of invincible smugness (though perhaps it was just his invincible cocaine habit), and was as lucid as you could expect the product of generations of northern European inbreeding to be.

Reggie smiled pleasantly as they came and stood next to us, though I sensed he wasn't terribly eager for their company. "Have you heard about the horse?" he asked Ronnie.

"Winged Victory?" Ronnie Highgate cocked his head

somewhat violently and his eyes bulged when he spoke.

"What? That great brown gelding was called Winged Victory?"

"Gelding? Good Lord no, man. I thought you were talking about the Belmont. Winged Victory should have won it, but the track was muddy. Saw the horse myself back in February, put ten thousand pounds on it to win the Triple Crown. Would have, too, if it hadn't been for that damnable rain storm. My family knows horses, you know."

"Yes, we know," said Reggie, already bored.

Highgate, however, missed the cue, and while the three of them continued to talk horses and muddy racetracks I tried to think over what Reggie had just told me. I was still reeling from it. All three murders actually suicides? Even apart from the supposed suicide cabal, the whole thing was almost unthinkable. And the cabal had to exist for it to be possible at all. So could there be anything in it?

Bella, it was true, could conceivably have killed herself. I hadn't been close to her for years, so of course I had no idea if she had been despondent enough for there to be anything to the idea that she had taken her own life. I had to say, marrying Micah Aaronson seemed like it would have to be a letdown after the life she had lived. But did she despair over it? Maybe Reggie was right, and it was some desperate reaction to romantic shipwreck with an earlier lover. And, if it came to that, she could have simply poisoned herself. The police hadn't even hinted at such a thing, but perhaps murder didn't need to enter into it at all. Max was certain she hadn't killed herself, she was too full of life and happy about her marriage, but the fact is Max probably wouldn't know any better than I would what was really in her mind. So it was at least possible that Bella's death had been suicide, but in that case there was no need to think anyone else had helped her along. But what about the others?

I was hardly an expert, but strangulation seemed like a horrible way to die. It was inconceivable to think of Charlotte choosing that, or even acquiescing to it, especially when things like poisoning were available. And even beyond that, where was Reggie getting his information about the Turners' finances? I hadn't heard anything of the sort, and in fact had reason to believe they were still doing quite well. Reggie's joke about marrying Speers was actually well-taken, but still. I knew Charlotte, and even if she were in such desperate financial straits she would have married Andrew a thousand times before she would have chosen death—much less to let herself be brutally murdered. And what did she need to worry about life insurance for in any case? She didn't have any great debts, and again it was simply impossible that she would have chosen to die like that so her family could pick up a little cash. That whole idea was monstrous!

And what about Jordan? It was even harder to imagine him choosing death. Reggie made it sound as if he would have no life to speak of without a fortune at his back, but that was nonsense. If anyone could live on charm alone, it was Jordan. And, as with the Turners, I had heard nothing to suggest the Wymarks were in trouble. Everyone had heard questionable things about Ossington, it's true, but half the stories were that the whole thing was a prank. Even if Jordan did lose money there, so what? Adam could pick up the bill, and if he had gone bust, it was hard to imagine Jordan feeling responsible for setting things right. He spent his life as the hedonistic black sheep of the family, and suddenly he decides to die so Adam doesn't have to settle his debts for him? There was nothing in it, even if he was destitute, which no one but Reggie seemed to believe. And then supposedly it was an easy death because he was shot, but that sounded like a theory advanced by someone who had never been shot. And how could Jordan be sure it would be quick? Especially if it was supposedly Bella shooting him—or really anyone else, unless he had hired Annie Oakley to shoot him. But it didn't matter anyway—Jordan would never have even considered any of this. Of course it would always be better for a playboy to have his pockets full, but Jordan always wore his family wealth lightly, and I was sure he could get on fine without it.

It was hard to tell who was less likely to act this way, Charlotte or Jordan. But even aside from the fact that the whole story was psychologically beyond belief, the notion of some kind of secret suicide pact didn't work. Suddenly an idea popped into my head: what if Bella killed the other two so her own suicide would look like a murder and her family could collect her insurance? But then of course I remembered that Bella was the one of the three who absolutely was not broke and did not need to worry about insurance money. No, I didn't know where Reggie had heard all this, or what had led him to fabricate it himself, but the whole thing was obvious hogwash. Still, there was something about it that nagged at me…

I was torn from my reveries when Highgate suddenly turned his head to look at Reggie with such force that his entire body convulsed. "Good Lord," he cried, "I just now saw what you're wearing. What happened to you, man? Are those long johns? Did someone steal your suit of clothes?"

"Yes," said Freddie, grinning triumphantly. "Fear not, partygoers. The mighty Iron Man is here to protect you!" He turned and gave Reggie a rather impertinent leer, but his brother took the whole thing with admirable stoicism.

"I'm Spider Man, Freddie, not Iron Man."

"No, it's Iron Man, surely? Look at the costume."

"Yes, do look. There's a large spider on my chest."

Freddie bent down and peered at it in the red light of the party. "No, I think not, dear brother. Unless I'm very much mistaken, that's some kind of iron monger's tool."

Reggie and I looked at Freddie while Ronnie Highgate rubbed his nose with great violence.

"Well, be that as it may," said Freddie, as if it were some abstruse question that we couldn't hope to answer. "Who would have thought that Reggie's superhero getup would pale beside Cousin Georgie's horsey stunt? I hope he didn't kick anyone."

"Good Lord," said Highgate, having granted his nose a reprieve. "Don't joke about that. Just in my lifetime two Highgates have been killed when they were kicked in the head by a horse. One of them was actually a Longbridge, but even so. It mostly comes to the same thing."

"Oh," said Freddie, "I meant Cousin Georgie. But you're right, the horse would do much more damage. Yes, good thinking, Highgate. You can tell your family knows horses."

"Hello, Balfour," he said, turning to me. "Good to see you out with a straight back and a brave face. Staying strong, the best one can."

I was floored. I admit I was not expecting Freddie Chapman to know much about the health of Balfour and Son, but I certainly didn't expect him to say anything about it if he did—much less to make me an object of pity! I stared at him.

"It's been a rough patch for you, old boy, but it will get better," he continued, serene and untroubled. "First there was Charlotte, the poor thing. Always difficult to lose one's intended. Then your cousin Wymark, so soon after. Just last week, wasn't it?"

My expression changed, but I stared at him still.

"Good heavens," cried Reggie. "I forgot Jordan Wymark was your cousin." He reached out and grabbed my arm. "Balfour, I'm so sorry."

I glanced back and forth from one brother to the other. Freddie looked merely melancholy, Reggie positively stricken. I also cast a quick look at Ronnie Highgate, who was staring urgently at the ceiling lights, seeming to commune with them in some strange, intense manner while we mere mortals struggled on well below the divided line.

"I tell you, old man," said Freddie, "I don't think I've ever in my life felt my age until I heard about poor Charlotte."

"Yes, it was awful to learn about that," I said. "But Charlotte wasn't my fiancé. She was engaged to Andrew Speers. She and I dated, but it was many years ago now." I looked sideways at Reggie to see if he at least understood this much. Freddie frowned and began to speak, but I pressed on.

"And Jordan Wymark wasn't my cousin. No connection at all between our two families, really."

"But the resemblance is so strong," said Reggie.

"And surely your mother married Adam Wymark's brother," said Freddie.

"No," I said. "She married my father. His name is

101

Balfour."

Reggie Chapman seemed very pleased with this explanation. "Yes, of course it would be, wouldn't it?" he said, and looked encouragingly at his brother.

Freddie still seemed befuddled by the whole matter, but he gave a good-natured shrug. "Well, I suppose she could have married anybody, really."

"The important thing," said Reggie, "is that Balfour here isn't bereaved."

"Yes," agreed Freddie. "Bully for you, I say, though I suppose strictly speaking you didn't really do anything."

"No, not really," I said. "Not much at all besides being myself."

"Well that is quite enough for any of us most of the time," said Freddie. "That is to say, not that being you would be enough for us. I'm me."

"But are you really, Freddie?" said Reggie. "Perhaps—"

"Good Lord," Highgate suddenly cried out, with a wild-eyed fervor to which we had all become accustomed at that point. "You're talking about those killings! I've heard about those. You have a popular uprising on your hands. If you insist on staying here, you had best all be on your guard."

"Oh, that. It's nothing," said Reggie, somewhat dismissively.

"Yes," said Freddie, with sudden vehemence. "We won't be going anywhere or changing any of our usual habits. Let the rabble come! I stand ready to face down all the green grocers and dress makers the city has to throw at me." And with that he thrust his head forward in an oddly defiant manner, his hairless jowls quivering in the red light.

I tried to imagine Freddie Chapman in a time of revolution. All I could see was an image of him being docilely led to the guillotine, thinking all the while that he was being fitted for a new shirt.

"I beg your pardon," Highgate objected violently. "If there's one thing we Highgates know, it's the danger of plebeian discontent."

"I thought you knew horses," Freddie asked innocently.

Highgate glowered at him. "Besides horses. Need I remind you of the terrible life history of Edward Highgate?"

"Perhaps you might," said Reggie dryly.

"He was married to a French royal at the time of the Revolution. Good Lord, what a time! In the midst of the most terrible scenes he managed to escape from Paris, dressed as a peasant, riding a donkey. He was caught out in the open deep in the country one night. It was so cold his donkey died. He cut the ghastly beast open and crawled inside to keep from freezing to death."

Reggie interrupted him. "Isn't that a scene from a Star War," he asked ingenuously, but with a clear note of skepticism.

Highgate glared at Reggie Chapman even more intensely than he had his brother. "He was blasted lucky to last the night! In the morning he made his way to a nearby village—he lived to regret it! The peasants recognized him as a noble. For weeks they kept him captive, had their way with him. He eventually made it back to Britain—don't ask me how!—but he was a broken man. It was all he could do to walk under his own power, and he *certainly* never rode a horse again."

"Yes, but surely," began Freddie.

"Take my word for it," cried Highgate. "Or don't—but I would advise you to lay low, practice the arts of blending in with the commoners crawling through this godforsaken city.

"Ah, it's too much!" And with that he hurried off to the bathroom.

We all watched him go, somewhat surprised at his sudden departure, then stood looking at each other, a bit unsure of how to follow that.

"Perhaps he's right," said Reggie.

"Oh, yes, surely what's needed here is for all of us to blend in with the so-called 'common man,'" said Freddie. "Come, Reggie, it's time to don some short pants and 'tee' shirts," he continued with boundless contempt, "then let's procure a jeroboam of Coors Light and take in a match of one of those concussion sports. Behold, you all, I am a populist *bon vivant*!"

103

"I don't know if all that will be necessary," said Reggie.

"You're right. —we can content ourselves with going about making loud, vaguely illiterate affirmations of our support for the syphilitic kleptocrat running the country."

"Now, Freddie, you know the whole family has asked you to stop referring to father that way," said Reggie.

"The New York Stock Exchange is not the country, Reggie, as I've told you countless times before. I fear for what it will take to make you realize that."

But then our attention was drawn to a scene unfolding on the other side of the room. Ronnie Highgate had emerged from the bathroom and was standing in a rapidly widening space on the dance floor, doing an especially energetic version of the running man. A few girls who had at first looked at him with a sporting appreciation were now backing away, and others were following suit after throwing quick glances, at first curious and then uneasy, over their shoulder at what they sensed was some kind of commotion.

"We'd better go collect Ronnie," said Reggie.

"Yes," said Freddie. "In fact, I think I've had quite enough of this place."

They bade their farewells and were surprisingly quick in convincing Highgate to leave with them. I went back to the bar, got another glass of champagne, and wandered off to a different part of the massive room.

Throughout the hall there were giant martini glasses, maybe ten feet high. The stems were thick cylinders of glass that, whether by design or accident, reflected the ceiling lights in new colors that flashed and spun out into the room. In the tops of the glasses were dancing girls. Some wore lingerie and lacy corsets, in appropriately lurid shades of pink and purple, and moved about alone in their glasses, arching and gyrating above the party goers' heads like so many PG-13 Tinkerbells. The ones I noticed, however, were moving in odd ways, throwing their arms and legs about in strange, abrupt patterns which tended to draw one's thoughts away from anything libidinal and towards concern about exotic medical reactions. Their routines looked like they belonged more in an experimental interpretive dance than in a strip club floor show, though I suppose my experience with either is quite limited. A few of the glasses had two girls in them, along with a couple feet of water (or, if whoever set them up had a flair for the literal, possibly gin and vermouth). The girls splashed about merrily, looking more happy and natural than their dancing counterparts, or indeed than anyone else in the room.

Not too far from me there were two middle-aged men, both looking rather dumpy and disheveled in ill-fitting suits, gazing up at one of the girls. They exchanged a few words with each other and then started trying to clamber up the stem in a strange tandem. The girl at the top was lying on her back, kicking her legs up in the air. They had an unnatural flushed glow in the pink and purple lighting, like great fluorescent pork loins waving and wafting their fleshy essence out upon the sad American night. The two men, for their part, may have been fighting each other to get up the stem, but I suspect the flurry of jostling and turmoil was just garden variety drunken ineptitude. Suddenly one of the men jumped back and moved away from the glass. His legs remained strangely planted as his upper body moved spasmodically in one direction, then the other, almost as if here were dancing to the music. Then he lurched forward, put his hands on his knees, and began vomiting on the floor in front of him. The other man kept trying to make his way up the glass stem, now making somewhat more progress without the interference of his compatriot, but still slipping back down. The entire glass was beginning to rock a bit, side to side, and the girl at the top was now aware of the man trying to get up there with her. She was still lying on her back, but now her legs were kicking much more rapidly, and she made me think of an insect flipped over on its shell. Suddenly another man, slightly shorter and thicker than the other two, strode purposefully onto the scene. He was tense around the shoulders like the man who had vomited (and was still vomiting), but he seemed quite sober. He walked up to the man still trying to climb the stem and punched him in his lower back, just above his belt. The would-be wall crawler fell back off the stem, his arms and legs flailing in pain in a way that recalled the girl's frantic movements, and crashed into the floor, in an area that must have been covered with the other man's vomit. He recoiled with obvious disgust and tried to spring back up, but the newcomer struck him again, this time in the face, and with the full force of gravity behind him. The man went down and did not try to rise again. The defender of the martini girl's honor (or perhaps just of the giant martini glass's integrity) grabbed his collar, then turned and grabbed the collar of the other man, who had just begun retching violently again. He dragged them both away, the beaten man's limbs twitching and casting about like he was being electrocuted, the sick man slumped down and apparently insensate, liquid spurting out of him as if he were a ruptured water balloon. The girl had moved from her back and was watching all of this with concern, her hands perched on the edge of the glass and her legs tucked up under her.

I found the whole spectacle strangely dispiriting, and turned and walked off in the other direction. I came upon two men standing next to each other, talking to one another with a strange air. One man was rather short and, with gray hair and a somewhat leathery face, looked rather old. He was clearly interested in what the other man was saying, though he seemed as if perhaps he was trying to act nonchalant as he listened to him, occasionally asking questions. The other man was tall and lean but had strangely puffy eyes. The music stopped for a moment and I could hear their conversation. "So yes," puffy eyes was saying, "the island is shut down, at least for the time being, but yes, of course the operation is still running." But then, aware of the sudden silence and the fact that his voice was carrying, he looked over his shoulder, saw me standing there, and gave a dirty look. He took the arm of his companion, who studiously kept his face forward and pointed away from me, and moved a little further away. My glass was empty and I decided to leave the party.

The atmosphere in The Old Hundredth was swampy and fetid, and the night air felt good. I walked about for a bit, not

106

really thinking about anything, just happy to be out in the open and seeing the city. I was rarely in Midtown at that time, and there was something both charming and a little melancholy about how deserted it was. I ended up on Fifth Avenue, just outside of Rockefeller Center. There was a guy packing up his hot dog cart, another guy playing the saxophone, and otherwise the street was empty other than a few people walking up and down. The guy with the saxophone started playing "New York, New York." Ordinarily I may have thought it was corny, but that night it seemed like a perfect moment. I wandered southward, looking in the windows of the various shops, stopping here and there to take a closer look at the Cartier or Burberry displays. I was standing outside a new outpost of Lewis & Ransome that had just opened, lost in my own thoughts, when I realized there was someone standing beside me. I looked over at him, somewhat startled, but he just kept gazing at the suits in the window. He looked to be homeless, his clothes torn and dirty, his face smudged, and a bottle in a brown paper bag in his hand. His face was rawboned and mournful and his expression as he stared up almost reverent, though he didn't really seem to be contemplating the clothes hanging in front of us. I assumed he had approached to say something to me, but he just stood there in silence, looking at the window, though he seemed to be aware of me and indeed to have somehow established some kind of silent communion. The hot dog cart and the man with the sax were gone now, and the street was completely empty and silent, save for the occasional movement of the wind or the sound of a car passing by on the next block.

We stood there for a few minutes like that, gazing at the soft, rich folds of fabric, the way they hung there gravely in the half-light, gray-green like wooded hills opening onto dark, forgotten fields rolling on beyond us under a comfortless night.

The spell was broken when we heard voices down the road, emerging from a side street a few blocks above 42nd Street. There was a man's voice, loud and vacuous, and a couple of women's voices chirping along under it like some sort of mindless counterpoint. They came out onto Fifth Avenue and headed south. There were three of them, all clustered together, the man walking in the middle, his arm embracing a woman on each side of him, both gripping him back. They were obviously drunk and moved together like that, tramping energetically down the street like a clutch of demented marionettes. "Thank God for Tinder," the man called out, and they all laughed loudly. They walked a little farther and he added, "I might start an account on Grindr, just to celebrate social media!" Only one of the women laughed at this, but he guffawed loudly enough for all three of them. So they continued to move down the street, stomping and groping and gabbling. I turned away, deeply annoyed, but when I did I saw my companion looking back up the street to the north, seemingly staring at something on the east side of the avenue, though I couldn't see anything there.

"Heard a man talk about them four things once." He paused for a moment or two, and the silence seemed to have returned. "Didn't care to hear no more." He kept looking up the street, but held out his paper bag to me. I declined. Without changing his expression or bearing, he took a drink. He held it in his mouth for a while as he continued to stare, then swallowed it. His mouth pulled into a slight sneer, as if it were bitter. "You ever wonder, maybe this is hell?"

I stood there for a moment, alarmed and dumbfounded, but didn't say anything. He didn't look over, but a subtle change in his demeanor told me he was waiting for me to say something, even more observing my wordless reaction, somehow taking my measure in the darkness and silence. It suddenly seemed to me as if he were moving in some ghastly, ruinous pall that was reaching out to swallow me like an amoeba. I started away from him with a shiver, and though I caught myself I still set off quickly down the street. "I can't, uh…" I called out over my shoulder, quickening my pace. He replied with something clearly directed at me but too garbled for me to understand, his voice somehow both despondent and menacing.

Chapter Six

A Truly Unforgettable Dinner Party

So Tuesday night of that week ended up being little more than a series of odd conversations and false starts, though it somehow felt very eventful, even like some kind of narrow escape. Wednesday was a welcome change of pace, a quiet, productive day at work and an early bed. Thursday was progressing much the same way when Dad came into my office around four o'clock. He was holding his cell phone in his hand like a breadbox and had a flummoxed look on his face.

"Ethan," he said, with a self-doubting quiver in his voice, "have you seen this?"

He held his phone out to me. On the screen was a tweet from President Ivan von Clapp:

We always say that we can't dee fault on our national debt. That only "weakens" our bargaining position!! I have gone through bankruptcy many times' and always come out "stronger". Y NOT DEE FAULT??? #SLAGGAT

"What the hell is 'SLAGGAT,'" Dad asked. Not what I found most remarkable about the tweet, but I answered his question in a spirit of filial piety.

"It's an abbreviation for 'Start Living America's Great Greatness Again Today.' You'll remember that during the election he kept referring to America's 'Great Greatness,' and various media types mocked him for it. So he embraced it as his campaign slogan, and he still uses it."

"Yes, I knew about the slogan," Dad said. "I didn't realize he used that abbreviation."

"Yes, he does. That symbol in front of it is a hashtag."

"Yes, I know about hashtags, at least in general terms." He paused for a moment. "The abbreviation seems poorly thought out."

"Yes, his supporters liked the slogan less when others started calling them 'slaggats.'"

"Well, he still seems to be using it with gusto," Dad said.

"Yes, he is undaunted, or at least uncomprehending, about so many things." Dad gave me a quick look, and I remembered our clipped exchange the other night. We both let it pass.

We turned back to the phone and stood there, gazing dumbly at the screen. It was time to acknowledge the fact that the president was tweeting about defaulting on the national debt. "Is there any way a default could actually help us," Dad asked, though his tone of voice expressed complete perplexity at what he was saying, not any attempt to gather information.

"I...have no idea. I don't think anyone really knows what would happen if the government defaulted."

I left work shortly afterwards to go home and prepare for a dinner party, where I feared this latest outrageous tweet would dominate the conversation. Genevieve Hastings, the hostess, was not terribly political herself but she had invited Kate Watson, a rising star in the Democratic Party's consultancy class who had worked on the last presidential campaign. I didn't look forward to the parade of po-faced clichés I imagined would pass for conversation on the topic. But Genevieve was eager to show off her new apartment—the hand-written invitations came in the mail on thick paper and promised "a truly unforgettable dinner party"—and I had already told her I would be there.

We all knew the political story of the past few years. Even so, I recounted it to myself frequently—it was still so hard to believe when you stopped and really thought about it, and it always distracted me from the grim dismemberment of the family business.

It had perhaps the most implausible starting point imaginable. In the late '50s Benvolio Euphemus is born to an

American woman and her Greek husband when they're both students in Baltimore. The husband, though a Greek national, is himself an immigrant from Ethiopia, a self-made man who goes on to become one of Greece's first billionaires. But by then he is long since estranged from his wife and son, who now live in an artists' colony in New Mexico. Strange rumors swirl around him, including occasional murmurs of devil worship. When he drowns some people suggest suicide, others murder, a few something more diabolical. But the important thing for our story is that he never reconciled with his family back in the U.S., and young Benvolio grows up intrigued, almost haunted, by his lost father. He follows his footsteps and becomes a businessman, travels the world, and despite having grown up surrounded by hippies and visiting artists, himself becomes a polished, debonair cosmopolitan who speaks six languages, has business interests on every continent, and never appears in public wearing anything less than an Armani suit. He eventually finds his way back to the United States, where he attracts notice for his great wealth and soon becomes a national figure known for his good sense, even manner, stately speech, and gentle humor.

He announces that he will run for president, though his campaign focuses more on his life story and personal beliefs than on any questions of policy. With apparent candor but in perfectly measured cadences he speaks about the sense of loss and confusion that came from not knowing his father, but also about the redemptive power of hard work and a simple, humanistic faith in other people. It is drab, even banal—a mixture of daytime television confession and Horatio Alger platitudes—but it resonates with the American public. Perhaps it is the historical moment, or perhaps the quiet certainty of the speaker, but people begin to rally around him with a strange energy. Pundits insist he can't win, they literally laugh on television when his candidacy is mentioned. He's too foreign, they say, too cultivated and soft, Americans will never trust him. He has no political experience, and his ideas are edifying but completely impracticable. Euphemus promises to end the Iraq War, talks

111

about restoring America's promise and leadership in the world, about a new civic order at home and abroad based on mutual respect and hope. He wins the presidency in a landslide.

He governs for eight years, and although some grumble his only achievement was keeping anyone on Wall Street from going to jail after the financial meltdown, he remains very popular with Democrats, especially the urban, professional, Republican-lite wing of the party.

Enter from stage left Ivan von Clapp, who seems almost engineered to be Euphemus's polar opposite, the smelly afterbirth of the man his supporters call "The American Dream." Von Clapp makes his fortune in New York real estate, or rather his brother Otto makes a fortune for both of them. Occasionally Otto gives him small side projects that Ivan inevitably bankrupts, usually within the year. Ivan is mostly a figure of fun, a Billy Carter character, who at one point bankrupts the family business in under three months when Otto hands it over to him while he battles cancer. Otto manages to right the ship, and Ivan is put out to pasture, sent around the country to open casinos and given a role promoting beauty pageants, a kind of real-life Fredo Corleone. He is eventually given a television show where he invites contestants to compete for chunks of "his" money, usually with bizarre and whimsical strings attached. Someone presents a detailed business plan or a new app to him, but then they have to play "Dixie" on a kazoo or let tarantulas crawl over them or swim through a pool of Campbell's cream of mushroom soup, while Ivan merrily eats a bowl in another shot, mugging for the camera. Eventually he creates massive controversy when he tries to use the show to legitimize a white supremacist militia. There are widespread calls to cancel the show and fire Ivan, but the ratings are too good, and the network in fact gives him a raise and issues a mealy-mouthed statement that seems to exonerate the militia. He emerges from this confrontation empowered, and decides to run for president.

Von Clapp is a virulent reversal of Euphemus in every

important way: loud, vulgar, thick-witted, unable to express himself except in the crudest terms, thoroughly base in moral conduct and personal tastes. At some point, for reasons no one entirely knows or comprehends, he conceives a strange antipathy towards President Euphemus. He begins taunting him, first on his show, then on his new but hugely addictive Twitter account. Quickly, however, the taunting turns to something darker, as von Clapp begins spreading a conspiracy theory that President Benvolio Euphemus is not Benvolio Euphemus at all. He seems to believe that someone, whom he calls "The Hatchet Man," killed Euphemus at some undisclosed point in the past, grafted his fingerprints onto his own fingers, and had reconstructive surgery to look like Euphemus. Many of his fans and followers on Twitter become convinced of this theory, and they along with von Clapp begin demanding that Euphemus release current dental records to be compared with those procured from a dentist's office in Albuquerque. Cable news channels begin hosting heated debates on whether von Clapp's allegations are possible, with doctors and surgeons explaining patiently that they are not, while Republican lieutenant governors and retired generals tell strange, seemingly completely inapposite stories that somehow conclude that perhaps there is something in it after all. Von Clapp's accusations begin to take an even darker turn, as he claims that The Hatchet Man is in fact a high priest in a secret Aztec cult that survives to this day and continues to practice human sacrifice. He suggests that The Hatchet Man was involved in the disappearance of two American airmen in Juarez, that he offered them as live sacrifices, cut their chests open and removed their hearts, and this is what enabled him to become President. At other times von Clapp insinuates that The Hatchet Man is part of some kind of sinister *Reconquista*, and begins reminding people of the stories about Euphemus's father and devil worship (despite the fact that he seems to believe Euphemus is dead and The Hatchet Man is a complete stranger who has taken over his identity, this strikes a powerful chord with many of his supporters and followers, who by now number in the millions). His charges become more strange and confusing, and therefore even harder to refute. Among other things, he speaks (and tweets) as if he thinks that Africa and Latin America are the same place, and at times even as if he thinks the original Benvolio Euphemus and The Hatchet Man are actually the same person, so that all the parts of his story run together to create one terrible menace.

Someone releases a cellphone video clandestinely taken of him at home, crying like a small child, whimpering over and over that "The Hatchet Man is coming to kill me." Far from hurting him with his supporters, this just further convinces them of his sincerity and of the reality of the threat. "He has all the money in the world, but he's chosen to risk his life and set himself against The Hatchet Man, who is pure evil. All just to keep us safe," a woman in Texas tells CNN. It is a common sentiment.

In an absurd spectacle that involves him wearing a bald eagle costume and being lowered onto a stage on a von Clapp Properties construction site in New Jersey by a crane, he declares he is running for president. This is of course a bad joke. He has no chance of winning the Republican nomination, and in any case Cynthia Grubwell, President Euphemus's Vice President, is waiting in the dove-white wings of the Democratic Party, which by now has become a shining beacon of well-scrubbed professional class virtue.

Von Clapp dispatches with the other Republicans like a fox moving through a henhouse. In the debates he alternates between insults and flatly stated facts that no one can contradict but which leave the other candidates stammering and, occasionally, choking with rage. The connection between his conspiracizing and the worst elements of American society, never really concealed, now rises to the surface. He does nothing to disavow the connection but this, like everything else, seems only to play to his advantage. He refuses to condemn the Ku Klux Klan when they show up outside one of his rallies, and CNN and Fox News feature serious, chin-stroking debates about whether the Klan is actually bad.

The final Republican debate is between von Clapp and

114

Orlando Flaccide, the governor of Florida and the party elders' candidate. The debate begins with von Clapp wearing a joy buzzer when he shakes Flaccide's hand. Flaccide jumps back, and von Clapp holds up his hand, proudly displaying the buzzer and grinning wildly for the cameras. Flaccide spends most of the debate denying that the Iraq War was a mistake and insisting that all Americans who are willing to work are happy with the economy. Von Clapp clinches the nomination the following week.

In the general election the still-popular President Euphemus campaigns strenuously for Grubwell, as does most of the political and journalistic establishment. Nothing von Clapp can say seems to hurt him. I remember one television interview that made a brief public impression before being swallowed up in the ever churning sea of outrage and stupidity that our public life had become.

"What, you think we're so innocent" he asked the interviewer, a popular cable news "reporter" who looked something like a constipated ceramic elf. "We put FDR on the dime, but—boy howdy! What do you think happened in all the Southy Americas when they wanted to elect their own FDR? We killed him, every time, and about 50,000 of the people around him just for good measure. You like JFK? Very sad, how he was killed, wasn't it? Everyone thinks it was sad. Make some shows about it, be sure to show the people crying. Well, they had JFKs all over, in all the places I can't remember the names, but the point—you won't be telling the people what happened to them. Very bad ratings— people will stop watching. Worse than that, you'll lose your sponsors. The sponsors won't like those stories at all. Let me tell you, we have something called the CIA, and they are not nice people at all. Look into it sometime, but trust me, you won't be talking about it on here.

"You will lose your show, your place here. And then what? If you're not on tv, you're nothing. If someone else isn't looking at you, then you have to look at yourself. And that's no good. I don't like to do that at all, and looking at you right now, I know you don't either."

In a sign of increasing desperation outlets like the *Primrose* report his comments with all the hesitations and conversational roughness of their original expression, refusing him the usual courtesy of polishing his spoken comments. His supporters are outraged at what they see as intentional linguistic assassination, his opponents that someone this inarticulate has made it this far in "the process." It is a fact that his spoken comments are stranger and more incoherent than those of almost any other politician, but amidst all the fuming and sniggering everyone seems to miss the rough, indomitable truths shaken loose in his strange staccato fumblings. Euphemus and Grubwell are never as clumsy or inarticulate as von Clapp is in nearly every sentence, but their clipped and polished mendacities—born of natural eloquence and a statesmanlike pose in Euphemus's case, of painfully crafted and triangulated campaign stratagems in Grubwell's—never even brush up against the truth. It is as if some half-mummified old gentleman from the eighteenth century has somehow been kept alive somewhere in the artificial recesses of the Harvard Club, and goes on murmuring his favorite phrases without noticing that his body has shriveled and decayed. And then one day he is wheeled out into the sunlight and carted around town, decrepit and lecherous in his powdered wig and lead face paint, never noticing what a disgusting figure he cuts as he tries to make love to the young women he meets, tattooed baristas and freelancers suffocating under crushing mounds of debt, suffering his advances as he dodders and drools on about the unbreakable bond between commerce and liberty.

To the shock and dismay of everyone who thought they counted, von Clapp wins the presidency easily, then immediately sets about embarrassing the office beyond even his worst critics' expectations. He proposes televised executions, with himself as a kind of ghoulish emcee. "The ratings will be great as we eliminate these ANIMALS," he tweets. The Chief Justice of the Supreme Court, widely considered a loyal Republican who would gladly repeal the entirety of the New Deal if possible, issues an unprecedented public rebuke and a promise to strike down any such innovations. After a torrent of hysterical tweets, von Clapp abandons the proposal. He demands that the government rebuild the White House and Capitol building and give Otto's construction company the contract, but his advisors convince him this is impossible because there is no open space for development in Washington. He gives an official presidential endorsement to a revenge porn site, and allows it to use the Presidential seal for promotions. When his Chief of Staff objects, President von Clapp throws his favorite bust of John A. Quitman at him.

Gone is the peculiar mix of decadence and optimism, the cloying, ironic wink as everyone acts badly. Here is a much rougher beast on the prowl. A secret, gurgling rage erupts like a rash across the soapy skin of our fair republic, and the Hatchet Man stalks the empty catacombs of the splintered national mind.

Genevieve's apartment was on the Lower East Side and I arrived in her neighborhood a little early. I had to admit to feeling a certain resentment about being the only wage slave among our little dinner party, especially given the character of the work I had been doing. I stopped in at The Marble Cod to have a drink and sand down whatever edge I may have been carrying with me. When I arrived the after-work crowd was mostly gone and the evening crowd was just beginning to arrive. The bay windows were open onto the street, and despite the fact that it was already early evening, the light was full and warm streaming into the bar. People were coming and going, the air was fresh, and I found myself, rather unexpectedly, feeling good just to be alive. I walked to the bar, where the bartender looked exactly as I expected. Black vest and white shirt, sleeves rolled up tightly to display the sleeve tattoos on both arms, beard long but clearly shaped and groomed, hair parted and laying exactly in place. He was youthful and fresh-faced beneath his carefully cultivated scruff, striking the perfect balance between the studied archaisms of the bar and the exacting trendiness of its

117

patrons. He greeted me by suggesting an Old Fashioned, a proposition to which I thought it only courteous to consent.

As I sat there drinking, I thought about the place. The barkeep's getup, the carefully cut Old Fashioned glasses, the zinc bar top, the Billie Holiday playing as ambient music—everything was meant to conjure up the 1930s. And this for a crowd that had never seen a polio victim or gone to bed hungry one night in their lives, for whom the Great Depression and Hitler were no more real than Sauron or Voldemort. They had lived through two wars, were still living through them, and probably no one in that room had ever met someone who fought in either. Ordinarily reflections like these would make me bitter, but the drink was as pleasant as the summer air blowing in off the street, and instead I just felt detached and reflective. The music kept playing and I ordered another drink.

Fresh drink in hand, I turned around in my stool and, to my rather pleasant surprise, saw Freya Kittredge. She was with Jocelyn Prosser and Lily Chang. We all exchanged greetings, then Jocelyn and Lily moved to the back of the building where they apparently had some kind of event. Freya lingered with me. Fortunately, I happened to be wearing an Hermès cashmere jacket, and the Old Fashioned had helped me unwind a little. My smile was relaxed and genuine.

"Fancy seeing you here," she began archly. "I was beginning to think you were all work and no play." She was wearing a tangerine dress that only added to the overall feeling of warmth and lightness in the place.

"Well, things have been busy, but I try to get out every once in a while." It was a leaden reply, and I tried not to wince visibly. It seemed like so long since I had felt this kind of desire or excitement for anything, I barely knew how to act. I glanced at her, trying to keep that relaxed smile in place. Freya's mouth was small, and that, together with the curious and ironic expression she often wore, made it difficult to tell if she was smiling or not. She seemed to be smiling now, but the intent behind that smile was opaque.

"How are things at Balfour," she asked, gamely following the line of discussion I had oafishly plunked down. "Are you taking good care of your clients?"

"We're trying." I noticed, with some alarm, that I could barely even rally myself when discussing work. Freya's hair was pulled back and her cheekbones and eyes really did look beautiful. I thought for a second about saying so, but immediately realized it was both too forward and too corny. In desperation, I offered up, "Of course, some are easier to take care of than others." It didn't even make sense, but I was just glad I hadn't blurted out something about how dreary our second quarter numbers had been. It didn't help that her dress showed her figure to such subtle but unmistakable advantage. It was all I could do to form complete sentences.

But the gods smiled on me. "I'm sure they are," she returned graciously. "But I wonder about your investors. I've been looking to invest a little recently. Maybe Balfour would be a good place."

"I can only imagine what kind of assets you'd have to invest, but based on what I do know, I'm sure they're very valuable. We'd certainly see to it that they received the attention they deserve."

Her smile widened and passed into the territory of the unmistakable. "I've been somewhat disappointed with the investments I've made in the past. They start out with a lot of noise and activity, promising great things. But then they fade quickly, and leave me with very little return on my outlay."

"That's unconscionable. They should recognize a valuable investor when they see one."

"They'd have to know their business much better than most of these New York boys seem to. You can't recognize a valuable investor, much less know how to please one, when your fundamentals aren't strong. I'm not even expecting long-term yields at this point, just something more than a flash in the pan and a short sell."

"I certainly like to think we're more capable than that. Just off the top of my head I can think of some good strategies for you, and I'd be happy to explore them with you in more depth sometime soon."

At that point Jocelyn appeared in the doorway of the back room and motioned to Freya. "Well, it looks like my presence is required," she said. "But I'm certainly impressed by what I've seen so far, and I'd like to look into working with you in the very near future."

She made sure I had her number then joined the party in the back. I finished my drink, gave the barman an exuberant smile and an even more exuberant tip, and went out into the street and the warmth of the early evening sun.

The tattooed teddy bear's Old Fashioneds had been deceptively potent, and after two of those and my talk with Freya I was feeling a little too elated to go straight to Genevieve's party. I took a walk around the block, stopped to buy a bottle of wine and some flowers for the table, and then headed up to Genevieve and Franklin's new digs.

They were in the penthouse apartment, and I knew from speaking with Genevieve that theirs was the only unit that had been completed and that they were living in the building basically alone at this point. The nameplates in the outer lobby were made of an elegant ivory, rich enough to remind everyone that this was now a luxury apartment. In a somewhat comically deflating touch, the buzzers of all the empty apartments were covered with tape, with only Genevieve and Franklin's uncovered at the very top. As I buzzed them I noticed that their names were written in a kind of gold leaf cursive that subtly, tastefully, but very surely signaled their distinction even among this august group of names floating among clouds of purest ivory. I suppose I was happy for Genevieve and Franklin, but this still all struck me as rather amusing as I went in and headed up the elevator.

Franklin opened the door when I arrived at the apartment. I liked Franklin, who was quiet, bookish, and somewhat nervous. He never really seemed comfortable or even in the right place at Genevieve's gatherings, but he soldiered through them all manfully. He smiled at me with a mixture of relief and apology as he welcomed me in. He seemed to find the whole occasion a little ridiculous and to regret his part in it. I greeted him heartily, still feeling the Old Fashioneds, and presented him with the flowers and wine I had bought in the street.

The new apartment really was impressive. Franklin showed me around it a bit, somewhat sheepishly, seemingly a little embarrassed to be showing off but also happy to have my company and be spared the general hubbub of the gathering that was already going strong in the kitchen, where Genevieve was finishing the dinner preparations. From the small vestibule we entered into the middle of a long room furnished in mahogany. This large room basically wrapped around this part of the apartment in a large, square C shape, enclosing the kitchen and dining room. At the other end of the C a hallway led back to the bedrooms. The entire C was paneled in rich brown and red wood, and in the long room that ran parallel to the kitchen and dining room the windows opened onto a view of the river and the Manhattan Bridge.

The kitchen and dining room, perhaps in a nod to the building's somewhat more working class past, were relatively simple by comparison, chiefly furnished with white tile with blue accents. Franklin and I went in to join the others.

The kitchen and dining room were unassuming compared to what I had just seen but still quite large. The rest of the group had assembled in the kitchen and were standing around an island while Genevieve moved all manner of food in and out of various pots and pans. Kate Watson was there, as expected, with her boyfriend Zach. I wasn't sure what exactly Kate was doing now, but she must have been buzzing around the Democratic Party's establishment in some way or another. I had gotten trapped in a brief conversation with Zach at a party recently, and so knew that he now "worked in venture capital," an even more meaningless occupation than that of his wife, and one that apparently required even less effort. Still, I suppose it was a step up for him after spending ten years getting a Master's in Creative Writing from Columbia. Hannahlore Sampson was also there. I didn't know her well but gathered from things Genevieve had said that she was an aspiring actress or something of the sort. She was rather pretty, in a vacuous, well-fed kind of way, but other than that didn't make much of an impression. It seemed like she might have been there with Bradford Coxcomb, another peripheral figure who was, so far as I could remember, part of the Keith Halwood set. Finally there was Clarkie Kipner. Clarkie had dated my sister for years, so I knew him well. His mother was a Cravath and his father wrote for *The New Contrarian Consensus*, so the general ineffectiveness of the trust fund kid was compounded in his case by a doughy enthusiasm for gimcrack intellectual fads. Still, he was harmless, like the Dauphin in *Henry V*. Other than Clarkie I didn't know these people well and, as you might be able to guess from these descriptions, I was happy to keep it that way.

The only people I really liked in this group were our hosts. Genevieve was basically a socialite, though genuinely kind and intelligent. She liked to describe herself as the "curator of a lifestyle Instagram," a phrase that always amused me when I considered how confusing it would have been to anyone ten years ago. Franklin was the only one among them who worked in any real way, though he mostly did freelance editing, purely out of personal interest, and kept very quiet about it.

As Franklin and I entered the kitchen he instinctively shrunk off to the side of the room and I followed him without thinking about it. I found myself standing in front of one of the speakers playing music. The music was low, but standing a few inches from the speaker it affected me (it occurred to me that Franklin may have purposely chosen a spot in front of the speakers to have a reason to beg out of conversation). Nina Simone's "Sinnerman" was playing, directly at my back, and it made me feel rattled and fractious. The group around the island continued their conversation and barely took note of Franklin and myself. I smiled an apology to Franklin and slipped back into the main hall, where I poured myself a drink from a display of bottles I had noticed on our way through. Having taken care of that I went over and opened a window. Bourbon in hand and evening breeze on my face I felt pretty good. I stood there for a couple of minutes, having recaptured that feeling from earlier, then steeled myself to reenter the fray.

As I walked back into the kitchen Genevieve immediately saw me and greeted me warmly. "Ethan! So glad to see you! I didn't even know you were here." Franklin was leaning against the wall with his hands behind his back. He said nothing.

I drifted over toward the island, smiling at Genevieve then scanning the other faces, which mostly offered a choice between vacant, exaggerated smiles or muted hostility and confusion. I returned Genevieve's warm greeting, then cast a glance back over my shoulder at Franklin. He met my gaze with a tight smile and remained leaning against the wall, as if his hands behind the small of his back were attached to some vital life source he couldn't possibly leave.

We hugged and Genevieve asked me if I had seen the place. "Yes, Franklin showed me around a bit. It's beautiful, Genevieve. You're going to be very happy here."

"You know the building still has the original metal fire escapes," she said. "I love them! They give the place so much authenticity."

Then she fell back into dinner preparations and I was subsumed by the horde. Clarkie and I smiled at each other. He was talking to Hannahlore.

"I found a really great source for activated cashews," she said. "You can tell the difference for hours after eating them. And it's only twenty-five dollars per cashew, which is such a good price."

"Oh, yeah," said Clarkie. "You have to activate your cashews." Bradford took a sip of wine and gave Clarkie a less than friendly look, peering at him over the rounded glass. The conversation about activated cashews continued and I wondered if the evening might venture into jade egg territory.

Franklin glided up silently and poured me a glass of wine. I gave him a friendly smile and he and I stood there quietly for a few moments while the others chirped away happily. Then dinner was ready and we all repaired to the dining room.

Genevieve was clearly enjoying handling all the details of making and serving the dinner herself, and I have to say she did it well and without being at all fussy about it. The first course was served and we all settled in and politely waited for our hostess to direct the conversation.

"Oh my God, you guys," Genevieve began, flushed with pleasure at how well the evening was progressing, "have you heard about these murders? And the police theory about what's happening?"

Probably the only thing I wanted to discuss less than von Clapp was the murders, though I had known they were likely to be a topic of conversation as well. I was vaguely aware that word had begun to spread that there might be some connection between the three high society murders of the past three weeks, and that the connection might be the Vows column in the *Primrose*. But no one was taking it very seriously, and certainly no one expected it might continue along those lines. So it didn't really give anyone pause that Genevieve and Franklin's marriage had recently been announced in the column, and that Clarkie had just been featured the past Sunday. It was something unusual and interesting but obviously too far-fetched to mean anything, and could still be discussed lightly, sitting comfortably under the sunny sky of Marcel Duchamp's epitaph, "Besides, it is always someone else who dies."

I of course had some connection with each of the victims, but no one there knew me well enough to know that except Genevieve and Franklin, in whose discretion I trusted, and possibly Clarkie, on whose oblivion I counted. So I took a page from Franklin's book and pretended to be too engrossed in my antipasto to speak, and let the conversation bubble along, hoping it would soon move on to something else.

"Murders? I don't think so. I saw that model was killed. Such a tragedy—she was so beautiful."

"Jordan Wymark was shot a few weeks ago, too. Right here in Manhattan."

"Oh, I do remember hearing about that. I didn't know Jordan very well, but that was pretty shocking."

"Yes, and another girl was killed the week before Jordan. Each of them had either just been married or were about to be married. And they had all been profiled in the Vows column of *The New York Primrose*."

"Really? What a bizarre coincidence."

"Yes, but is it a coincidence? I've heard the police think there may be some connection."

"What connection? The fact that they all appeared in the *Primrose*?"

"Yes, exactly. Maybe there's a murderer out there, picking his victims out of the wedding announcements in the *Rose*."

"That's ridiculous. That doesn't happen in real life."

"Yes, I think so too. You have to have an actual reason to kill someone. No one does it because a voice told them to go shoot the person they saw in the paper."

"Well, one idea is that the killer is targeting them because they're wealthy. They all have the same basic background— wealthy families, old money. Private schools, lives of comfort and glamour. Maybe it's someone lashing out at all that."

I made a bid to put an end to the discussion. "Bah," I said, "that's all nonsense. I doubt it's someone out there who has paranoid delusions about people he sees in the paper, but that's at least possible."

We were finished with our first course. Genevieve and Franklin gathered the plates and took them into the kitchen. The main course was still baking in the oven, and a delicious odor of mushrooms, lemon, and basil was beginning to drift out into the dining room.

My intervention was mostly successful—conversation turned to the question of economic inequality.

"Do poor people actually read the Vows column in the *Primrose*? It doesn't seem like they would."

"Do we even have poor people any more? I thought we had universal basic income now, and everyone was doing alright."

"No, there's no UBI. A lot of states have legalized marijuana. Maybe that's what you were thinking about."

"Hmm, maybe. But then what am I paying all these taxes for?"

What began as genuine confusion soon darkened, and the mood of rancor against the resentful plebs rose while our hosts were in the kitchen drizzling raspberry vinaigrette over our spinach salads. It passed through decrying their ingratitude to wondering why they refused to get jobs and work if they wanted money. As Genevieve and Franklin returned with our salads it passed on to suggesting they might like things better in Mexico.

I glanced up at Genevieve and saw her brow furrowed as she lowered a plate in front of Hannahlore. She seemed to be trying to think of how to bring the conversation back under control. Franklin gave me a concerned look as he gave me my salad, apparently wondering what could have happened during the three or four minutes he and Genevieve had been gone.

"No, actually it's nothing to worry about," Clarkie said exultantly. "We're really all just living in a computer simulation. The poor aren't even real!"

"Well," said Genevieve, swinging herself down into her chair as if there wasn't a moment to lose, "things certainly got lively while we were in the kitchen. Did you guys see that Walt Heil was in town this weekend?"

"I can never keep my Silicon Valley supervillains straight," I said, trying to help her restore order, "which one is he?"

"He's one of the richest men in the world," Bradford said importantly. "He founded the most popular website on the internet, Outrage.com." He took a sip of wine then added sententiously, "You have to admire the innovative mind." Perhaps instead of jade eggs we were going to get bitcoin.

"Last year it brought in more than ten billion dollars," Clarkie added. Bradford half winced, half scowled when he said this, having apparently conceived some kind of rivalry between the two of them. Clarkie was completely unaware of it, which of course just made the whole thing more entertaining.

"Is he the one who drinks baby's blood in his mushroom-ayahuasca coffee," I asked. "Or funded that militia?"

"No, but he has been sued for sexual harassment like fifty times."

This of course led on to recollections of the countless similar cases that had emerged just in the past few months, which spurred a rare foray into the conversation by young Zachary.

"It's so difficult to be hearing about this all the time," Zach lowed. "People don't really think about that, how hard it is for good men like me to be bombarded with all these details all the time." I leaned back from the table a bit. Zach had six very hard eyes on him, but he was oblivious.

"You know this opioid crisis is huge right now."

"I've heard something about that, but I'm not sure what it is. Do you know?"

"Yeah, I guess people start on pain-killers, get addicted, and then go over to heroin."

"Wow. Where do they get the heroin?"

"I don't know. They buy it on the street, I guess."

"I mean, where does it come from?"

"Oh. That's a good question. Mexico, I guess."

"No, I'm pretty sure heroin is made from opium, which grows in Afghanistan or Australia or some place like that."

"Well, I thought at some point it came in from Mexico."

"Careful, Bradford" I said, trying to lighten the mood of general befuddled consternation, "von Clapp is getting to you."

Kate let out a contemptuous snort. "Can you imagine what our neighbors think? Especially Canada!"

"Yes, if only we could elect a brain genius softboy who's spent half his adult life in blackface."

I was worried this was going to lead us onto the topic of von Clapp, but the mysterious specter of the opioid crisis was not a topic to be abandoned so easily. Hannahlore asked Clarkie if he had talked to his dad about it, thereby irritating both Bradford and Kate, who apparently felt that her policy expertise had been slighted. She placed her phone on the table and began typing and scrolling.

"Well," said Clarkie, looking around at each of us, prolonging the moment, "It just so happens that I asked him about it just the other day. He said he really didn't know, he hadn't had time to look into it. But he said that if people don't like where they live, they should move to a place where there's more tech and less heroin." This was something of an anticlimax, and the disappointment was palpable. Hannahlore frowned. Bradford beamed. Clarkie tried to rally with more inside information. "He's working on a piece for the next *New Contrarian Consensus* right now. It's about the von Clapp Backers controversy."

Some of the other guests looked at him strangely but I knew what he was talking about. A group of Republicans who abhorred von Clapp's antics tried to mount some kind of resistance to his rise in their party, calling themselves "Never von Clapps." Then someone suggested they were "clapping back" at Ivan, and they should call themselves "von Clapp Backers," so they did. Unfortunately this made them seem like supporters of von Clapp, and a series of bitter recriminations ensued, punctuated by the occasional desperate insistence that the meaning was perfectly clear. Between this and the slaggat fiasco it was a difficult season for snappy political nicknames. But it gave everyone exactly what they wanted, a chance to talk endlessly about words and meanings and misunderstandings and the history of things on the internet, and to completely ignore all those real things with sharp teeth and open mouths just outside their doors.

In fact the media, or at least the media any of us in that room were likely to follow, had given far more attention to the von Clapp Backers "controversy" than to the opioid crisis, and Clarkie Senior knew his business in writing about that. Even so, I don't think anyone was quite expecting that response, and we all kept looking at Clarkie, expecting he had something more to say. Then Genevieve cut in. "I saw that longread he wrote about vintage alarm clocks," she said helpfully. "So cool that people can write about that!"

The conversation about opioids resumed, with something

of the air of a group of adults turning back to their confab after briefly humoring a child's interruption.

"The other day," said Bradford, "I heard someone say that von Clapp won because of the opioid crisis. They didn't really explain, but I assumed they meant something like people being too high when they voted and picking von Clapp by mistake. Is that why he won, Kate?" Bradford gave her a smolderingly interested look as he said this, apparently meaning to provoke Hannahlore by lavishing his attention on Kate.

"That and racism," Kate nodded, without looking up from her phone. Sadly for Bradford, this new stratagem seemed to be working about as well as his pronounced enthusiasm for activated cashews.

Genevieve had slipped back into the kitchen and now reappeared pushing a cart. Inside a silver dish was the main course. "We'll just leave that in there to finish cooking and then reabsorb its juices. It should be ready in about ten minutes," she said.

Clarkie excused himself to go wash up. The conversation fell into a bit of a lull, as we all cast our eyes on the gleaming silver dish and inhaled the lovely aroma that was slowly filling the room.

Eventually Hannahlore broke the silence. "You know," she said, "I saw a flyer the other day for a lit class at the New School that was supposed to help people understand the von Clapp voter, or something like that. It was mostly Southern fiction."

"Are you going to take the class?"

"I thought about it," said Hannahlore. "But I looked at the reading list. They just wanted us to read a bunch of bro authors. Faulkner, some guy named Flannagan Connors, Cormac McCartney, probably that Tony Morrison everyone always talks about—all just bro novelists."

Franklin looked at me desperately. I gathered he might have been nervously contemplating a correction, though he looked like he was about to attempt a jailbreak. "Oh, yeah, total bros," Genevieve tutted sympathetically, making a light signal to Franklin, who said nothing.

"Yeah, that's terrible," Kate agreed. "Wait, was Faulkner black?"

"Oh, uh, I don't know," said Hannahlore. "If he was, then he's not a bro, of course."

"No, of course not," said Kate, then turned to Zach. "Well, was he?"

"Huh? How should I know?"

"You spent like eight years in that writing program!"

"Oh, Columbia, yeah. But a lot of that time I was just working on my final project. We didn't really talk about that kind of thing anyway, specific writers. I mean, of course it's important to be diverse, but I don't think I've heard of that guy, Fowler or whatever. So I really don't know."

Kate scowled, but Genevieve swept in and chirped happily, "What did you learn then?"

"Mostly the rules of writing. Things you can't ever do if you want your writing to be good."

"Oh, like what?"

"Like don't use adverbs. Adverbs are really bad."

"You mean 'bad,'" Genevieve smiled. "Terrible," she added and grimaced playfully from the strain of her adverbial abstention.

"Adjectives aren't much better," Zach said glumly.

Another conversational lull ensued. Our attention again migrated to the chicken in the silver dish, but it wasn't ready yet. We all seemed a little unsure of how to handle this dire situation.

"I think maybe I should go check on Clarkie," I said. Between the Old Fashioneds at the Marble Cod, the drink I had poured myself when I arrived, and the few splashes of wine I had drunk with dinner, I was feeling rather heady (though I'm happy to say I was able to stand up and set off without incident). I passed out of the dining room and back through the kitchen, not entirely sure where I might find Clarkie or what he would be up to. A few seconds later I came rushing back into the room. Bradford was sitting with his back to the door, and I grabbed the back of his chair as hard as I could, staring wildly at the others.

No one seemed to notice the manner of my reentrance at first, and Bradford kept holding forth. "You see, I haven't just travelled to Machu Picchu, I've really studied it. Watched a couple of movies about it, even read part of a book about it. And I can tell you—"

But at that point Genevieve realized something was wrong. "Ethan, what is it," she said, and as my eyes met hers she seemed to get some inkling of what had happened. "Where, where's Clarkie," she said standing up from the table, her voice rising in panic. The others remained oblivious, and for a few seconds Genevieve and I were locked in a silent communion of horror. "We need…call the police," I was finally able to get out. "What is it," Bradford asked, half turning around in his chair, obviously irritated at having been interrupted. Genevieve was up and beginning to move around the table to go through the kitchen. "No," I cried, and stepped in front of her. "Genevieve, call the police! *And no one go through that door!*"

After a couple of minutes I recovered my composure and remembered Detective Allison's card, still in my wallet. I called him and he arrived only a few minutes after the first uniformed police. Two beat cops had answered the initial 911 call, and although there was some confusion getting them into the building and up to the right apartment, they followed my directions to the body, which was lying in the hallway leading back to the bedrooms, and then secured the rest of the apartment. One of them was fairly young and, when he reemerged from the back rooms of the apartment, looked pretty shaken. Just as they came back to the dining room and were trying to figure out how many of us were there and who we were, Allison arrived and quickly took control of the situation.

Genevieve was hit the hardest. Every few minutes she seemed to buckle and shrink a little more, the full enormity of what had happened coming home to her like a series of hammer blows. Franklin was doing his best to comfort her and keep her focused on something outside her own mind, but was also in far worse shape than I would have expected.

Allison, meanwhile, demanded my attention. He left the two beat cops in the dining room with everyone else while he pulled me out into the front hallway to find out who the various members of the dinner party were. I tried to give him a quick rundown of each. He listened intently, often interrupting me with questions, about half of which seemed pertinent and about half of which made little sense to me. In any case, just as I was finishing my disquisition for him another set of police arrived, this one including both more uniforms and a couple of detectives in suits. I noticed Detective Leo was not among them.

"Detective Leo isn't coming tonight," Allison said, apparently reading my thoughts. "Would you believe it? Tonight's his anniversary."

Allison directed the new arrivals to various points around the apartment. Then he turned back to me. "So what happened here, Mr. Balfour," he asked, his manner somehow both open and penetrating at once.

I stared at him for a moment, unsure of how to answer. "I'm pretty sure Clarkie is dead," I finally said, and looked at him uncertainly.

He nodded sympathetically, then something seemed to click for him. "Did you find him, Mr. Balfour?"

I just nodded back at him and, rather foolishly, gulped.

Allison looked over to his right where the hallway opened onto the main room, then reached out his arm and piloted me down the hallway and into a chair. He pulled up another one and sat a few feet in front of me. His eyes were surprisingly soft and sympathetic, and seemed genuine. "What happened, Mr. Balfour?"

"I don't know, Detective. I suppose he might have shot himself, but why would he do that here? And he obviously didn't seem like he was about to do anything like that. So I think someone else must have shot him."

"So you think he was shot?"

"He must have been. There was so much blood,

Detective."

He nodded benevolently but in the way you do when you're humoring a child.

"So he got up from the table, and was gone for, what? A few minutes? Or longer?"

"Something like that. Probably five or ten. He used to date my sister so I knew him fairly well. I knew he could get distracted and forget about himself and others. Genevieve was about to serve the main course so I wanted to go get him, to make sure he'd be there and wouldn't hold things up. I saw him lying on the ground in the hallway. At first I didn't realize what was happening, but something made me stop. I thought the blood was a red rug or something. Then I realized what it was, and why Clarkie must have been lying on the ground. I froze for a second or two, or maybe half a minute, I really don't know, then ran back in to the dining room."

"So you thought he had been shot? Did you hear anything in the dining room?"

"No, not at all…So I guess it must have been someone else then. They must have used a silencer."

Allison shook his head slightly. "That would have suppressed the sound a little, Mr. Balfour, but you still would have all heard it in the dining room. Unless you had something else making a lot of noise."

"No, nothing. But the blood, Detective…"

"I know, Mr. Balfour." He got up and called one of the other officers, who came in from the other end of the long room. They consulted briefly then Allison returned to the seat across from me.

"I'm going to take a look myself in a minute, Mr. Balfour, but it looks like the wound was made with a knife. I don't want this to be too upsetting for you, but that could definitely account for the blood, especially if it had been a few minutes before you saw him.

"Mr. Balfour, I understand you're shaken. I've worked a lot of homicides at this point, and they still sometimes get to me. And it's never been someone I know. So I can only imagine what you must be going through right now. If you'd

133

like, I can just take a brief statement from you and send you home." It might have been my imagination, but I thought his voice seemed to lilt up a little at the end of that last sentence, as if he were hoping I would decline his offer.

"Actually, Detective Allison, I really don't think I want to be alone right now. I just need to pull myself together a little, but I'd rather stay here a bit, assuming I wouldn't be in the way. You might have more questions, and I might remember more. I might even be able to help you a little talking to the others. I know that might be interfering, but I remember our earlier conversation and how you seemed to be looking for help in understanding some of what's going on here."

"That probably would be helpful, sir, assuming you're up to it. You're right that we'll probably have more questions and that you'll probably remember more. And you could maybe sit in on our interviews. But I don't want to push you, Mr. Balfour."

"No, no, Detective, I think that'd be best for me." I paused for a moment. "Detective, you know that Clarkie was featured in this week's Vows column in *The New York Primrose*?"

Allison took in a breath and his shoulders tensed up, but he nodded as if he had been expecting this. "I didn't know who the deceased was until just now, Mr. Balfour, so no, I had no idea. But I'm afraid this isn't really surprising to me."

"I think until now," I said, "I was still somewhat frightened, afraid that whoever had done this was still in the apartment, and we might be in danger. But in the back of my mind, I remembered that and I think I knew what had happened, and no one was going to come after the rest of us."

We both paused and looked at each other. I took a deep breath and straightened myself up. "So that was…Clarkie was stabbed?"

"Something like that, Mr. Balfour. We don't need to worry about details now. But it looks like it might have been done with a knife from the kitchen here. Whoever did this was a pretty cool customer."

"But how did this person get in here—" Suddenly I

grabbed the arms of my chair violently. My whole body almost spasmed, then I looked at the window. "Detective—I —the window."

"What's that, Mr. Balfour?"

"I opened the window. When I came in—I had a drink in here while everyone else was in the kitchen. I opened the window because I felt warm and thought it was too stuffy. That's how they got in. It's my fault!"

Allison held his hand up to calm me down. "Let's not jump to any conclusions, Mr. Balfour. Let's wait and talk to everyone, then we'll have a better picture of what happened. It's very helpful to know the window was opened, and when. But we have no idea whether the killer used that window. We really don't know anything at this point. I once arrested a cat burglar who robbed dinner parties like this. He would jimmy the front door and get in that way. We just have to wait and see.

"I really shouldn't be dragging a civilian into an investigation like this, but these are extraordinary times. If anyone asks, you're just staying and sitting with us during these interviews to help us keep track of everyone and to make them feel better."

That gave me a little more courage, so I told Allison what I had noticed coming into the building, that Genevieve and Franklin's place was the only one with a nameplate as of yet. He had noticed the same thing, and reached the obvious conclusion—anyone who had followed Clarkie here would know which apartment he would be in. But he cautioned me not to assume this had happened.

"Here's my advice, Mr. Balfour—let's keep as open a mind as we can for as long as we can. When we've gotten as many facts as possible about what happened tonight, we can try to piece together what happened, or at least rule out what didn't."

Allison's caution was quickly vindicated. Genevieve and Franklin were the first to be brought in to the makeshift interview room that the main room had become. Genevieve wasn't able to say much, but they both told us that the air conditioning in the building didn't work yet, so the windows were frequently open. In fact, that night Franklin had opened all the windows in the back of the apartment, and had opened two in the main front room. Genevieve had asked him to do that, since she thought the apartment would get too hot with her cooking. They were both surprised that I had found all the windows in the main room closed when I slipped out of the kitchen to have a drink.

As for the building, both Genevieve and Franklin confirmed that none of the other units were yet occupied. There were people going in and out all day, dressed both in work clothes and in more professional attire. Allison asked them if any workmen or other strangers had been in their apartment recently, and they said no. He asked who else might have known who was coming to the dinner, and neither had any real idea who, if anyone, they may have told about the guest list.

Allison asked if there was any way into the apartment besides the front door and the various windows. It was then that Genevieve seemed to realize that someone had likely come in through one of the windows, perhaps the window of the master bedroom, which had been open. She started to break down completely, saying she would never spend another night there. Allison tried to calm her down by asking Franklin if he had locked the front door after I arrived. He had not. The thought that a murderer might have walked through her front door, however, did little to comfort Genevieve. Franklin quickly told the detective that there were no other means of entry of which he knew, then one of the uniform cops who had been hovering took them both back into the dining room.

It was awkward and tight maneuvering, with Clarkie's body blocking the way back to the bedrooms, and visible just around the corner of the main room where we were sitting. Allison tried to keep things moving but also to get everything he needed out of each witness. We had been joined by another detective, who at first gave me a quizzical look but was assured by Allison that my presence was kosher.

The next guest to be ushered into our little salon was Zach. He flopped down into the chair opposite Detective Allison and, after a quick peak at the three of us, dropped his eyes to the floor.

"I'm probably not going to be of much help," he said, somewhat sullenly. "I'm not always real keyed in to my surroundings. To be honest," he said, glancing briefly at me with a mixture of embarrassment and hostility, "I didn't know there were two other guys here tonight."

"You didn't know?" Allison, for once, was unable to control his reaction.

"You know there were three," I said.

"Oh, well Franklin. I know him. He and I went to school together."

"So you didn't know how many people were at the table?"

"Not really, no. Trying to keep track of other people's names and life narratives is a definite stressor for me."

"Did you notice anything during dinner?" Allison couldn't help himself. "Did you not notice there were different men speaking at different times?"

Zach shrugged, seeming slightly resentful. "I try not to listen to what other people say. It mostly just bums me out."

Allison asked him a few pointed questions but got nothing in return. Finally he asked Zach if he had closed any of the windows in that room.

"Windows?" Zach looked up at the row of windows in front of him. He registered their existence and seemed almost offended to find them there, staring back at him with their glassy, blue-black eyes. "No, I didn't close any. Why would I do that?"

"I suppose you wouldn't," said Allison, and dismissed him.

"You said he works in finance," Allison asked when he was gone.

"I think that just means he receives an allowance from his father, who is a hedge fund manager."

"That's all we get nowadays," said the other detective, who was standing behind the chairs where Allison and I sat.

"A bunch of doughy retards who have never done anything but stare at their phones."

"I don't know, Gilly," Allison said. "Maybe some of these kids will invent a better CPAP machine for you and me."

"Bah, the hell with it," returned Gilly, "I'm ready to go."

At that point the uniform returned with Kate. She had as little of interest to say about any of this as she did about anything else. We did learn, however, that she closed both windows.

"Yes, after Franklin showed us around and the rest of the group went into the kitchen I lingered in here to admire the view. I thought the breeze was too strong, though, so I closed the two open windows."

"You closed them," asked Allison. "Just like that? Was there any other reason?"

"Like I told you," said Kate, oddly defiant, "it was too cold in here and the wind was blowing in. So I closed them."

Suddenly a strange, up-and-down whistle seemed to emanate from the windows themselves. After a couple seconds' confusion we realized it was Gilly's phone.

"It's my brother," he said, and his pocket released another whistle. "He's at the Mets game, must want to keep me informed."

"Maybe you could silence your phone," said Kate.

Gilly gave his head a single, stoic shake. "Got to keep it on for when the chief buzzes. And he will buzz, oh yes, believe you me, young lady. So you were saying, you closed the windows. And did you lock them?"

"Lock them? No."

"Was that because you didn't have the strength or because trying to turn the locks hurt your hands too much, miss, or did you not want to lock them?" Allison made a slight motion to him, and he dropped it.

"No, I didn't even look for the locks. I just wanted to close the windows because of the cold air. I—"

"Cold air," said Gilly, "it's mid-June, miss. If you're using illegal narcotics, it will catch up with you, young lady. Maybe not tonight, but you won't be so young and carefree

138

forever. Think it over while you have the chance, missy."
Kate stared at him. His phone gave off another whistle.

"Must be a good game," said Allison.

"Joey always wanted to be a play-by-play guy," Gilly said
seriously.

"Thank you, Ms. Watson," said Allison. "You've been
very helpful."

"Well," said Kate, drawing herself up, "I'll have you—"
but the uniformed officer loomed. She gave me a look and I
indicated she had best return to the dining room. As she was
walking away Gilly took out his phone to steal a quick look
at the screen. As he did so it whistled again. I could see Kate
clench her fists and try to look back, but alas she was too far
gone, and the uniformed officer kept her going. As she
walked away I had a vision of her slipping down the greasy
pole of Democratic consultancy before she could reach
Robbie Mook levels of untouchable incompetence, marrying
Zach and moving to Westchester county, making
schoolmarmish social media posts about how everyone
needed to get a flu shot. It was poignant, in its way, except
for the fact that I cared not at all.

Soon Bradford was sitting across from us. He cut a
slightly less ridiculous figure than Zach but was no more
helpful. He was so caught up in admiring his hosts'
magnificent apartment that he barely took note of much of
what was going on around him. He had, in fact, barely
noticed Clarkie at all. He was obviously lying, but I doubted
he could say anything useful, so I didn't bother to contradict
him or give any indication to Allison that he should try
probing. Soon he was gone and we had our last interview,
Hannahlore.

The exchange was brief and predictable. Like the others,
she had not noticed anything unusual, but also had no real
idea what would have been unusual. She was mainly focused
on herself, with an all too familiar mixture of narcissism and
anxiety, and then on the people and events around her. None
of them seemed peculiar or even remarkable. Now that we
knew what happened to the windows, there wasn't even that

to ask her about. She said she would continue to think about it and let the detectives know if she remembered anything that seemed important or even slightly curious.

As Allison was finishing up with her Genevieve and Franklin returned to the room. They were leaving to spend the night at Franklin's parents' townhouse on the Upper East Side, and wanted to let Allison know where they were going and make sure he was done with them for the night. As they came in Hannahlore was getting up to leave. She stopped and hesitated for a moment, seemingly unsure about something.

Allison leaned forward slightly with an expectant look on his face. "Ms. Sampson," he said, "is there anything else you'd like to say?"

"Well…no," she said, still clearly undecided.

"Are you sure," said Allison, "anything you might remember or be thinking about right now could help us." He didn't really look it, but at this point I had been around him enough to know he was really quite eager.

"Well," she said, looking uncertainly at the floor, then eventually sweeping her gaze up to Genevieve. "Genevieve, that chicken smelled so good and…we never got a chance to try it. Do you think we could take some home? In a bag or something?"

Genevieve said nothing. Gilly's cellphone whistled.

Chapter Seven

The Letter

I don't know how late Allison (and eventually Leo, I'm sure) were at work that night, or who made what decision at what level, but sometime the next morning the story began to appear online that the police believed a serial killer was responsible for all four murders. The police themselves held a news conference around noon. Allison was there, looking slightly bedraggled and uncomfortable with all the attention (in fact he cut exactly the figure I would have expected). The point of the news conference seemed to be just to put the word out that there was almost certainly a pattern to these killings, and to let everyone know that the police were taking the killing of four of New York's socioeconomic elite very seriously indeed. They didn't seem particularly interested in information from the public, which wasn't all that surprising given that in place of a suspect they merely had a list of newspaper clippings. They didn't even suggest a motive for the crimes, and dodged the question when a reporter put it to them.

But I suppose they knew their business. The bare notion that someone was stalking and murdering the city's patrician class was enough to set everyone abuzz. I understand it became national news, but just in New York I know everyone was instantly obsessed by the idea. Once the story had fully circulated after lunch, everyone at work either avoided looking in my direction or stared at me like I was some kind of endangered exotic bird they had never seen before and expected to vanish before their eyes.

I didn't know when the police might contact me to talk to them again, or if they would at all. So I went about my day as usual, though I was half-expecting the police to call at any minute. When I saw the press conference at noon I figured their dance cards were more than full and I tried to forget about them and the murders generally. It was then that my thoughts returned to Freya. It was only the previous night that I had seen her, but these were extraordinary times, not least for me. I thought I would call her and see if she was free that weekend.

Somewhat to my annoyance, I got her voicemail. I left a message and she texted me about an hour later:

I'm sorry I missed your call. I woke up with a terrible summer cold—it happens every year. I'm afraid I wouldn't be very good company this weekend, unless you want to see a real-life reenactment of the Typhoid Mary saga. But I'll get back to you when I'm feeling better, maybe the middle of next week. My regrets on this weekend!

I was staring out the window feeling sorry for myself when I got a call from Detective Leo, asking me to come down to the station as soon as I possibly could. He said they wanted my opinion on something they could only show me there, and then stressed again that it was urgent. I told him I would be there posthaste, and went to tell Dad I had to go. He had been hit rather hard by Clarkie's death, and although his habitual reluctance to let me leave the office resurfaced for a moment, when he realized it was for the murder investigation he merely nodded his head wearily and lowered his darkened face back to his desk. I was worried about him but, to be frank, I was also eager to get out of the office. As for what was waiting for me at the police station, I was a little apprehensive but generally keen to work into the police's enquiry.

When I asked for Detective Leo at the police station I was informed he was in the Situation Room and that I should wait for him to come fetch me. The Situation Room turned out to be rather newer and sleeker than the room where I had met with Allison and Leo previously, but still seemed to me surprisingly familiar, not terribly different from a conference room you might find in any office building in Manhattan. Somewhat to my surprise, once Leo led me into the room it was just the two of us. It was the first time I had ever been alone with him, and although I of course remembered our exchanges in the earlier interview, this somehow felt like the first time that he had ever spoken to me directly. I assumed that Allison would join us momentarily, but when he didn't I asked Leo about him.

"Detective Allison is in court today. Had to testify in an older case. So it's just me—hope that's not a problem for you." Then he gave me that sleepy, cryptic smile that might have been friendly, amused, or icily ironic.

"No, of course not," I said, trying to give him a pleasantly reassuring smile. "I'm happy to help in any way I can, working with whoever I can."

Leo gave me a curt nod and his face became serious. "No point in beating around the bush here, Mr. Balfour. We've received a communication that claims to be from the killer. We believe it may be genuine."

Leo's face remained blank and impassive, but I must have looked alarmed. "It's alright, Mr. Balfour," he said evenly, "this sometimes happens with serial killers. It doesn't make them any more or less dangerous, though it usually adds to their legend."

I have to admit I felt a strange thrill when he said that. "Serial killer? I guess that's what this person is."

"Yes, and it's not unusual that they contact the police or the media, especially when the case is getting a lot of public attention. We've received several notes and such since yesterday's story, and most of them are obvious cranks. But this one, we think, may really be from the killer.

"I'm sure I don't need to tell you that this is an extraordinary measure we're taking, showing it to you. But we're really at a loss as to who this person might be and how he keeps getting access to the victims. I hope it goes without saying that you cannot tell anyone about this, and definitely not that we've shown it to you."

I nodded seriously and he took a plastic sleeve out of the folder he was holding and gave it to me. Inside the sleeve was the letter.

143

To my admirers,

Isn't it time we make a proper acquaintance? I know you've been wondering about me for quite some time, and now that you've finally decided I must be real, it seemed only polite to send you a little note introducing myself. Not that I'm going to give you a name, of course—what fun would that be? But it's only fair, after all, since I don't know any of your names. I suppose that I will learn them, once you've learned mine. I hope it won't seem rude if I say that I'm not looking forward to that little engagement, and I'm going to do what I can to postpone it.

I don't know if you admire my handiwork or are repulsed by it, but either way I think it right to tell you my reasons for what I'm doing. And the truth is, I'm saving New York! Do you remember our city, gentlemen? I'm sure you do, and I'm sure you know what I'm talking about, hard-working men that you are (and women, too, of course!—I even understand the detective in charge of my case is a woman—O brave new world, that has such creatures in it!). The New York of jazz musicians and writers, mobsters and tycoons, the Empire State Building and the Yankees, immigrants and blue bloods. The center of the world for everything that mattered. And now what do I see when I look around me? An endless parade of moneyed mediocrities, whey-faced and chinless, choking the streets of Manhattan with their trust fund airs. A colony of pompous cretins in Brooklyn, devoting themselves to the endless, breathless celebration of sanctimonious ephemera. A couple of dingbat billionaire sociopaths who can't stop snivelling about having to pay taxes. Jareth Kucker, van Clapp's right hand (it doesn't take much imagination to know what old Ivan is doing with that hand when it's Kucker), a half-wit slumlord who is somehow not even able to do that effectively. And then the old, rotten upper crust, the would-be aristocrats of the city, fey and listless and mewling like gelded kittens. Well, it's time someone started clawing something back for the old New York, and I've started with this last bunch of brainless parasites.

But one must have order! So I've been picking my subjects

144

from the Vows column of The New York Primrose, *as you of course know by now. Think about it, they should be grateful. They thought they were just getting a few moments of preening among their peers, while anyone else who noticed mocked them mercilessly. Instead I've immortalized them. Now they will forever be part of the history of New York, and one hopes of the beginning of a new chapter of rebirth and vitalization!*

You will of course want details that prove I am in fact the killer. Charlotte Turner was wearing a green dress when she was killed. She was also wearing a string of pearls that she herself took off (or at least, you would not have found anyone else's fingerprints on them). There was a vase of flowers on the table behind the couch, which she knocked over—that was indeed almost her last act before shuffling off this mortal coil. Jordan Wymark was smoking a cigarette when I approached and shot him. You no doubt found it near his body, though I'm afraid I didn't notice the brand. He was wearing one of those white and blue checkered shirts that everyone has on these days. The fatal poison was given to Bella Jacobs at a public event, so no points for knowing she was wearing a demure little diamond necklace. Clark Kipner was at a dinner party in the penthouse apartment of an otherwise as yet unoccupied building. His throat was slit with a kitchen knife and he was found beneath a landscape painting—unless he had more life left in him than I thought and dragged himself a little ways down the hallway. I take it those facts are enough to prove my bona fides.

Of course you could never say so, perhaps not even to yourselves, but I know your hearts are with me. So we both continue our work, simpatico in so many ways, until one day we must meet, face to face.

With kind regards,
5

I finished reading it and held the note for a moment, unsure of what to say or even whether I could maintain my composure. I looked over at Leo, and he seemed to pick up on my fear.

"Are these details about the murders..."

"They are all correct," said Leo. "That's why we think this is genuine."

I stared at him for a moment. "Detective," I told him, "I have to say that reading this I have chills running up and down my spine. All I can think of is Jack the Ripper, the Zodiac Killer. And now...I guess there's another one. And I'm holding his letter."

Leo nodded patiently. "It's okay if you need to take a minute."

"No, no," I said, "of course I'm fine." I cleared my throat and glanced back down at the paper. "Why would he sign it with just the number five?"

"Yes," said Leo calmly, "he seems to have wanted to leave us with a riddle. Does that mean anything to you? Do you think it might have any particular significance in your social circle?"

I thought for a moment. "No, not really. Nothing I can think of. Fifth Avenue, maybe? But that hardly seems his style."

"No clubs that feature the number five? Any groups of five you can think of in symbols or emblems, anything like that?"

I tried to think of anything that might fit the bill, but came up blank. But something else did come to me. "Is it the number of murders he's committed?"

Leo's face was calm as ever. "He's committed four so far: Turner, Wymark, Jacobs, Kipner." He paused for a moment, as if to let that register, then added, "Four that we know of."

"You mean..." I said quietly, and my eyes widened.

"He could have killed someone else we don't yet know about. Maybe some time ago. We're looking back through past columns and seeing if there have been any other suspicious deaths. But," he added, apparently trying to calm me, "don't be too alarmed, Mr. Balfour. That's just one possible meaning for the number five. There's no particular reason to even think that's what it's about."

"Maybe it means he'll kill five total?"

146

"It could," Leo agreed. "He may believe he'll do that and then stop, if he thinks he's made his point. But the reality is he won't be able to. Serial killers can't stop like that. And he seems to know that, since he talks about our inevitable meeting."

"Why do serial killers contact the police like this," I asked. "To taunt you? Maybe he does want you to know about another murder he's committed."

"Maybe," Leo said, unimpressed. "Remember, Mr. Balfour, this is just one possibility, and one we don't want to get too hung up on. If he wants to direct us to another murder we haven't connected to him yet, this is a pretty subtle way to do it. And this guy doesn't seem big on subtlety."

"Yes, maybe you're right," I said. "I suppose he couldn't resist the chance to get more attention by mentioning another murder, especially since everyone thinks he's only killed four so far."

"We don't want to overcommit to that theory, but we can't really dismiss it, either. People like this don't always think in ways that make sense to you or me. It's a possibility at this point, nothing more or less."

I had to hand it to the police, they were not ones for rushing to judgment, no matter what evidence you presented them with. Then again, their man was still at large, so maybe a little more boldness in drawing conclusions would have served them well.

Leo looked at me for a minute, like he was considering something. "Something else did occur to me with the number five. It was Joe DiMaggio's number. This is a bit of a shot in the dark, but with this whole 'Old New York' thing this guy has going, maybe that's it. Can you think of any connection that might have to anyone in your world, DiMaggio, the Yankees, anyone who might really identify with that in any way."

Again I dutifully turned it over in my mind for a moment or two. "Andrew Speers was at a Yankees game when Charlotte was killed. Other than that, not really. I can't think of any particular connection to DiMaggio or that era of

147

baseball, Yankees or otherwise. At least not among anyone I know."

Leo nodded. "What about this," he continued. "There are a couple of Shakespeare references in the letter. Does that ring any bells? Anyone in your social circle that may have a theater background, or anything like that?"

"No, I don't think so. You may find a few patrons of the theater among these families, but I don't know that anyone has any particularly strong connection to Shakespeare. But you're right, it is odd that he fits two lines from Shakespeare in this letter. What are they from, *The Tempest* and *Romeo and Juliet*?"

"The mortal coil line is actually from *Hamlet*," Leo replied. "The famous 'To be or not to be' soliloquy."

I looked at him uncertainly. Perhaps he had looked up the lines earlier. I glanced back at the letter laying on the table, but he wasn't finished.

"He misquotes the line from *The Tempest*," said Leo. "Miranda says 'people,' not 'creatures.'"

Without thinking about it I shot him a look that must have betrayed my shock. After Allison's *schwab da zebra* comment, I was hardly expecting Leo to be quoting Shakespeare, much less knowing the name of the character who said the lines. I realized at once my reaction was probably offensive, but he merely shrugged. "College boy," he said blandly. I gave him a serious, understanding look, trying to make up for my initial rudeness. Somewhat unexpectedly, he continued. "City College, double major in English and Anthropology. Neither seemed to have great career prospects, so I became a cop because I like to solve puzzles."

"So maybe you wrote the letter," I said, and to my pleasant surprise he actually laughed.

"What makes you think someone in my social circle wrote this letter," I asked. "It seems to me, if I can be somewhat blunt about it, to be written by someone from a different class."

"Oh?" Finally he seemed genuinely interested, wanting to hear my thoughts rather than just pump me for particular details.

"Well, yes. I don't know how to put it exactly except to say that he's trying too hard. Italicizing 'bona fides,' for instance. Someone in my circle might use the term, but they wouldn't italicize it to show they know it's Latin. To be perfectly frank, most of them probably wouldn't know that. And generally, there's just a sense of overdoing it throughout."

"Yes, he definitely has a dramatic streak. That's why I wondered if anyone in your circle, even your extended circle, had acted or done anything of the sort."

"No one I can think of offhand, but I will think about that more, maybe ask around. But I would have thought the author comes from more of a working-class background. The celebration of an older, tougher New York. You're right, Joe DiMaggio does fit this letter. But he was not really a hero of the upper classes. And then the hostility to the rich—I mean, what does he call us? "The rotten upper crust." And whoever wrote this is clearly acting on that sentiment." I looked over the letter again. "And then look at this: 'I know your hearts are with me.' Maybe because of class loyalty? Maybe he even has some kind of family connection to the police, some familiarity?"

Leo nodded. "All good points. But it's hard for me to imagine someone who would fit in at a cop bar somehow getting into Charlotte Turner's apartment, or into the engagement party where Bella Jacobs was poisoned. It almost has to be someone of your general background."

"Fair enough, Detective," I conceded. "Maybe the truth is somewhere in the middle—someone with more middle-class, maybe upper middle-class origins. They've experienced the world of the Turners and the Jacobs, but they feel like obvious outsiders, maybe above all because of their personal wealth—or lack thereof. But they have some education, which they're eager to highlight in this letter, and they feel superior for that reason—which of course just makes their obvious social and economic inferiority all the more galling. They identify with an old, idealized working class New York, but above all with the cultural heyday of the city, the jazz music and writers and such."

Leo was looking at me thoughtfully. "That does all fit together, Mr. Balfour. You may well be right. Even so," he added, almost sheepishly, "I would appreciate it if you could, as you suggested, ask around about whether anyone in your extended social circle has that theater background." I looked at him, a little surprised. "We'd have a lot smaller haystack to sift through if our suspects just included members of the Union Club rather than all the disgruntled creative types in New York," he added.

"The author seems to be partial to Manhattan. Maybe you could start there."

"That may not be as much help as you think," he returned, and for a second I was worried he was actually irritated, so dead was his pan. I looked over and realized he was also joking. We both smiled, then I picked back up the thread.

"Really, though, I think I can start to see it. He moves to New York, he's intelligent, well-read, he has big ambitions of writing the Great American Novel, or maybe making a splash in the theater. Maybe both. But he gets here, and quickly realizes his ideas about the city, and about the success awaiting him here, bear little relation to reality. Instead of F. Scott Fitzgerald and Duke Ellington, or even Jay McInerney and Lou Reed, he finds Gawker and Upworthy. Manhattan is full of the 'moneyed mediocrities,' as he calls them, and he somehow falls in with them. He's quick, witty—a little melodramatic, but no one holds that against him, they even find it kind of amusing. No one cares about what he takes to be his real talents and abilities. He's just a kind of court jester, a hanger-on, spending time with people he secretly despises who treat him with a faint but unconcealed contempt. Eventually, his resentment and rage boil over, and he conceives this plan to start killing them…"

I flatter myself that Detective Leo was listening intently to all of this, at least by the end. I trailed off here, and he quickly jumped in, eager to pick up the thread. "That's good," he said, "very good. My only question is about the idea that the killer moved here from somewhere else. That makes a huge difference in who we're looking for. Maybe you just used the phrase without thinking about it, but do you really think he moved here, maybe recently? Whoever wrote that letter seems to identify pretty strongly with New York, especially the New York of old."

"Yes," I replied. "But you know how that is. You meet someone who starts railing against the demise of the authentic New York, then a few minutes later you learn they just moved here six months ago from Duluth or someplace."

Leo gave me another sleepy, distant smile and nodded.

"I have to say, Detective, I've seen this kind of thing before, the starry-eyed newcomer hitting the glass ceiling of class and becoming embittered. Sometimes it plays out romantically, sometimes socially or even in business connections. And, to me at least, it feels right here."

Leo looked at me carefully. "There is one other thing," he said. "Since you've already seen the letter, we might as well go over everything. You'll notice that the letter has very specific details of Charlotte Turner's murder, details only the killer could know. With Jordan Wymark's murder, on the other hand, the letter is pretty vague. It says we probably found a cigarette near the body in an alley, and says he was wearing a shirt with a very common pattern."

"Yes, I believe he means the very shirt I'm wearing," I said, and looked at him uncomfortably. "You think the writer is just bluffing on Jordan?"

"Could be. Could be that whoever wrote this killed Turner but not Wymark, and wants to make us believe otherwise, for whatever reason."

"But he'd be taking quite a chance, wouldn't he? This is a popular men's shirt just now, but what if Jordan had been wearing a green or yellow shirt? Then it would have been obvious that whoever killed Charlotte didn't kill Jordan. If that's true, and that's what whoever wrote the letter wanted to hide, he's taking a big chance."

Leo nodded, unperturbed. "He may have seen Wymark earlier in the night. May have seen a picture of him from that night somewhere on social media." He looked at me, apparently trying to gauge whether people like Jordan Wymark would ever appear on Instagram. "Then again, maybe not," he continued, though I don't believe I had done anything to discourage him.

"Did you find a cigarette near Jordan, with his DNA on it," I asked, trying to be helpful. I immediately felt like an idiot, asking about DNA tests like someone whose entire knowledge of criminal investigations came from CSI and the OJ trial. But it turned out they had.

"We did. Apparently he favored Marlboros, at least that night. Of course, the killer might have seen him smoking earlier, or known him to be a smoker. But you're right, bluffing like this would be a risk." He seemed to be wrapping up this line of thought, apparently thinking it had run its course. "Maybe the writer did in fact kill both, and just doesn't have any better details about Wymark."

"But what about the others? You said those details were accurate too."

"Ah, yes," said Leo, and shifted uneasily. "We actually don't know if Ms. Jacobs was wearing a diamond necklace that night. We're trying to run it down. It could be another reasonable guess."

"Yes, not hard to believe she would wear diamonds, but nothing flashy enough to upstage Evelyn. But surely this is all too risky? And what about Clarkie? Are those things true?"

"It's a little more complicated with Mr. Kipner. He was killed with a kitchen knife, but there was no landscape painting anywhere near him. And he didn't seem to move at all from where he first fell."

I paused for a moment and looked back down at the letter. "So his throat was slit," I asked without looking back up. "I thought maybe he had been shot, then Detective Allison let me believe he had been stabbed. I had never seen so much blood...I didn't know what to think."

"Detective Allison told me he was amazed at how well you held up last night. That's tough for anybody. And he said you were extremely helpful."

I played embarrassed, but of course I was happy to hear that. "So," I said after a moment, "he's lying about that one? But how would he know about the knife?"

"He's not necessarily lying," said Leo. "Whatever happened, it must have been very quick, and he was running an enormous risk. You wouldn't necessarily expect him to notice paintings. In high-stress, high-adrenaline situations like that, some of your perceptions and memories might be off.

"Then again, what he said wasn't right. And there were a lot of people there, including several cops who otherwise wouldn't have been at a murder, much less a murder from this case. So maybe he just heard something from someone who was there.

"I lean toward thinking he did it, and overall he's telling us enough true things about all the cases that it seems like he's our guy for all four. But the bottom line is that he's very detailed about Ms. Turner, and all of it is accurate. So that does leave us with some questions."

I nodded uncertainly, really not sure what to say. "Yes, I suppose it does. But then he would have had more time in Charlotte's case than Clarkie's, as you've pointed out, and I suppose there would have been fewer telling details outside in a back alley than in Charlotte's apartment.

"But," I added, thinking this would be like catnip for the good detective, "some people I've talked to do think Charlotte's murder seems different. Much more personal. And it's so hard to see any real motive for it. It's the same with Bella's murder, really, but that also almost seems like it could have been random. So…I guess what I'm saying is I really have no idea."

He chuckled briefly, and I set the letter in its sleeve down on the table.

"There is one other thing, Detective. You've probably thought of it, but…"

"Really, Mr. Balfour, if you have any thoughts at all, please share them. As I said, you've seen the letter now, so anything that occurs to you, please don't hold back."

"Well," I began, a little hesitant to proceed, "we've been talking like the letter writer must be a man. But really, couldn't all the murders have been committed by a woman? I don't know the details of Charlotte's death, and I'm happy to say I don't know much about the physics of strangulation in any case. But certainly the others could have been committed by a woman. It's…just a thought," I concluded, somewhat embarrassed.

"That's a good point, Mr. Balfour, and we've had the same thought. With that in mind, can you think of anyone who might fit this profile now that we're including women?"

Again I puzzled over his question for a few seconds, feeling somewhat stupid. "No, I don't think so. But I will keep thinking about it, and of course I'll contact you at once if someone does occur to me."

"Yes, please do that," he said. "And please, Mr. Balfour, at the risk of beating a dead horse—whatever you do don't mention this letter to anyone. Again we have to ask you to trust that we know what we're doing and have good reasons for not wanting this letter to be public knowledge at this point.

"But since you're here and you've seen it now, I wonder if you could do us a favor and look over the columns that featured the victims. You might see things we haven't, especially in light of this letter."

Chapter Eight

The Columns

Detective Leo led me over to a long table standing against a wall. On it were the various columns featuring each victim, cut out from the newspaper and laminated.

"You're using the print versions," I asked. "Do you think they have some significance for the killer?"

"Personally, I doubt it," said Leo. "Though now with this old New York angle, maybe. But either way they give us more information about how the newspaper presented them than the printouts. Those are in that folder, if you want to see them," he said, pointing to a red folder sitting at the corner of the table. "I think one of them has an extra picture, but otherwise they're the same."

"I think these will work," I said. "Shall I?"

Leo motioned to the first column, the one announcing the impending marriage of Charlotte and Andrew. I picked it up and began reading.

Charlotte Turner and Andrew Speers are to be married on June 17th at the First Presbyterian Church in Manhattan.

Ms. Turner, 30, is an entrepreneur and philanthropist. She graduated from Columbia with a degree in General Studies and travelled widely after graduation. She has since settled back in New York and become known for her advocacy for several charitable causes, especially shelter animals and rooftop gardening.

She is the daughter of Barbara and Edward Turner of Manhattan. The bride's father owns several businesses and manages a family trust. Both of the bride's parents are active philanthropists, known especially for their support for wetlands conservation and the performing arts.

Mr. Speers, 32, is a financier. He graduated from Harvard University with a degree in Finance, then received an MBA from the Wharton School at the University of Pennsylvania. An avid baseball fan, Mr. Speers was a trainer for the Harvard baseball team and once tried out for a minor league team. He is well-known among his friends for his ambition to one day manage what he often calls "an elite hedge fund."

He is the son of Georgiana and Lawrence Speers of Manhattan. The groom's father manages a family trust and several business interests. Both of the groom's parents are active philanthropists, known especially for their support for cancer research and the performing arts.

The couple first met at a lawn party in the Hamptons. Ms. Turner noticed Mr. Speers when he lit a cigar with a hundred dollar bill. "I remember him just waving the burning bill in the air once his cigar was lit, and looking at me and smiling," says Ms. Turner. Unfortunately Mr. Speers' admiring gaze did not take in the open flame in his hand, and he singed his jacket and shirt and burnt his fingers. That probably would have brought a very quick end to the courtship, but Keith Halwood, a mutual friend, had noticed the interest and introduced them to one another before artfully disappearing.

"The conversation was a little awkward at first," recalls Ms. Turner. "I just remember him saying something like, 'Stupid fire, thinks it can go where it wants and have fun at my expense. I hate it!' I thought I had some aloe vera in my purse, but then I didn't, and he seemed annoyed that I was talking about how he had just burned himself...even though he had just been doing that."

Happily, however, the couple soon discovered they had something in common. "Then I mentioned I was from a Mayflower family," says Ms. Turner. "He said he was too, and I gave him an uncertain look for a second. I couldn't remember a Speers on the ship. Then he explained that his mother was an Allerton. We laughed and laughed." A bond was forged, and they parted that night planning to meet again for dinner the following evening.

And yet the two new inamorati soon hit a snag when they realized they were distantly related. "A Turner had married an Allerton at some point, and we were something like sixth cousins once removed," says Charlotte. "At first I was a little creeped out, but then we just said, 'Pretty sure the Habsburgs got closer than sixth cousins, and they turned out fine!'"

Yet according to Lincott Bowles, one of Mr. Speers' oldest friends, the groom was not quite so easily reconciled to the idea, or at least to that formulation of it. "He wasn't sure who the Habsburgs were," says Mr. Bowles, "but when he found out, he was irritated. 'What, it's only good enough if it was done by a bunch of Germans no one's ever heard of,' I remember him saying. I naturally didn't have the heart to tell him about the hemophilia."

Mr. Speers' attraction to Ms. Turner eventually won out over his hostility to the idea of following a trail blazed by moderately deformed Europeans of yore, but not before a lively episode out on the town one night. "He tried to get into it one night with these British guys," Mr. Bowles relates. "He thought they were German, and I guess that Habsburg comment had been eating at him for a few days. I don't know what he was thinking: they were pretty hammered, but there were like four of them. I certainly wasn't going to back him up just because he was jealous of some inbred monarch from the eighteenth century. Fortunately, England had just qualified for the World Cup that night, and they were all in good spirits. They just laughed the whole thing off and sent him on his way."

Mr. Bowles is more enthusiastic, however, about Mr. Speers' engagement to Ms. Turner. So is Penelope Lane, a friend of Ms. Turner. "I hope they'll be so happy together," she says. "Charlotte is a great friend and such a fascinating person—she always has something thought-provoking to say about her great interests, like yoga or tapas, and of course rooftop gardening."

The way was not completely clear for them at first,

however. Both Ms. Turner and Mr. Speers were involved with other partners when their relationship first kindled. But after a little luck and a lot of perseverance, they are going to be married in a few weeks. Ms. Turner beams with joy when she thinks about it all. "After everything we've been through," she reflects, "nothing can stop us from being together now!"

I glanced up from the end of the column to the photograph in the middle of the page. It was the two of them smiling at the camera, taken in a park. It was about as straightforward and unimaginative as you could get, which somehow seemed appropriate. Andrew was staring directly at the camera, his face stretched into a strained, bitter rictus that was apparently meant to approximate a smile. I remembered from previous occasions taking photographs with him that he thought he looked like an idiot when he smiled naturally. And on this point, at least, Andrew was correct. The effect of his self-conscious smile, however, was not to make him look serious or virile but like he was receiving a rectal exam, or perhaps had been possessed by a demon (which had perhaps entered him during a still-ongoing rectal exam). Charlotte, meanwhile, was holding his hand awkwardly and staring off into a space a little to the left of the camera. I suppose Andrew's facial expression could at least pass for a smile, but Charlotte looked stunned, as if she had just been presented with some terrible realization. I had a strong sense that whoever had chosen this picture intensely dislike the couple, or at least the idea of their union.

Having finished my perusal of the column I set it back down on the table, a little unsure of what Leo expected from me. He must have read that in my expression.

"If anything seems strange to you in any of these," he said, "definitely let me know. But more than that, we're just looking for you to read them all over and see if you notice any patterns, or anything that seems a little out of place or possibly significant that keeps cropping up."

"I can do that."

"I had one question for you," Leo said. "It says here Ms.

Turner was an entrepreneur. But we don't know what that's about."

I shrugged, a little unsure myself. "I think she sold jewelry on Etsy," I said. "That's really the only thing I can think of."

"I guess they embellish a little," Leo said laconically.

I suddenly remembered my favorite example. "Two Medical Professionals Will Now Heal The World Together" —he was a plastic surgeon and she sold new age detoxes and health foods online. I thought about recounting it to Leo, but I somehow wasn't sure he would see the humor, at least not like I did. So I just moved on to the next column, Jordan's.

This time the first thing that caught my attention was of course the picture. Jordan's fiancée was achingly lovely, and Jordan radiated joy and vitality. They were also outside, sitting in a park, her in front with Jordan embracing her from behind. It was perhaps the best-looking picture in the history of the Vows column.

Rather than stare at this indefinitely I turned to the column itself.

Sophie Fontana and Jordan Wymark are to be married on June 3rd in a private ceremony in Bryant Park.

Ms. Fontana, 27, is a model and photographer. She graduated from Northwestern University with a degree in German Literature, and later received a Master's Degree in Film Studies from UCLA. Her photographs are held in several collections in the United States and abroad.

She is the daughter of Janet and Louis Fontana of Bunghole, California. The bride's mother is a retired speech therapist and professional baker. Her father is a retired importer who owns and operates a small vineyard in northern California.

Mr. Wymark, 31, is a junior partner at the venture capital firm Ossington and Associates. He graduated from Princeton University with a degree in Marketing. An avid water polo player, he competed with the American national team at the 2012 Summer Olympics in London, where they won a silver medal.

He is the son of the late Eleanor and Adam Wymark of New York. The groom's mother, who passed away in 2009 after a battle with cancer, was a writer and conservationist perhaps best known for her 1979 book Singing Tree, Dancing Bush, *a record of her travels in Africa. The groom's father is a senior partner at the brokerage firm Wymark and Hathaway and a philanthropist best known for his long support of the Metropolitan Opera, which named its performance space after the Wymarks in 2011. The groom's stepmother, Liv Wymark, is a former actress and noted vaccination skeptic.*

The couple met when their paths crossed during an evening on the town last year. Mr. Wymark remembers it vividly, and swears it was love at first sight.

"We were at Lucian's one night," recounted Mr. Wymark, referring to the exclusive bar in Tribeca. "About half of us had gone to Princeton, half to Yale. As good-looking girls came in, we tried to guess which school they had gone to, then we'd go up and ask them. It was a conversation starter, but we were pretty serious about the competition, too.

"I'll be honest," he continues. "When Sophie came in, I knew she was too good-looking to have gone to Princeton. But I pretend-insisted she must have, and went over to talk to her. It turned out she had gone to school somewhere in the Midwest, but she was so beautiful, I didn't care," he enthuses.

Ms. Fontana has slightly different memories of the evening. When Lucian's closed for the evening, Mr. Wymark invited her to an after-hours club for Princeton graduates and their guests, modelled on one of Princeton's eating clubs. "I grew up on a farm in Northern California," Ms. Fontana says. "But even I knew the words 'Princeton' and 'after hours club' didn't really belong in the same sentence."

But her curiosity, and perhaps Mr. Wymark's charm, got the better of her, and she and two friends accompanied Mr. Wymark and his compatriots to their secretive destination. When they arrived, Ms. Fontana's worst fears were realized: the "after hours club" was in fact just the apartment of one of Mr. Wymark's friends in the financial district. "It was really lame," Ms. Fontana recalls. "There was a bar of sorts with a couple of guys behind it, serving drinks. The Wolf of Wall Street was playing on a big screen tv. The host served me crème de menthe and tried to tell me it was absinthe (as if that was supposed to impress me). When I mentioned that my father owned a vineyard, he started lecturing me on wine. But he thought that Pinot Grigio was a red and that Malbec came from Australia." Her friends were similarly underwhelmed by the experience, and they all left together.

Mr. Wymark's friends were somewhat offended by the ladies' quick departure, but he broke ranks with the others and followed them out onto the street. "I knew I couldn't let Sophie get away," he says now, still with some animation. Somehow the group ended up down around Wall Street, and Mr. Wymark asked Ms. Fontana if she would accept his dinner invitation if he could jump over Charging Bull, the famous statue near the Stock Exchange. "I knew I probably hadn't made the best impression, especially after the pit stop at Eddie's, so I had to do something drastic to win her over," Mr. Wymark says. The suggestion did have an effect on Ms. Fontana, though perhaps not quite the one Mr. Wymark anticipated. "I remember we were down at Bowling Green," she says. "It was silent and empty, just an occasional cab going by back up at the top of the street. Suddenly Jordan told me he was going to jump over the bull for me, and it was obvious he was really going to do it, or really try. And I felt… concerned, and protective of him." She was surprised by the feelings, and as she paused to try to sort them out, Mr. Wymark made his charge at the bull. He approached it from the side and, placing his hand on the bull's neck as he went up, very nearly cleared it—on this everyone who was present agrees. But he did not quite make it, and although his momentum carried him over the great bronze beast he came down on his shoulder and face. "I was able to turn and absorb most of the impact into my shoulder," Mr. Wymark explains. "I've always been pretty good at falling. I scraped my face, and at first thought I might have cut it up a bit. But I *stood up and felt it and realized I was fine. My shoulder hurt, but with the excitement of the jump and the stinging pain in my cheek, I felt really excited and alive. But then I was worried what Sophie thought." Ms. Fontana had worries of her own, and she came running around the statue to see if Mr. Wymark was okay. "When I saw her coming running up like that, and the look on her face, I knew it had worked, and that it was worth it even if my collarbone was broken or whatever," Mr. Wymark says. They stared at each other in silence for a second or two, then kissed. Both agree that the courtship proceeded apace from that moment.*

I felt something for Jordan and his bride as I finished the column but tried not to show anything to Leo. "Any questions about this one," I said flatly as I set it back on the table.

"Not right now," he said, "but you know us. We always reserve the right to come back and ask questions later."

I smiled slightly as he handed me the next laminated column.

Again the photo commanded my attention. It was taken at the reception after their ceremony. Bella was dressed rather conservatively, her hair up in a bun, everything about her appearance subdued. It only made her more transcendent, her dark hair and pearl-colored dress perfectly framing her face. Her husband Micah was wearing a dark suit, a kippa, and wire-rimmed glasses. He looked like exactly what he was, a man who spent sixty hours a week doing a kind of financial analysis that you couldn't understand without a forty minute explanation and a PhD in systems theory.

Bella Jacobs and Micah Aaronson were married on May 20th at Central Synagogue in Manhattan.

Ms. Jacobs, 34, is a retired model who continues to work in film. She graduated from Oxford University with a degree in International Relations. For the past decade and counting she has been one of the most famous and successful fashion models in the world. She is now pursuing a career as an actor and director.

She is the daughter of Lilith and Max Jacobs of Manhattan. The bride's mother is a philanthropist and patron of the arts. The bride's father is a philanthropist and well-known real estate developer who was recently named one of the twenty-one most influential figures in twenty-first century New York by New York Magazine.

Mr. Aaronson, 31, is a financial analyst with the firm Cromwell and Sharpe. He graduated from Carnegie Mellon University with a degree in Mathematics. In addition to his work in the financial industry, Mr. Aaronson is an amateur violinist and a keen student of cryptograms.

He is the son of Annette and Allan Aaronson of Cleveland, Ohio. The groom's mother is a retired accountant who now manages an antique shop. The groom's father is a founding partner of Cleveland's largest corporate law firm, Aaronson and Zukowsky.

*Until her recent retirement Ms. Jacobs was perhaps the most famous and sought-after fashion model of the past twenty years—*Vogue *magazine once famously described her as "Helen of Troy but with better cheekbones." This creates a challenge for profiling her, since all the modeling agencies for which she worked are now embroiled in lawsuits alleging widespread sexual harassment and abuse. Most of the models who worked for them had to sign non-disclosure agreements as part of their contracts, and all of them are now required to remain completely silent as these various legal cases play out in court. Even describing how Ms. Jacobs and Mr. Aaronson met is difficult, since they were introduced by an attorney friend of Mr. Aaronson who had met Ms. Jacobs as part of his work on one of these lawsuits.*

"Modelling was fun," says Ms. Jacobs. "The best thing about it was definitely being able to travel so widely and see so much of the world, especially at such a young age." Beyond that she has no comments about her professional life up to this time.

Several of her former colleagues with whom we spoke for this profile did, however, share one well-known and well-

verified story about Ms. Jacobs. She is still fondly remembered by many in the industry for using krav maga to break the arm of a photographer whom one of our sources describes as "legendarily handsy" and another as "a pencil-dicked hipster perv."

In the past few years Ms. Jacobs has begun a career in film, first taking a few acting roles and recently branching out and directing a short film about soil erosion. Unfortunately, the directors and producers with whom she has worked in this new career have all been involved in lawsuits of their own, also alleging sexual harassment and assault, so Ms. Jacobs cannot speak about her time working with them either.

Mr. Aaronson's background is less shrouded in legally mandated secrecy. He studied mathematics, physics, and history at Carnegie Mellon, while also reading deeply in Jewish theology and mysticism. The quiet life he has made for himself in New York is quite at odds with Ms. Jacobs' past. Friends say it is a classic case of opposites attracting.

Mr. Aaronson is also fascinated by cryptograms, coded or encrypted forms of communication. He has long made a private study of them, his interest reaching back to his childhood.

"I remember my Uncle Nathan used to talk about the idea that the entire world was one enormous, infinitely complex puzzle. What was it trying to tell us? Or was it God himself, trying to communicate to us through the world, through all the chances and accidents that we could make sense of if we only had the key? Uncle Nathan would say that if we could figure out the code, we would know how to move the levers of the world, change the outcomes of history and history itself, even the fabric of reality itself" he says, stretching his arms out to indicate the vastness of what his uncle was saying. "Of course," Mr. Aaronson continues, "he was developing schizophrenia. But the idea has always stuck with me. What is being communicated to us that we can't comprehend, at least not yet?"

Ms. Jacobs says that Mr. Aaronson has devised several

elaborate codes himself and written a lengthy manuscript on the topic, "at least a few hundred pages." But Mr. Aaronson has no plans to make any of it public at present.

Of course like all couples, Ms. Jacobs and Mr. Aaronson have had their challenges. At one point they even thought about ending things, but Keith Halwood, a mutual friend, stepped in and convinced them to persevere. "I told them, 'You two can't just go your separate ways. I've got plans for you,'" he jokes now. His intervention worked, and after a few late-night heart-to-heart talks, they were back together, their bond stronger than ever.

"During those talks," Ms. Jacobs recalls, "Micah would play the violin to help him work through his feelings. It was adorable, and really helped me to see him in a new light."

"It also helped me to open up," Mr. Aaronson adds, though he says he doesn't recommend it to others "unless their partner is very patient—or very easily entertained."

"Hmm," I said as I finished reading it.

"What do you see," asked Leo.

"Well, here's Keith Halwood again. He was also mentioned in Charlotte's announcement. I don't think they mentioned him in Jordan's, but I know they're old friends. I didn't realize he was all that close with any of the others. It's probably nothing, just an odd coincidence that he keeps showing up."

I thought maybe I saw a glimmer of genuine interest shine through Leo's eyes for a moment, but he was basically inscrutable to me. "Interesting you should say that," he said. "We'll have to keep that in mind."

I looked at him for a moment, wondering if he was going to divulge anything else.

"They were already married by the time the profile appeared," he pointed out.

"Yes," I said. "I think that was about privacy, since Bella was a celebrity."

"It breaks a pattern," said Leo.

"Patterns," I said, and looked back down at the column.

165

"Maybe you should get Micah Aaronson in here."

Leo smiled, and we moved on to the next and final column, Clarkie's. It occurred to me, as I took it from Leo, that I didn't even know who he was going to marry.

Magdalena Belmonte and Clark Kipner, Jr. are to be married at St. Leo the Great Catholic Church in Baltimore on June 24th.

Ms. Belmonte, 27, is a PhD student in Comparative Literature at Stuyvesant University. She graduated from the University of Maryland with degrees in English and Philosophy. Her thesis is on the work of the early modern Spanish mystics Teresa of Avila and John of the Cross.

She is the daughter of Maria and Tomasino Belmonte of Baltimore. The bride's mother is a former social worker who now manages special education programs for the city's Catholic schools. The bride's father is a professor at Baltimore City Community College but is best known for his work as a poet and translator.

Mr. Kipner, 31, known to friends as "Clarkie," is a freelance writer and visual artist. He graduated from New York University with a degree in General Studies. In addition to his written and visual projects, he works as a consultant and editor in the field of arts and letters.

He is the son of Judith Cravath and Clark Kipner, Sr. of New York City. Ms. Cravath is a filmmaker and memoirist. Mr. Kipner is a long-time staff writer and associate editor for The New Contrarian Consensus.

The couple met at a literary event in the city. They found themselves speaking about recent novels over a glass of wine, a conversation that left them both intrigued.

"Clarkie had lots of strong opinions at first," recalls Ms. Belmonte. "It was the usual bravado you find at events like that, especially among men. But he was very open to hearing them challenged. There was something charming in how quickly he was overwhelmed and how honest he was about it."

Mr. Kipner also felt a spark during that first conversation.

"I've heard people talking about books all my life," he says. "There was something about Magdalena that was really unique. I remember she had a very moral approach to art that I really wasn't used to hearing, but it was more than that."

Genevieve Hastings, a long-time friend of Mr. Kipner, thinks she knows what it was. "Magdalena is very bright and perceptive," Ms. Hastings says, "but she's probably less interested in seeming clever than anyone else I've ever met. I think that was really refreshing for Clarkie, and even challenging."

As the couple got to know each other better, Mr. Kipner was always surprised, and further drawn toward Ms. Belmonte, by her relative indifference to the prestigious cultural circles in which he was used to moving.

"Usually academics are desperate for any kind of bigger audience," says Mr. Kipner, who knows this both from social experience and from his work as a consultant and coach for professors who want to expand the reach of their ideas. "But she didn't seem all that impressed."

"I think Magdalena was curious about the whole world of the NCC, and the various writers and artists Clarkie and his family know," says Ms. Hastings. "But I think once she looked into it a little, she found it all pretty wanting."

Indeed, although Ms. Belmonte is pursuing an academic career at an elite institution in one of the cultural capitals of the world, she often finds herself at odds with it.

Even those who have not always agreed with Ms. Belmonte respect her conviction. Henry Ocho-Coomer, a professor at Stuyvesant and the chair of the English department, remembers her opposition to the department's plans for a new Master's Degree program in Porn Studies.

"I remember she met with me about it. She was spearheading a movement to prevent the program from being developed, though I think the movement was really just her and a few other religious students scattered across the university. I appreciated her determination and professionalism," he says, stressing that professionalism is

the lifeblood of academic exchange.

"But," adds Professor Ocho-Coomer, shrugging magnanimously, "you can't stop science."

Ms. Belmonte has led other protests against Stuyvesant's policies and chosen directions for development, though these other protests have also been unsuccessful. They included an attempt to stop the development of Stuyvesant's new satellite campus in Abu Dhabi—which, according to Amnesty International, Human Rights Watch, and unguarded comments at the United Nations by the president of the UAE, was being built using slave labor—and the university's partnership with The Fairington Foundation for Free Markets and Race Realism.

"It certainly makes you question incremental reform and trust in the procedures we have for that reform," Ms. Belmonte sighs. "It can be a difficult balance, trying to keep doing good and not fall into despair, but also not forgetting who the prince of this world is," she adds cryptically.

Mr. Kipner, by contrast, takes a more optimistic view of the world and is happy to be in tune with its rhythms. He even sees himself as often calling the tune ahead of time, though in ways that are often not obvious.

"I was never a hipster," says Mr. Kipner, "but I anticipated a lot of the trends that came to define the whole hipster movement.

"For instance," Mr. Kipner recalls, "I tried to grow a beard, but couldn't really get it to come in. But if I could have, I'd have been way ahead of the curve. In fact, I was way ahead of the curve, even without an actual beard."

The couple look forward to seeing what new developments come their way, confident they'll meet them together even when they seem to be going in opposite directions.

I looked at the picture. Clarkie was smiling broadly, looking happy but basically vacant, which pretty much captured who he was. His fiancée had a look on her face that may have been a smile, though it may just as easily have been the set of her mouth. She didn't seem particularly happy. At first she seemed almost bored, but as I looked more closely she seemed more calm, indifferent, perhaps focused on something else that had nothing to do with the picture or her surroundings.

I had to say, Clarkie certainly seemed to have a type, though this Magdalena was obviously a significant step up from Alana. And she had apparently convinced him to be married in a Catholic Church. I could only imagine what Clark Sr. thought about that, though I suppose by this point he should have known how his son was with women. But then it was even more mystifying what this woman wanted with Clarkie, especially in marriage.

Reading the column I was sure this relationship was somehow asexual, something I had always felt about his relationship with Alana and a vague but unmistakable sense I had when I saw him with the one or two women he had dated in between the two. It occurred to me there was something a little irregular about most of these relationships, or at least about one of the partners. There were the rumors about Jordan, of course, and there were far less flattering rumors about Andrew Speers. Bella and Micah seemed fine, but I didn't know them all that well and didn't really move in the same circles. Then again, maybe these weren't really coincidences, just a commentary on the mores and abilities of my peers. I briefly considered mentioning it to Leo as a possible angle, but almost immediately ruled it out. It was absurd to think the letter writer would know about any of this, at least based on the profile we seemed to be working up, and any of it would have been far too tawdry to mention in any case.

"Anything stand out to you from that one," asked Leo.

"No," I said, shaking my head slowly, "nothing."

"No Keith Halwood," Leo said.

"No," I said, "but I seem to remember that he was going to be at the dinner last night. I think Genevieve sent us all a text a few days ago saying he was invited but wouldn't be able to attend. He had gotten his schedule confused and had something else he couldn't miss."

Leo seemed to take half a step backward, though his face showed no change.

"Do you think there could be something to this Halwood connection," I asked him.

Before he could answer me, Allison came into the room, seeming hurried and slightly discombobulated but still carrying himself as if he were in charge of the entire building.

He had news about the investigation. He greeted me then looked at me for a moment before speaking.

"Mr. Balfour, given the circumstances, I think I can let you in on this piece of information. We've had Keith Halwood under surveillance for the past few days. Last night he went to a fundraiser at Columbia. Plainclothes sat outside the building, didn't see him come out till he left for home sometime after eleven. Now, of course the building has other entrances, so it's possible he snuck out and made his way down to the Hastings' apartment. But there is absolutely no sign that he knows he's being followed, and no reason for him to suspect it. Oh, and one other thing: the fundraiser was formal. So while it's theoretically possible Halwood ended up down in the Lower East Side last night, his evening wear would have made entering the apartment harder, especially by the window, and would have made him stand out on the street. We have detectives canvassing the area around the Hastings' apartment, and so far no one remembers seeing anyone in a tuxedo. So, never say 'never,' but if they don't turn anything up I think we can pretty much cross him off our list."

"That's unfortunate," I said, "since, so far as I know, that's the only name on the list." Out of the corner of my eye I thought I had seen Leo deflate a little at Allison's news, and I felt much the same way.

We all stood there in silence for a moment, apparently all feeling the loss of what had seemed a rather promising lead. I suddenly remembered one of Maura's theories from our night at the gallery. "Something has occurred to me, Detectives," I said, in my usual diffident way with them.

"Once again, I'm afraid this is rather awkward and difficult for me. I'm always in this position where it seems like I must speak ill of the dead, and usually about people with whom I was once quite close." I hesitated for a moment, but then resumed before Allison's inevitable words of encouragement arrived. "You see, Charlotte—well, she certainly wasn't promiscuous, not at all. Quite the opposite, really. But…well, she could be easily impressed by new men, especially if they were handsome or charming. And Andrew, to be perfectly frank—which seems more than appropriate after four murders—is rather dull." I looked back and forth between them, each detective patiently humoring my scruples. "To continue in this vein of candor, gentlemen, I'm not really sure why she accepted his proposal. Almost everyone thought it a poor match from the beginning. Perhaps she felt it was time to marry, or it may be that she was just flattered by that level of attention and commitment. And Charlotte…well, just to be perfectly blunt, and I hope not too uncharitable"—here I could tell I was trying Allison's patience, so I pressed on despite myself—"she probably would have been too weak to break off the engagement just because she had lost interest in him, or even realized the match was unsuitable. It's even possible, you know, that she may have been looking for a way out, as well as someone to rely on during the inevitable ugliness involving Andrew and his family—and maybe hers. And all of that, after all, leaves someone in a difficult position to make good choices. So perhaps there was a gentleman caller at her apartment, and she let him in, was even quite relaxed with him…maybe the fact that she was sitting on the couch, apparently not suspecting a thing from her murderer, isn't as strange as we think. And perhaps it didn't even need to be anyone she had known especially well before. No one you would find in her address book."

"Also leaves it open whether the first murder is connected to the others," said Leo.

"That's helpful," Allison said, not even bothering to invest the words with any sarcasm. "Let me ask you this, Mr.

Balfour, and please think about it carefully. Do you think Andrew Speers is aware of everything you just said?"

I thought about it for a moment, and then gave him a slightly apologetic look. "There's no way to be polite about this. I don't think he's bright or perceptive enough for most of that to occur to him, or for him to be aware of what the people around him are thinking. But I think he has a strong jealous streak, one that could bring him to the same place even if he's blissfully unaware of why he's found himself there."

"So her fiancé sends someone to kill her and she lets him in because she's sick of the fiancé," said Leo. "Grimly fitting."

"I hardly think Andrew Speers would be able to appreciate the supposed poetic justice," I said with some feeling.

"Detective Leo still gets a little imaginative, even after some of the things he's seen," said Allison. "It's good—every once in a while, a criminal surprises you. We are certainly dealing with something extraordinary here, even if Mr. Speers is not that. But, let's not forget, we still have nothing to connect him to that first murder—and a lot to put him in the clear. We're certainly not ruling him out, but we're a long way from proving or even thinking he did it.

"Incidentally, Mr. Balfour," Allison continued, here adopting his conspiratorial tone, "I have a little information about the incident last night. You understand, of course, that this cannot leave this room." He looked at me meaningfully and I nodded. "Last night on our sweep of the building, we found the window on the floor below the penthouse open, just below the room with the window you had opened. The construction crew says they make sure they're closed every night before leaving."

"So…that was how the killer got in and out?"

"We don't quite know that. We didn't find any physical evidence confirming that anyone came through either window. But the fire escape connects both of them. It certainly would have been an easy way to get up there, slip in and out of the Hastings' apartment, then get back into the building at the lower floor and escape from there. The rest of the building was deserted at that hour."

"I suppose the killer could have just sat on the fire escape, waiting and watching for Clarkie."

"We don't know that any of that happened, sir," said Allison. "But it certainly seems possible."

Again I gulped like an idiot. "Earlier," I said, my voice faltering, "I was telling Detective Leo that I couldn't believe I was holding a letter from the killer. All I could think of was Jack the Ripper, the Zodiac Killer. They might as well have been Dracula or the Wolf-Man for as real as they were to me before that moment. And now all I can think of is how those other letter writers got away. Will this killer?"

"Lots of murderers write to the police, Mr. Balfour. They almost all get caught."

"But some…" I said.

Allison shook his head. "This is a compulsive killer, Mr. Balfour. He's committed four murders in four weeks, each week choosing his victim from the same newspaper column. He's not stalking people in deserted state parks or in dark alleys before electric lighting or police radios. He won't be able to stop himself, and we'll catch him. Soon." He looked back and forth, like he was making sure no one was around, or like he was trying to decide whether to trust me. "With cases like these, Mr. Balfour, as terrible as it is to say, we often can't do anything but wait until we have enough victims to see a pattern. Well, we have our pattern. Now the trap will close on our correspondent, and he won't be able to help himself—he'll run into it."

"He doesn't seem like a compulsive madman," I said. "He seems quite lucid and disciplined. How else is he still at large?"

"Sure," said Allison, "serial killers are lucid—they're not 'crazy' like we'd normally think of it. But they can't ever just walk away from it. Once you see the pattern, once you can read their signature, it's a matter of time. And this guy's next move is being broadcast in flashing neon lights in Times Square."

"But surely the *Primrose* is going to stop publishing the columns after this?"

"Yes, they are. We think he'll go back and target someone else from this past week. Again, he won't be able to help himself. We're going to give police protection to all of them, but we think he'll be compelled to act even with that.

"We appreciate you looking over all this with us, Mr. Balfour. Of course. We still think there's a good chance the killer knew at least one of the victims, or had some kind of connection that was more meaningful than just seeing their name and picture in the paper one day. But if all else fails, we're counting on him to reveal himself. The fact that he's writing us notes now just makes that all the more likely. The killer can't disappear now. The urge to make this turn out a certain way will just be too strong.

"And that's the thing about when they start writing letters like this. They want to be caught. They want the recognition. They get so comfortable with murder, they're sure there's a right way to do it, a right victim, and they're choosing them."

Chapter Nine

A Rumor of Class War

It seemed like I had been at the police station for the entire day, but in fact it had only been an hour or two. I still had at least a couple of hours work to do at the office, so on my way back I stopped at Youngman's Deli to get a sandwich. Almost as soon as I walked in I saw Max Jacobs and his wife at a table. Max waved to me, a friendly look on his face, and motioned me over.

"Ethan," he said as I walked up, "it's good to see you. I hear you've been working with the police on the murders, including Bella's."

It was typical of Max to cut straight to the chase. "I don't know if I would say that. I've been pulled in a little, I suppose. You've heard about Clarkie Kipner?"

Max frowned and nodded slightly. "Yes. Terrible. This needs to end, all of it. But you've been talking with the police?"

"A little. I didn't really have a choice—I was at the dinner party last night."

Max sat there, looking up at me, his hand barely moving over the little bundle of knife and fork rolled into a paper napkin beside his plate.

Mercifully, Davina noticed my obvious discomfort and intervened.

"Ethan, can you believe Max wants to order a brisket sandwich?" She turned to him. "You can't eat brisket because of your cholesterol. Ethan, explain this to him."

"I think he understands cholesterol, Davina."

"High cholesterol," said Max, "they've been telling me

that for twenty-five years. At this point, I think the malaria from the global warming is going to get me before the cholesterol does."

"You can scoff all you like," said Davina, "but we're living in a time of unrivalled scientific knowledge and progress. I think it's ridiculous that you want to turn your back on all that."

"Sure," said Max, "behold the glories of Western civilization. Me spending half a day drinking fruity sludge that empties my bowels so I can get up at 4 A.M. the next morning to go in and have a hundred yards of metal hose run up my—"

"Ethan," said Davina in a high, clear voice, "how is your mother? You know I really regret that we don't see her as often as we used to. I hope she's well?"

We made small talk for a few more minutes, then I went and ordered a sandwich and ate it quickly at the counter. I waved to Max and Davina on the way out. Max held up his brisket sandwich in return, like a victorious battle standard. But the look on his face told me I had gotten away with something. Walking out the door and into the street, I remembered a line from La Rouchefoucauld: "Death and the sun cannot be looked at steadily." I never heard Max's thoughts on death or saw him stare at the sun, but it occurred to me then that there wasn't much he couldn't stare down.

Max was sarcastic and dismissive of the world and its requirements, but I could see that he was recovering. His world was not shrinking to Davina, or to his health, and it wouldn't. He was bereaved but not maimed, and it had perhaps already occurred to him, as it just had to me, that he couldn't be because he was fundamentally a survivor. It must be a sad, dark, secret knowledge that would come creeping into his mind, to know that he had suffered perhaps the worst loss that he could but that he was really incapable of losing anything too important to him. I imagined it would be lonely for him, whenever the moment came, but I think I understood it.

But enough of such reflections. I needed to clear my head of everything as I got closer to the office. Trying to understand all the information the police had before them, and what I should do about it, had been taxing, but I had no time to relax or decompress. As I turned the corner of our street and was walking toward the door of the office, still chewing over everything I had seen and heard in the past twenty-four hours, I noticed a guy milling about near the door of the building. He had dark hair and a broad, open face that was made somewhat striking by his Roman nose. His body was heavy and rounded without quite being fat, and he was wearing a gray suit with a French blue shirt but no tie. The suit was not expensive but did look nice, and this somehow seemed in keeping with the rest of his appearance. He was not bad-looking, though he wore an expression of lax amusement seasoned with a faint air of mischief that I found annoying (and which seemed habitual for him). When he saw me approaching, he glanced over at the guy standing next to him and said something, then came rushing over to me.

"Mr. Balfour," he called out to me in a husky voice with a New York accent. "Is that you, Mr. Balfour?"

I didn't answer but just looked at him skeptically. Fatally, though, I did stop walking.

That was apparently all the confirmation he needed. "Eddie Balfour, everybody! Just like the clothes!" He turned back to his friend as he called this out, and it looked as if his compatriot was filming our little encounter on his phone. The fact that Balfour and Son used to deal in part in clothes, and that our downturn roughly coincided with our withdrawal from that operation to focus on finance (against my advice), only increased my irritation. It was like someone elbowing you on the subway and somehow managing to rub salt in an open wound in the process.

"And just who are you supposed to be, my good sir," I demanded, but the words weren't even out of my mouth before I almost winced at the absurdity of "my good sir." I never have handled this kind of unearned cheek well, and I was sad to see he was so quickly bringing this bristling formality out of me.

"Folks, we're here with Eddie Balfour," he said to the

177

camera, ignoring me. "Mr. Balfour, you're a member of the city's wealthy elite. Hey, who are we fooling," he said, glancing back to the camera with a grimace, "if you're in the wealthy elite here in the Big Apple, you're part of the wealthy elite of the entire country—the whole world. I don't believe your catalogues offer any diamond cufflinks, but I'm sure you've got quite a private collection. Now some sinister madman is stalking you and your ilk. And word is, you're helping the police try to track him. Do you have any comment, your eminence?"

I had been staring at him dumbly during his disquisition, unable to comprehend what was actually happening. But the snark of that last comment snapped me out of my daze. "First of all," I said with obvious irritation, despite my best efforts to hide it, "my name is Ethan, not Eddie. And the name of the clothing company is Bauer, not Balfour."

All the mischief and energy were instantly drained from him, his face falling like he was a child who had just been told there was no Santa. "But you're still with the clothes, right?"

"No," I said curtly, and felt further irritation that I wasn't able to control or even conceal my pique.

He recovered quickly, and that same look of unconcerned impudence returned. "Well, whatever the source of your boundless riches may be, your eminence, can you tell us anything about the investigation?" He could perhaps see I was becoming even more irritated. "What is your role with the police, sir?"

I looked at him sharply. "I'm obviously not going to comment on the police investigation—of which I am not a part!"

"Very convincing denial, your eminence," he said merrily. "Let me ask you this, sir: how many butlers do you have, and do you think one of them could have done it?" At this point his cameraman erupted in a witless cackle, and my interlocutor turned to him. "Tommy, keep the camera steady, now—we're a professional operation here" he said, laughing himself.

I glowered at him. "What do you think this is," I demanded, and instantly regretted it.

His face opened up in mock surprise. "Well, your eminence, this happens to be D'Ambruzzi TV." Then he turned back to the camera. "It's damn good TV," he shouted archly at the cellphone. "But seriously, your surly sirriness," he said, turning back to me, "if you don't make clothes and you're not working with the police, what is it you do? How would you justify your life of leisure to our many discerning viewers here at D'Ambruzzi TV?"

"I don't lead a life of leisure—in fact I was trying to go to work when you got in my way here. But I don't need to justify anything to anyone, least of all to the likes of you!"

"What are you contributing to this great common venture we call society, your hard-workingness?"

"I contribute far more than you do, skulking about in the middle of the day and waylaying actual adults on the sidewalk with your little cell phone cinematographer."

"You do more for the world than me? That's highly debatable, your eminence."

"It's not in the least debatable," I all but shouted at him.

"And yet I am debating it right now, therefore it is, *ipso facto*, debatable. Try to keep up, your surliness!"

He was having a grand old time, and it was clear there was no way I was going to come out of this exchange looking like anything other than a privileged dolt with a short temper. So I turned on my heel and walked into the building. I could hear him behind me: "Well, folks, I guess I hit a nerve. Maybe when I mentioned his collection of diamond cufflinks. He's probably dashing off to count them now, make sure they're all still there." His cameraman guffawed and I hated the world.

I was relieved to see he was staying outside on the sidewalk, but the anger didn't leave me easily. Inside I saw Maura, who had been watching through the window. She greeted me and seemed concerned.

"What happened out there," she asked.

"That jackass came up to me and started asking questions about the murders. He seemed to be playing the whole thing

179

for laughs. His idiot friend was filming it on his phone. I'm not even sure what I said, I was so angry."

Maura was nodding sympathetically. "Do you know who that was," I asked her, looking back to make sure he was still outside.

"I think it's Michael D'Ambruzzi. He's a columnist for *The New York Thoroughbred*. He also does these sort of ambush videos, just like this, and posts them online. He's actually been banned from City Hall."

"What," I said, and stared at her in disbelief.

"Yes. It's good you walked away quickly. I hope he didn't provoke you into anything."

"You mean this jackanapes does this regularly and is still employed? By a newspaper?"

"Well," she said, smiling slightly, "the *Thoroughbred* anyway. He actually has something of a following. His videos are usually light-hearted. He's not overly confrontational, he draws people into saying something embarrassing or unguarded."

"Well, I'm glad four murders is so amusing to him. And apparently to the *Thoroughbred*."

Maura shrugged. She looked like she was trying to be understanding, but also wanted to let me know how things really stood. "Since the announcement of the connection between the murders and the police's theory, there's been a lot of chatter. Online and everywhere else. A lot of it is... well, not always kind."

"Yes," I said slowly. "I suppose that's to be expected. But why is he targeting me? No one knows better than me how worthless most of the one percent is."

Maura gave me a searching look, as if she was trying to figure out whether I really believed what I had just said. "I'm serious, Maura," I said, somewhat exasperated.

She nodded ambiguously. "Well, I would really just let this whole thing with D'Ambruzzi go, Ethan. The worst thing you could do would be to give him any more attention or response. With any luck, you didn't give him anything to work with there, and this will be the end of it. Even if he does post a video online, no one important will see it." She paused for a moment and contemplated me with something that looked like pity, which I really didn't care for. "I'm sorry, Ethan. Best to just let this go and move on with everything else you have to do."

I knew from long and bitter experience that she was right, and that if I tried to spar with him I would just end up humiliating myself—"my good sir" would be just the beginning. That of course is why I find people like him so enraging, and why in the back of my mind I knew I wouldn't be able to completely let it go.

But once I got upstairs I had to forget about it completely for the time being. Dad needed me on calls with possible buyers for our properties in Philadelphia. Then the Russians he had talked to the previous week were suddenly back in the mix, and Dad wanted me on a conference call with them. After the business day wrapped up there was more work to do on inventories in the city and in Philadelphia, though Dad and I were both too burnt out to work much past six. I went to Maxine's for dinner by myself, and did little but stare at my plate and try to recharge. A brief postprandial stroll was cut short by the muggy weather and the return of all the day's events and revelations.

I went home and checked the *Primrose*'s website to see if there was any news on whether they would be pulling the Vows columns for that week (and perhaps indefinitely). They had eliminated their public editor, so I wasn't sure where to look. I checked the Vows columns—the previous Sunday's were still up, with no change or announcement. Perhaps the Opinion page? I went there and scanned the day's offerings.

"John C. Calhoun For President," by Blodie Uberweiss. I give a brave, iconoclastic rebuke of the recent spate of campus protests

"Private Prisons Are Indeed Like Slavery: Both Are Good Because They Efficiently Build Capital," by Matt Jenkins. My time as President Euphemus's Chief of Staff taught me the unlovable truth about the world.

"I Agree With von Clapp On This: Climate Change Isn't

181

Real," by Brent Dreck. I may be a von Clapp Backer, but when he's right, he's right.

"Immigrants—They Get The Job Done! But Do They Really?" by Fletcher Harrison. We all love Hamilton, *but let's not get carried away by political correctness.*

"Enough With the Social Media Abuse of Journalists," by Harrison Fletcher. I am tired of taking guff from internet personages like DoktorBoner420.

"This Is Really, Really, Really, Really Big," by Ron Piedmont. Does anyone realize how big this is?

Nothing. I got up and went to the window, where the last few traces of daylight were still visible in the street. Something was still eating at me, though I couldn't figure out what it was. Suddenly I remembered my unfortunate intercourse with the Italianate *Thoroughbred* columnist that afternoon. Grudgingly but ineluctably, I pulled myself away from the window and went back to the computer. I went to the *Thoroughbred*'s website and found their opinion section. The next day's had already posted, and I read down the list to see if D'Ambruzzi was among them.

"Everything Offends Me, Especially SNOWFLAKES," by Manley Cudd. Read this if you want to be angry.

"'Snapchat'? How About 'Get A Job,'" by Ray Lauria. Today's kids would rather "work it" online than line up to work.

"Please Support My Kickstarter To Send 1,000 Plexico Burress Bobbleheads To Tom Brady's House," by Sammy Shuttlecock. Happy birthday, Tommy Boy.

Then, at the end of the line, D'Ambruzzi's abysmal commentary on the events of the past few weeks. He even had his picture there, smiling benevolently like some shaven tabloid Santa. I clicked on the headline with a strange mixture of rage and resignation.

A Specter is Haunting the Knickerbocker Club
Have you heard the news, gentle readers? The 1% is now the .99%. Is this a clever attempt to blend in with the 99%?

No, sadly not, but our beyachted overlords may want to consider other ways to do that. You see, esteemed readers of New York's finest newspaper, the explanation for that missing one-one-hundredth of the one percent is much darker. Apparently, someone out there got tired of hunting for decent-paying work and decided to start hunting people with indecent riches. Someone has gone from Man Friday to Friday the 13th. Someone, it seems, is systematically murdering members of New York's ultra-wealthy. And there appears to be a method to their madness.

You may have heard of the Vows columns in The New York Primrose, *a generally lackluster publication that still has some reflected glory from sitting in the same publishing firmament as* The Thoroughbred. *It's a weekly column that details the upcoming nuptials of New York's highest society, the affluent, the effete, and the overfed, with an occasional token piece on someone who's actually done more with their life than take a few yoga classes. It's been mocked for years, but apparently now someone has decided to do more than write a withering blog post about it. In the past four weeks, four members of New York's finest families, the very crustiest and upperiest of its upper crust, have been murdered. Each week, the person murdered featured in the previous Sunday's Vows section in* The Primrose.

Of course, any loss of life is terrible. My heart goes out to their families, especially the parents who have lost children just about to create the next cycle of this beautiful, crazy, constantly repeating but always new and unique pageant we call life.

But my heart also goes out to the countless millions of Americans out there struggling, and dying, from the opioid addiction that writes the dividend checks for these besotted billionaires. My heart goes out to all the good, honest people out there trying to scratch out a living in the long shadow of shuttered factories and warehouses, left with less to raise a family than these children of privilege spend on a bottle of champagne. Heck, my heart goes out to all the hard-working New Yorkers, many of them no doubt reading these pages, wondering when they're going to catch a break, and wondering when the rest of us became indentured servants to a few obscenely wealthy families who make King Farouk look like Poor Richard. And my heart most definitely goes out to our brave men and women in uniform, serving overseas and running the greatest of risks so that these pampered scions and legatees can rest secure as they nibble on their gold-dusted cannoli (and hey, take it from me, gentle reader: if adding gold dust to your cannoli makes it taste better, all manner of things have gone horribly wrong!).

I know I'm getting a little serious here, more than what most of my readers are used to, but extraordinary times call for extraordinary measures, or at least slightly more earnest newspaper columns. But really, what do we owe these one percenters (and yeah, I know I'm talking like an Occupy Wall Street type, but don't worry, I've showered today). These guys pay their taxes like Carmelo Anthony plays defense. But instead of Melo's jump shot, their only real talent is wrecking the global economy. But of course they got even fatter out of all that. Remind me how this is fair again?

So people are fed up. But then maybe that's not even what's going on here. Maybe this killer is just looking for an easy target. Is it any surprise that someone who wants to kill with impunity might target a group of people who have to pay someone to start their car for them and who probably refer to opening a jar of pickles as "literal violence"? You can't make reference to people's wrists being limp anymore, and you can't make reference in print to anything else being limp. But I can't say I'm surprised to see someone targeting the readership of the Primrose *rather than* The Daily Bread. *When you've got so many trust fund kids and lifestyle bloggers to choose from, why would you go after our readers, people who hear the word "Jets" and think of a football team —highly debatable, I know, but bear with me, dear readers— rather than what they got for their sixteenth birthday? I've met some of the readers of this column, and they're tough as nails. Callouses on their hands, limbs like steel rails, and a grip like a bear trap. Forget about murder, I'm afraid to look at them funny—and that's just my grandma!*

But really, folks, I don't care if someone wants to use six different forks at dinner, and gets the vapors if someone uses the wrong one for the salad course. Use all the forks you like, just stop speaking with a forked tongue. That whining, stringy sound you hear isn't the world's smallest violin playing for you now that you're actually in danger—it's the sound of you fiddling from your Park Avenue penthouse while the rest of the country burns. So stop telling us that everything is going to be alright, that you were born into your filthy rich family because of your merit, and that all your free trade deals and bank bailouts are really somehow good for the rest of us. Just stop, and try telling us the truth for once. Or don't, because for all you want to think of yourselves as "thinkfluencers" or "thought leaders," the fact is no one is listening to you. Well, except that one mysterious figure stalking you from the shadows, who is watching and listening very intently indeed. But I have a feeling you'd be perfectly happy losing that audience.

So instead of just mourning the dead and searching for a killer, we need to debate fundamental questions of fairness in this nation, still the greatest in the world but in serious need of whatever Jefferson and Lincoln had in their water. That's where we are, folks. And that's why, despite all the ups and downs of his still young administration, I continue to support the programs of our President, Ivan von Clapp (that and the fact that his brother Otto still owns the building in Queens my parents live in—so how about it, Mr. Otto, can we finally get that hot water heater repaired?). We'll probably never know what actually happened on that state visit in Hamburg, whether President von Clapp really fell down those stairs and soiled himself or not. The reports that say he did are, in my always humble opinion, unreliable because they come from certain segments of the German press that resent not just President von Clapp but American power generally (and by the way, if the Germans now somehow have a problem with American global leadership, they can go ahead and start paying back all that Marshall Plan money...with interest).

But what happened in Hamburg is beside the point, unless you really need to make a joke about dirty laundry. The point is that this country doesn't just need rejuvenation—it needs serious, fundamental reform. Reform that actually helps all Americans realize the promise of this great land, even the ones who wouldn't know Wall Street from Rodeo Drive. So come on, everybody. Let's come together and start living America's greatness again—today and together.

It gave me some comfort to see these two birds of an imbecile feather flocking together.

My first thought after that was something like, "So this is my nemesis," but of course that was absurd. With the murders I had far greater problems than being jeered at by some fool on a city sidewalk while his idiot sidekick filmed it in iMovie. Still, I had an unpleasant feeling that I would be seeing him again. But there would be time enough to worry about that.

Chapter Ten

A Marriage of True Minds

After everything that happened Thursday and Friday I spent most of Saturday in bed, not so much sick as exhausted and fuzzy-headed. It was just as well I wasn't trying to go out with Freya that night, I reflected shortly before dozing off at 7:30 in the evening. I slept fitfully on the couch for a bit, then went to bed for good before it was full dark out.

I was awoken early Sunday morning by my phone buzzing mercilessly again and again. I finally accepted defeat and picked it up, fumbling with it as I brought it to my ear and croaked out a groggy "Hello?" I was immediately answered by my father's waspish voice: "Where have you been?"

It took me a few seconds to process this strange request for information. "Hello," Dad demanded. "Yes, I'm here. What do you mean, where have I been? I've been in bed, asleep."

"It's almost 9:30!"

"It's Sunday morning, Dad. Surely I'm allowed to sleep in a couple of hours." I wasn't sure where we were going with this, but I didn't expect this perfectly reasonable defense to be the end of it.

"Have you seen today's *Primrose*?"

"You know, that whole miserable thing has taken over my life so much that yes, I think the other night I did actually dream about—"

"Alana's announcement was printed!"

I stopped dead for a second, then remembered how impatient he was this morning. "What?"

"You heard me. Alana's announcement is in the paper this

morning. They went ahead and printed it."

"Dad, that's impossible, they——"

"There's a note explaining it. Hers and one other were printed, but that's not the point. You need to get on to your contact in the police, tell them to take her into protective custody."

I raised myself up in bed a little. "No, we should take her out of town, someplace the murderer won't know about and won't be able to learn about or guess. I'll do it. I'll take her up to Vermont, just stay in a hotel someplace for the next week."

"No, Ethan, you need to go to Philadelphia. Tonight, and for the next two weeks."

"Dad, come on. This could be Alana's life. The sale can wait."

"No, it can't," he said, the waspishness coming back into his voice. "Whatever future this family has is riding on the sale of Balfour and Son, Ethan. We cannot delay, and we cannot trip up here. Besides, we don't need you trying to protect your sister from some lunatic murderer. The police will do a better job than you ever could. So just call your contact and get someone over here right away, okay?"

"Alright," I said, and hung up. I was still far too drowsy to deal with Dad in frantic mode. I needed to wake up a bit before I called Allison, so I got out of bed and made coffee. While it was brewing I opened the *Primrose* on my phone to see what had actually been posted. I went to the Vows section and the first thing I saw was a special announcement from the editor, complete with a picture next to his name, which somehow made the whole thing seem even more unreal.

The editor of the Vows column looked exactly as I had expected: a pink, porcine, bald little man wearing a blue blazer, a salmon bowtie, and an inordinately self-satisfied simper. The image was completely out of place alongside the somber announcement he had to make.

Our readers are no doubt familiar with the terrible events of the past few weeks. A series of murders has been committed,

seemingly targeting ordinary members of the public featured in our Vows columns. Although we have yet to see conclusive evidence of a link between our columns and these ghastly attacks, we have been advised by the police to suspend publication of our Sunday columns. Although the safety of our readers and the general public is of paramount concern to us, we also understand the importance this recognition often carries for the subjects of our profiles. We have accordingly reached out to all those that were to be featured in this week's columns, apprising them of the situation and the possible security concerns and leaving the decision to them. All but two immediately agreed to have their profiles withdrawn. One couple insisted on pressing ahead with the appearance of their profile. The other did not respond to multiple attempts to reach them; in the circumstances, we chose to interpret this as unconcern with the police theory and a refusal to consent to the withdrawal of their profile. As always, we wish nothing but the brightest felicitations for all of our subjects, and indeed for all of our readers.
—Joel Cairo, Vows Editor

Having borne witness to Mr. Joel Cairo's ritual ablutions, I proceeded on to Alana's profile.

Alana Balfour and Bolivar Henderson are to be wed in a private ceremony in Manhattan on June 27th.

Ms. Balfour, 29, is a Manhattan socialite and advocate for various charitable causes. She graduated from Vardley College with a degree in General Studies. She is currently writing a novel-cum-memoir titled The Time Of Our Lives, *about her experiences growing up and spending time among what she calls "the youthful cream of society in the tempestuous hothouse navel of the world, madcap Manhattan."*

She is the daughter of Marie and Ronald Balfour of Manhattan. The bride's father is chief executive of the investment firm Balfour and Son. The bride's mother is a former actress and singer who is now primarily active as a philanthropist.

Mr. Henderson, 26, is a poet who has attracted a considerable following on Instagram. He graduated from the University of Washington with a degree in English. He currently lives in New York and is working on a first collection of poems.

He is the son of Eileen Meyer and Joanne Henderson of Palmerston, Washington. They own and manage a health food store and small book shop together.

Ms. Balfour and Mr. Henderson are looking forward to their marriage, but their first meeting began rather inauspiciously. They were introduced at a party by a mutual friend, but Ms. Balfour had trouble with Mr. Henderson's first name. This caused her some irritation, but Mr. Henderson was undeterred. In fact, he quickly spied a silver lining in her "unhinged rancor," as a mutual friend who was present described it: if she was unfamiliar with the name, she wouldn't make a common mistake about Mr. Henderson's identity.

"I'm not Latino," Mr. Henderson explains. "My mothers really wanted an indigenous person for the sperm donor, but that was hard to find. They thought they might have to settle for a Latino, but then they decided to have my uncle do it so the DNA would come from both families. He had travelled to Mexico on business, a few times actually, so they figured it was pretty close. And that's how I got my name."

Despite his name and his close brush with exotic parentage, Mr. Henderson does not today have a strong sense of identity with the Latinx community. "Growing up in Palmerston, I never met anyone who was Latinx or indigenous. Never met a black person either. But I have since moving to New York. Well, not formally 'met,' really, but I've seen them. Several of them, actually. And I'm very much looking forward to officially meeting one of them someday, whenever the universe decides the time is right and puts one in my path."

One thing the universe has bestowed on Mr. Henderson is a steady and growing prominence as an Instagram poet. Although he began writing poetry around the time he moved to New York, it took him some time to establish an audience for his work, and indeed to establish his own sense of who he is as a poet. *After some early work that he says he has long since deleted, Mr. Henderson's first successes came with poems that evinced what he now describes as a "Free Speech Playboy" persona. These poems appeared mainly in online outlets which have since removed them at Mr. Henderson's request. We were, however, able to find a few titles, which Mr. Henderson confirms are representative of his work at the time: "I'd Rather Get A Handy Than A Speech By Gandhi" and "Check Out the Skulls on Those Dolls."*

"I had recently moved to the city," he explains, "and was trying to figure out who I was and how I fit into the world at large and New York in particular. I was immature, and none of that represents who I really am, especially now."

Mr. Henderson soon began exploring new themes in his work, further developing his poetic persona to express skepticism about religion and an embrace of sensualism, such as in this untitled short poem:

By Jove—no, no
Bi Love—yes, yes

This work brought Mr. Henderson some attention and even notoriety, though he disavows most of it now. This led to rare opportunities like being chosen as a sponsored poet by New York's largest chain of vape shops.

He finally found his voice, however, and an enduring audience, with a body of work largely devoted to chronicling his struggles with Irritable Bowel Syndrome across various locations in the city.

"Rock-A-Feller"

Dashing into
Number 30

                                     Center
                    Rockefeller
      D.
John
66 floors
But where's

The john?

"IBS Blues"

Girlfriend wants me
To go
Look at
Art.

But I
Don't want
To, afraid
I'll
Shart.

As his poetic fortunes rose Mr. Henderson proposed to Ms. Balfour during a romantic trip to Taos, New Mexico. He still enthuses about the visit: "Taos is amazing. I read somewhere that 'Taos' is the plural of 'Tao,' and man that is so right. You can just feel it. I definitely picked the right locale to propose to Alana."

Ms. Balfour is less sure. "I had heard all these things about the place," she says, "but it was not Insta-worthy at all. Kind of a dump, really. All these squat little buildings made of mud for some reason, and they expected us to stay in them."

Mr. Henderson allows that Ms. Balfour did not share his experience, and for good reason. "I think I was really just attuned to the place because it's Native American, and I have that connection because of my Hispanic heritage. Someone told me they're not the same...still not sure how that works. All I know is Taos really blew my mind—I could feel all the Taos just vibrating in the air there."

Although Ms. Balfour was unimpressed by Taos she has long been looking forward to her wedding announcement appearing in the Primrose. *"It's not just for the attention," she explains, "I have an important announcement to make, and this is the perfect format.*

"I, too, suffer from IBS," Ms. Balfour says with a mixture of pride and trepidation. "I used to think it was just a few colonic cleanses that had gone really wrong—I wanted to believe that, to deny my true identity because the world is just so against us. But I've come to accept who I really am.

"My people have suffered so much that I'm hesitant to say anything publicly, but with the support of so many good friends and family, and especially Bolivar, I'm finally able to speak my truth. We mean to work together to remove the unjust stigma around our condition and improve life for our people."

With such a shared sense of purpose and understanding the union is bound to be a happy one.

Of course I knew what had happened—Alana had been in touch with the *Rose* and demanded they run the profile. But why was there another one? Who were these people?

Bridget Callahan and William Shields are to be wed at the Abyssinian Baptist Church in Harlem this Saturday.

Ms. Callahan, 27, is a freelance writer and editor whose journalism has appeared in many publications. She is also an adjunct instructor in New York University's Journalism program. She has recently completed her first novel, Grieving on Strange Shores, *about a family of refugees from Syria. It was published last autumn by White Whale Books. She graduated from the University of Chicago with a degree in Comparative Literature and History and later earned an M.A. in Journalism from Columbia.*

She is the daughter of Josephine and Michael Callahan of St. Louis, Missouri. The bride's father is a community organizer who founded the St. Francis Hostels, an organization that provides food, shelter, and financial services to homeless people in St. Louis. The bride's mother is an attorney who left a high-flying career in corporate law to specialize in immigration law and, more recently, founded an adoption agency.

Mr. Shields, 26, has just completed law school at

Columbia. He has a bachelor's degree from Vanderbilt University, where he studied Philosophy and English. He is also a musician who has recorded two albums and plays several instruments, most notably the piano.

He is the son of Antonia and James Shields of Memphis, Tennessee. The groom's mother is a high school English teacher and former dancer. The groom's late father was a musician who played trumpet in the Memphis area and on several acclaimed recordings, including albums by B. B. King, Allen Toussaint, and Tom Waits.

Ms. Callahan met Mr. Shields at a community event aimed at slowing the progress of gentrification in Harlem. She was struck by his intelligence and lack of cynicism, while he was drawn to her creative approaches to the problem.

"Most people our age—really, most people generally—are either oblivious or jaded," says Ms. Callahan. "It was really remarkable to me how Will had such a clear-eyed view of the problem, and what a tremendous historical loss we're facing, but didn't seem to have a trace of bitterness or resignation about him."

Mr. Shields plays piano, which his father taught him as a child, and various other instruments that he has mostly taught himself. "Some of my earliest memories are of my dad teaching me to play piano, then accompanying me on his trumpet as I banged away," says Mr. Shields. His father died somewhat suddenly when Mr. Shields was ten years old, succumbing to pancreatic cancer. "It was painful, at first, to keep playing the piano," Mr. Shields confides, "but it also brought me great solace. A lot of what I learned on the piano I figured out myself, just plunking around after he was gone." Mr. Shields's father's passing left the family in somewhat dire financial straits, and soon Mr. Shields was playing piano at various locations in Memphis to bring in extra money for his family. "I was still learning a lot, making mistakes, though these gigs were mostly in bars and other places where no one noticed. Eventually, I guess I learned the basics," says the ever-modest Mr. Shields. In addition to the blues and jazz he played around Memphis, he was also exploring classical music, particularly Chopin and Rachmaninoff. "I was mostly on my own with that stuff," he recalls, "just trial and error—mostly error. But the music itself just kept pulling me along. I wanted to be able to play with that mixture of precision and emotion." This spring he performed in a solo recital at Carnegie Hall.

The couple plan to move to Memphis, Tennessee after their wedding, where Mr. Shields will work as a civil rights lawyer and Ms. Callahan plans to work with the local homeless population and write a second novel. "We really wanted to go to New Orleans," explains Mr. Shields. "That city, besides all its history, has a special place in my heart because that was where my father played on some of his absolute favorites among his recording credits, especially an Etta James album at Sea-Saint Studios. But we're going to go to Tennessee, to be closer to my mom and grandparents...which is fine. Plenty of work for a civil rights lawyer in Memphis."

"We'll make it to New Orleans one day," Ms. Callahan adds.

Ms. Callahan conceived the idea for her first novel after a chance occurrence during a group trip to Greece. "Shortly after I graduated I took a trip to Greece with some friends," she recalls. "When we were in Lesbos, just lying on the beach, a raft full of refugees washed ashore. We rushed down to help them out of the water and wrapped them in our towels.

"The rest of the group continued on their tour of other islands," she continues. "Of course I wanted to go, but they were mostly just going to be beach trips. So my best friend and I decided to stay on the island and help at a local shelter for refugees for a few days."

Ms. Callahan and her friend met back up with the rest of their group in Athens, which Ms. Callahan had always looked forward to as the cultural high point of the trip. "I'll never forget those two days in Athens, especially visiting the Acropolis," she says. "But I'll also never forget the faces of the people I worked with in the shelter in Mytilene."

The idea for her first novel came to her before she even left Greece. "I knew I had to do something to try to help," she

195

says. "Various people have told me I have some ability as a writer, so I thought I would try to contribute something to making people better understand their experiences, and maybe even something to the larger world of letters." The book, published last year, won the PEN/Hemingway Award for a Debut Novel and was shortlisted for the Booker Prize.

"I am really wishing for the best for Bridget and Will," says Edith Campion, Ms. Callahan's best friend who stayed with her on Lesbos to work at the refugee shelter. "They are two extraordinary and giving people, and I know their marriage will be fruitful for them and for the world."

Of course the *Rose* sometimes ran profiles likes this, of more or less ordinary but highly accomplished people, to make the whole enterprise seem less ridiculous. But they made for quite the pairing with Alana and Bolivar. I finished my coffee and sent Alana a text. *So you got them to publish your profile despite everything?*

It was rare that she replied to my messages at all—and, to be fair, rare that I sent her any to begin with—but she responded in less than a minute.

Bolivar has had so much attention since the profile published! He just posted a new poem today. I know you don't have Insta, so I'm sending you a screenshot.

Despite myself, I paused for a moment to read the poem in the attached image, bizarrely thinking it might be relevant.

"Respecting Women Is The True Art"

Was Fra Angelico a Bra Angelico?
Was Michelangelo a Michelangel-bro?
No, no, Fra Angelico.
No, no, Roth-ko.
No, no, Picass-o!
No, no.

No.

"What the hell was that?" I said to myself, before realizing this was exactly what I should have expected, and that neither Alana nor Bolivar had any idea how much danger they were in.

I sent her a text. *Alana, what did I just read?*

Again she replied quickly. *I know, not one of his best, but I thought the Picasso part was powerful. He had to get something out there fast to make up for that "free speech playboy" stuff. His profile is higher than ever, but he is in serious danger of being cancelled over that.*

I needed more coffee to reply to this. I was pouring my second cup when the phone buzzed with another text from her. *We also have to deal with this Gandi thing. Googling now to try to find out who he is. Help?*

I took a deep breath, then a sip of coffee, then replied. *No, I mean the profile. Call me now.*

She didn't call and didn't reply to my message, so after a few minutes I called Allison.

"Mr. Balfour," he answered, already sounding a little on edge.

"Detective Allison! What the hell is happening!"

"I know, Mr. Balfour, it's thrown us all for a loop. Apparently your sister called the paper and insisted that the column be run. Just between you and me, sir, I understand she threatened them with a lawsuit."

"And what about this other couple? There should have been no columns this week, instead there are two!"

"Yes, sir. I just got off the phone with them maybe ten minutes ago. They were hiking the Appalachian Trail together and couldn't be reached. They only got back into town today, to prepare for the wedding. They had no idea what was going on and are totally shocked. They would have agreed to pull the column if they had known about any of this, but it's obviously too late now."

Now it made sense. I all but knew Allison was right and Alana had threatened to sue the *Primrose* if they didn't run her profile. I guess after that they were skittish about pulling the other one without some kind of explicit agreement from the subjects.

"Surely they'll be leaving town now? Scattering, going into hiding?"

"I really don't know. It was a lot for them to take in; I'm not sure they know what they'll do yet. They've got family coming from all over the country for this, and I think the family will be their first call, not us."

"Well, I suppose they don't really fit the profile anyway. I'm sure they're safe. It's Alana and Bolivar we have to worry about."

"Oh, I wouldn't be so sure, Mr. Balfour. The fact that they were featured in the columns at all makes them elites in the eyes of our killer, especially if the letter is genuine. And if it's not, the murderer may just be picking a name out of the columns at random, and feels compelled to continue no matter what.

"No, Mr. Balfour, I'm afraid our killer is going to make his attempt and either be captured or—more likely—die trying. But I don't think there's any doubt about this. *One of these four people is in danger for their life.*"

It was an eventful morning, but by midafternoon I forced myself to go to the train station and travel down to Philadelphia. I had half a mind to go get Alana and take her away, Dad's insistences be damned. But I knew it was unlikely she would come with me, at least with him clearly opposing it, and we'd be unable to maintain the necessary secrecy in any case.

I arrived at the offices of Balfour and Son in Philadelphia on Monday morning, though the offices were basically just a warehouse, mostly deserted at this point. There wasn't much of a staff left, but the receptionist was there every minute I was. I never quite learned her first name, she was simply "Ms. Graham," and I found her a rather unnerving presence. Certain of her mannerisms made her out to be middle-aged, but she had a plump, youthful face that seemed to always have an alert expression on it. This was probably due to the natural arch in her eyebrows, combined with the contrast between her brown skin and bright blonde hair, but she was always looking at me as if she had just discovered something and was half-surprised, half-amused about it. She mostly just sat at the front desk, quietly playing Etta James and Barbara Lynn songs on a small radio, and I tried to avoid her.

Monday was unremarkable. Tuesday morning around ten o'clock I received the news that Alana had been murdered. It was Maura who called and told me, and she kept the conversation mercifully brief and businesslike. I waited a few minutes and called Mother, but couldn't get through. I went back to work and then eventually left for lunch, avoiding the conversation with my parents as they seemed to be doing with me.

When I returned from lunch Ms. Graham was at her desk. We exchanged what seemed to me fairly strained nods of greeting as I passed her and went into my office. Just as I settled in at my desk there was a knock at the door. I called out for whoever it was to enter, and Ms. Graham's neatly-bunned head coiled around the door. "I'm sorry, Mr. Balfour, I forgot to tell you. A Detective Allison called from New York. He said he was driving down and should be here around two o'clock. He asked you to please be sure to be here to meet him. He said it was urgent." Now her hand appeared from behind the door, holding a small piece of paper which she read. "He said he needs to talk to you about the windows at the Hastings' apartment." She looked down at the paper again. "He also said new information has come up about Ms. Turner's case, and he needs to talk to you about it as soon as possible."

I thanked her and she slipped back behind the door, closing it again. I got up and walked over to the window. Down on the street below was a young man unloading a truck. As he passed back and forth from the building to the truck he was strutting so much he was almost dancing. All around him was the red brick of the new buildings, clean and bright in the sun against the rumpled gray of his uniform, and I stood there at the window and watched him for several minutes. Eventually, though, I went out to Ms. Graham's desk.

"Ms. Graham," I began, somewhat awkwardly, "I have some important instructions for you about this Detective Allison. When he gets here, I want you to tell him that I'm away in a meeting and you can't call me back. Tell him I got his message, and will be back as soon as possible, but unfortunately he'll have to wait. No matter what he says, keep him here and keep him waiting. An hour after he's arrived, tell him that I've had to go back to New York City. Can you do all that exactly as I've said?"

"Yes, I can," she answered.

I started to leave, stopped for a moment, then turned back to her. "And can you remind the detective that E is the fifth letter of the alphabet?"

She paused and gave me a look, and I couldn't tell if it was surprise or fatal comprehension. "Of course, Mr. Balfour."

So now here I am, back with you, telling you everything you didn't quite know but which I think you must have felt, or at least that you feel is right now that you're hearing it.

When I had to go to Philly, I genuinely feared for a moment that the whole thing might be up. Of course I was going to get back to the city, to try to make it happen without being detected, but it would be so much more difficult than the others. Then I thought of you. I knew that after everything you had seen and heard, you would want her dead, and that you would make the necessary choice. I was sure you felt the same as I did, about all of it—that you almost saw Alana through my eyes. Tell me you didn't feel a thrill of satisfaction and relief when you knew she was dead. You had your own reasons, no doubt, slightly different from mine—perhaps wholly different—but I knew I could count on you to want her just as dead as I did.

And of course you know why I wanted her dead. And you know now what all the other murders were for…but perhaps you don't know the "how" for each one? We have a little time, so it seems only fair to gratify your curiosity after the favor you've done me.

Charlotte was easy. She had indeed been in touch with me, and of course it was because she was sick of that angry dullard whose proposal she had made the mistake of accepting. Everyone seemed to suspect she might have been having some kind of affair, but no one knew who it might be. Needless to say she used a different phone to communicate with me (and who knows who else). I switched over to a burner myself for our clandestine communications—she didn't think to ask why, she just found the whole thing exciting. She told me about the private back entrance, of course, but I went in through the front that evening. Once I was in her apartment, I told her I had to go out again to get something. I made a point of banging my arm on the desk on my way out, drawing the attention of the doorman. I then doubled back around to the rear of the building, snuck up to Charlotte's apartment, strangled her and took the phone she used to talk to me.

Jordan was even easier. I had seen him recently and he told me he was trying to "stay clean," but of course that never took with him (honestly, the whole thing seemed like embarrassing play-acting). So I called him that night and told him I was going to buy some cocaine, and invited him to meet the dealer with me. He was a little surprised to hear the offer coming from me, but of course he didn't need much convincing. And fortunately it's easier to buy a gun than a bottle of wine in this country, so I had bought a pistol off the private market that no one could trace back to me. It was a little risky doing it in the open like that, even late at night in an alley, but with a little preparation it went off without a hitch.

Bella was a bit trickier. I arrived early to the Cravath party, expecting that she would arrive sometime after it had started. I was standing nearby when Evelyn froze her out, and I came up and offered to get her a drink. It was a simple matter to poison hers while I stood with my back to everyone else, pretending to survey the table. She was already talking to Hannah Sloan when I returned and gave her the drink, but I guessed, correctly apparently, that a few flattering comments to Hannah would make her forget anything else. So she wasn't able to tell the police I had given Bella her drink. Higher risk, but I had struck again, and again no one seemed to have any idea who it was.

Of course, Bella was easy to pull off but much harder to live with. I lost my nerve after that, or at least after the visit to see Max. Still, I was able to pull things together for Clarkie. It took some daring, but overall it was quite simple. I stopped the elevator on the floor below Genevieve's and opened the window next to the fire escape. She had already been enthusing about the fire escapes before I ever saw the building, so I was able to plan all that out in advance. Then I got Clarkie alone for a second as we moved from the kitchen to the dining room. I told him that I needed to talk to him, and that he should leave the table sometime before the main course and go wait for me in the hallway. Once he had done that I excused myself and, on my way through the kitchen, picked up the knife with a towel and wrapped the towel around the handle, to keep my prints off the knife and to keep me from cutting myself. I hurried out into the main room, carrying the knife behind my back. Clarkie was standing there in the hallway, grinning like an idiot. He didn't suspect a thing. I actually told him to look up at the painting on the wall, and of course he did. I cut his throat quickly, and he slumped to the ground almost instantly. I honestly don't think he was able to register what had happened before he blacked out. The towel had some blood on it, so there was no putting it back, but since I had used it earlier to wipe my hands there was no reason why it shouldn't have my DNA on it. So I dropped both the knife and towel and ran back to tell the others what I had "found." I suppose I felt a little bad for Clarkie, but honestly, it was like euthanizing an annoying cocker spaniel. I felt a little worse when I realized I had ruined Genevieve and Franklin's new apartment for them, but in an operation like this there is bound to be a little collateral damage.

Alana was the easiest to plan and set in motion but, it turned out, the hardest to control and bring in to harbor. I told her to insist that the *Rose* publish her profile, even told her to threaten to sue them if they didn't. I was pretty sure she'd do it with only the slightest prompting, but just to be certain I reminded her of the various stars who shone more brightly in her social firmament who had been featured before her. "It just doesn't seem fair," I said wistfully, and of course she was fool enough to seize on that and not think twice about the oddity of my being so sympathetic to her. Alana was never the sharpest tool in the shed, but she could think of little else once you had stirred the worm of envy in her. And of course she would never admit to anyone, much less volunteer the fact, that I had put her up to forcing the newspaper to run her profile. Then when the column was published I asked her about it via text and demanded she call me. I knew she would never accede to an order like that from me, nor would she reply to the text. So I had written evidence suggesting I was surprised at how she had acted and that I had tried to intervene.

Oh, and I killed that woman in Washington Heights, the one I dangled before the police, who of course had no idea about any of it. I had been up there to examine the building, which was empty, so I knew how to find my way in. Naturally I chose the easiest target, a prostitute I found on the street there, who didn't think anything of following me into the dark building. The whole thing was so sordid, dragging me down into nothingness—I had become a mere cliché. But I thought I needed the practice. A few days later I read in the paper that the police had arrested someone, her pimp or some man from the neighborhood, and extracted a confession from him. I doubt they'll ever figure out it was me, and if they do they'll probably cover it up to spare themselves the embarrassment. So I take that victory with me.

So there it is, my friend. That's how I did it, and of course I picked each of them just for the simple reason that I had easier access to them. That made it more difficult on a personal level, but I had to be realistic, think about the cold, hard facts of the case and act accordingly. I gave them no more sympathy than the world has given me. They were victims of chance and opportunity, in other words, which I suppose is unfair. But you really can't insist on fairness when your family's fortune rests on some forebear having shown up at the right time to slaughter some Indians, or to force a million Chinese into opium addiction at gunpoint.

What did I say earlier, just a bit ago? Charlotte was easy? Is that really true? I did feel bad for poor Charlotte. She was boy-crazy, but she was fundamentally weak, timid, insecure. She didn't even cry out! But she always liked it a little rough, and it was only a few seconds between when she figured out what was happening and when she lost consciousness. As for me, I just pretended to myself, just like I did to her, that it was all just a little kinky foreplay. Then at the very end I closed my eyes and just kept squeezing long after she had stopped moving, just to be sure. The woman in Washington Heights had been a stranger, and I had partaken of various medications to make sure I was both number and more manic than usual. But with Charlotte I had to be sober, and of course she was no stranger. That was a rough night—a terrible night, full of things I had never known or dreamt existed—but I got through it. Charlotte was weak, vain, shallow and annoying in all kinds of small ways, and really, when you took away all the high-end make-up and clothes and hair, not even all that attractive. But I had loved her once, and it was almost inhuman to do that to her, to hear that gasping, whimpering death rattle come snaking out through her red lips.

After that, I suppose it got a little easier, but I still didn't really want to do any of it. I really believe Jordan only cared about himself and his own pleasure, but he was always great fun to be around and I couldn't help but like him. Quite a bit, actually. But then he went quickly, two gunshots to the chest, and a swift, painless death is really all anyone can ask for. Bella was so beautiful, I felt like I was destroying a great work of art, but again I picked a poison that acted quickly and didn't cause suffering. It was probably better for her to die now anyway than to eventually fall victim to that awful bone disease that killed the women in Max's family. Clarkie was no great loss to the world, and at that point there was no going back in any case.

In retrospect, I have to admit, it's a little hard to believe I carried it all off. When the police called me in I was a little nervous, but I quickly adjusted and was able to play them fairly well. The real horror and fear of the actual murders somehow faded completely once the routine of the workweek began again, and what anxiety or disgust I may have felt in the moment or the hours after seemed like an absurd dream when I was sitting there, matching wits with the detectives. It was distressing how often I lost my nerve around them, but of course they didn't think anything of it. Fear and other unpleasant emotions would be perfectly natural in someone whose friends were being stalked and killed by some unknown lunatic. Very quickly it became a game, in the first place just to see if I could avoid detection myself, then to see if I could put them on to the wrong scent. I mostly succeeded, as I think anyone would have to agree. The letter was my masterstroke—enough genuine detail to convince them it was real, enough misdirection to keep them looking elsewhere. I had hoped signing it "5" would enable the murders to stop after Alana without any suspicion falling on me, but I like to think Detective Allison will be a little shocked when he realizes its meaning. It really was a good run, far better than anyone would have had a right to expect, but of course every great run has to end at some point.

Speaking of which, it really is too bad Balfour *père* didn't make better decisions, or couldn't just hold the ship steady until I could take over. None of this would have happened if he hadn't wrecked the family fortune then expected me to bear the brunt of it all. Every day in New York, surrounded by these hordes of people, hurrying to work in the morning then hurrying home to their families at night—I never really wondered who they were, what the world was to them, why they did it all. But now, as I saw a future as a permanently peripheral, déclassé member of a fallen family, I began to understand how things must look to those great unwashed masses. And, to be frank, I didn't much care for it. I don't know how—or more to the point, why—all those people are so accepting of their fate, but I decided such meek resignation was not for me.

So why am I giving up now? Does Allison actually know anything about either case he mentioned to Ms. Graham, anything that would bring them back to me? Was he just coming down with more routine questions that he had turned into some urgent matter in his usual way…or was he coming down in person to arrest me? I don't know, and to tell you the truth, I don't care anymore. I feel sure he and Leo would figure it all out eventually, there are just too many loose ends, too many places for them to work their way in. And once they've solved one murder they'll immediately see how they all connect. But, again, I don't care if they're there now or if they ever get there. I'm just tired of the whole thing. I do regret not having satisfied my curiosity about Freya Kittredge, but maybe some things are best left in the realm of imagination and anticipation.

I do feel bad for Mother and Dad, of course, losing Alana and now me, and in such unfortunate circumstances. And Dad an only child. A rather inglorious end for the New York Balfours, I suppose, but then there seems to be rather a lot of those going around.

Of course the police have no idea about you as of yet, though I'm afraid that might soon change. But since they don't know I'm here now we've been able to have this little talk, for which I'm grateful. It seems appropriate, even necessary, to me that this whole story gets out. And I think you're going to be sticking around even after you turn that last page on me. Though in fact, I think I'll beat you to it— I'm going out the window here. The quicker an end the better. I don't know what comes next, but I hope it's nothing. I imagine I'll have a lot to answer for if it's not, but at this point everything people say about God seems faintly repulsive to me, so I don't think I'd want to end up next to him anyway. So there it is. And now the rest, I sincerely hope, is silence.